SYNCHRONICITY

The Other Place Series, Book 4

By Elizabeth Roderick

SYNCHRONICITY

Limitless Publishing, LLC
Kailua, HI 96734
www.limitlesspublishing.com

Formatting: Limitless Publishing

ISBN-13: 978-1-64034-056-5
ISBN-10: 1-64034-056-4

Dedication

For Grandma Jeanne

And for Phoenix, of course,
Who sat with me in the wildflowers under the
cottonwood
Drinking off your death.
You were there, I think,
All of us finally free of the need for your judgment.
After all, you taught me how to live
Not like a lady, but like a woman

Chapter 1

Liria and I lie on the hard wooden floor of our new apartment, encapsulated like peanuts in our borrowed sleeping bags. I stare at the splashes of streetlight on the ceiling and listen to the man in the next apartment. He seems to be having an argument with his television, or maybe the television is having an argument with him.

Liria's sigh hisses through the empty corners of the room. "Arty is such a fucking asswipe."

I twist the slick fabric of my bag between my fingers. "Arty is a very cunning and deliberate person."

Liria rolls over, and her sleeping bag shoots little static sparks into the darkness. She regards me with her beautiful lips pulled into a frown, very close to mine. "I wonder what game she's playing."

"It's a game of the Dark Energy. You must see the patterns and parallels in this situation. They're lined up like wolves' teeth, along with Mom's petition and what Rebecca did. They're ready to bite us."

She puts her arm around me. She paints little tickling strokes on my neck, and her breath fills my lungs so that I'm dizzy with it. "I don't think those things have anything to do with one another," she says. "It's just a lot of shitty things happening all at once, that's all."

We're together in the Dark Energy, and I know Liria would never hurt me or trick me. But I don't know if she's right this time. She may be misreading the signs.

We lie in each other's arms. It's peaceful, but it also makes my heart ache and twists me up, because how I feel about her isn't how I should feel about her.

"Liria," I say, very carefully so as not to disturb the calmness, "Arty wants you back. She still loves you."

Liria is silent. My statement hangs in the air like a puff of vinegar-flavored smoke, slowly dissipating, dismembered by tendrils of Dark Energy.

"I don't think that's true," she says in a voice that's tiny, like a bug. "I think she just wants your money."

"But my money is a thing that doesn't exist in the Physical World right now, so her wanting it wouldn't be a strong enough force to compel her action because Other Place things don't have gravity like that, usually."

Liria sighs. "Justin…"

"I think it was a miscommunication between you two, and that you really love each other." My heart beats painfully. I twist and twist the sleeping bag until the zipper squeals in fear, and Liria gently pries my hands free.

She cradles both my hands in hers, tracing my fingers with her thumb. Her head is bowed and I can't see her face. "I…Arty's a jerk, Justin."

Her tickling thumbs make a bad environment for my agitation. "Everybody is a jerk sometimes, when the Dark Energy is telling them to do things that other people don't understand."

She looks up at me, her big eyes shining in the light that comes through the bare, warped windows. "I…I don't want to be with her anymore."

"Liria, I…" My words bunch up and form a lump in my throat, and I swallow them.

"Justin, what's wrong?"

I can't talk about the wrong feelings that are making garbage smells in the trash compactor of my stomach. "Liria, I need you in my life," I say instead. "I don't want to lose you."

"There's no way you're going to lose me." She hugs me tighter, all her curves pressed against mine. "I need you too, Justin. I need you."

Slowly, I take deep breaths of her good smells. It's enough. It has to be enough.

Eventually, her warmth seeps into me, and I fall asleep.

***

We dream that night of sitting together on the banks of a clear creek fringed by willow trees. The wind whistles through the grass and hisses through the branches like fizzing soda bubbles. Fish with tiny, fleshy wheels attached to their bellies chase each other along the muddy banks, their lips wooing, their eyes emotionless.

Crouching amongst the bendy top branches of the trees are a flock of vulture businessmen. They watch us silently, their unsettling stares piercing the Dark Energy.

Liria peers up at them through the rustling leaves, chewing on her lip. "Who are they, anyway?"

The businessmen jostle closer on the branches so they can hear.

"I don't know," I say. "But I don't think they have good intentions."

A shadow passes over, making us jump and cling tightly to one another. A creature of some sort is circling overhead, its large wings dark against the silver-blue sky.

Movement on the ground catches my eye. It is a construction paper heart, tumbling past us on the wind. It makes a memory mutter deep in my brain, but it wanders off, its voice fading, before I can hear the words.

***

A knock echoes through our empty apartment, jerking us back into the Physical World. Liria and I blink away the bleariness. We're in each other's arms with our sleeping bags twisted around us, and the morning sun bursts through the big, uncovered windows.

The knock comes again. Each rap feels like the

sting of a gigantic bee in my spine. I imagine an angry thug bee smacking the door with his brass knuckles, and I get the jitters. Then reality snuggles back too tight around me, and I realize it is probably not a huge, murderous bee, but something much, much worse. It is probably Arty, who said she was going to come over this morning.

Liria tosses her sleeping bag and pillow into a far corner of the room and tugs her fingers through her tangled blue hair. I pull on my jeans and go to the door, opening it quickly before I can change my mind.

Arty stands with her hands in the pockets of her sleek, red slacks. Their color makes me taste pomegranate. There is a moment in which her expression is vulnerable and sad, then it freezes over and she gives me a smile I could shave with. "Good morning, Justin."

"Good morning, Ms. Kopanis. Please come in."

She wrinkles her nose. "Please, call me Arty. The only people who call me Ms. Kopanis are checkout clerks and the police."

"I'm not a checkout clerk or the police." I step aside and she strides past me. Her eyes take in the sleeping bags in opposite corners, and I'm glad Liria thought to separate them. Even though Liria and I are not together like that, I know Arty would think the wrong thing, and I'm pretty sure it would turn her into a demon who transmits the sickness.

"We should go get breakfast," Arty says. "We have a lot to discuss." Her eyes flick to Liria, who stands picking her cuticles with a face that tells me she smells all the bad smells in this situation. "You should come with us, Liria," Arty continues. "I know how you like free meals, and I'm paying."

Liria's fists clench at her sides. "Let me get dressed and brush my teeth." She stomps over and causes a commotion of flying clothing at her suitcase, stalks off into the bathroom, and shuts the door hard.

I'm alone with Arty, who examines me with a blank look. She's difficult for me to figure out. She must know about the Dark Energy, though, because I have never seen anyone that can control it the way she does.

"Arty," I say, "I don't understand what kind of test this is. If it's not against the rules, maybe you could give me a hint."

Her green-blue eyes lose their blankness, like television screens turning on, but they're only showing static. "I guess I don't understand what kind of test this is, either, Justin." She gives me a little smile. It's not a friendship or happiness smile, and I'm not sure what kind it is, but she must give it a lot because it activates the little wrinkles in her freckled cheeks.

I lick my dry lips. "I'm not sure I'm even supposed to pass it. Maybe the Dark Energy doesn't want me to reach enlightenment."

She frowns. "What was that, Justin? I didn't hear you."

I shift on my feet. "No, nothing. It was nothing."

Liria comes out of the bathroom and stops in her tracks, gazing back and forth between the two of us. She scowls at Arty. "What's going on?"

"Let's go," Arty says.

It is a beautiful day outside, the grungy San Francisco streets steaming in the golden sun. Liria walks beside me, squinting off at nothing with a pained look. I want to take her hand. I want to find some way to smooth the emotions out for her and make her feel better, but I don't know how, especially with Arty watching.

Arty jerks her thumb down a side street. "I saw a little diner down here. You know if it's any good?"

Liria shrugs, shoving balled fists into the pockets of her Kelly green shorts. "Never been there. We just moved in a few days ago, and don't have money for eating out."

"Let's give the place a shot," Arty says.

The restaurant has big windows and smells like fried ham. A waitress leads us to a booth with pinky-red vinyl seats, which must be what's giving off the smell. I'm uncomfortable with the prospect of sitting on a fat slab of pig, but I realize that Liria and Arty and the waitress are staring at me so I scrunch my guts up against the grossness and slide over the greasy surface.

Liria slides in next to me. Arty sits across from us, her eyes fixed on us like a wolf watching a pair of rabbits. I try not to twitch my ears and little nose and beguile her into a bloodlust pounce. I try not to think about the fact she is probably carrying a gun somewhere on her person, but that thought is there, sitting heavy on me, so if she does pounce I probably won't be able to hop away in time. I shift my butt on the squishy ham. I'm uncomfortable all around.

The waitress takes our orders for coffee, then

waggles off into waitress land where the food happens. Arty smiles suddenly; I twitch, startled.

"Well," she says. "Your opening was a gigantic success, Justin. Every single last one of your pieces got offers, some of them multiple offers. You'll be buying me breakfast pretty soon."

Liria sits up straighter. "Really? That's awesome."

"I'm glad people like my pictures," I say.

"Well, it doesn't surprise me that they do," Arty says. "You're truly a genius, Justin. I mean, I'm not really an art person and even I can see how good you are."

"When are you going to give Justin his money?" Liria asks. "And don't try to take more than your forty percent, Arty, because that's what the contract says."

Arty cocks an eyebrow at her. "Calm down, Liria. No one is going to try to steal Justin's money, or at least I don't plan on it." She gives Liria her sharp little smile, and Liria crosses her arms and glares. Arty rolls her eyes back to me. "But we're not going to sell most of the pieces right now."

"What do you mean?" Liria says. "If people want to buy them, then let them. Justin needs money. I mean I...I'm barely making enough to cover rent." Liria picks at her cuticles and stares at her lap. The green, embarrassing haze of our money situation settles on us like fart smell.

Arty blinks. Her wolfish slyness seems to have been startled off. "You're working?"

Liria huffs out her nose. The waitress comes up with our coffees and smiles around at us, asks if we're ready to order.

We remember we're in a restaurant, and that our purpose in being here is supposedly to eat food. Arty and Liria stammer out vague requests including bacon and sides of fruit. I try to picture the type of food that belongs in my stomach in this situation, and can't. I ask for oatmeal in the hopes it's slimy enough to slide in between my other stomach slime.

The waitress's cheerful presence withdraws, leaving us to bask in squirminess. "Yes," Liria resumes. "I'm working."

"Where at?" Arty asks.

"A coffee shop."

Arty studies her for a few more moments, then looks back at me, frowning slightly as she tries to rearrange the shreds of her wolf costume into order. "If we sold all the pieces now, you wouldn't have anything left for other shows. And we can get even more money if we hold out. Your popularity is already growing, and if I know anything about business, increase in demand means increase in price."

"He'll paint some more pictures by the time he has another show," Liria says. "He gets them done really fast, a couple a week sometimes."

"So he wouldn't have many. I've set him up another show in New York in two weeks."

This statement drops onto our heads like a piano. Liria and I look wide-eyed at each other.

"New York?" Liria says quietly. "But, Arty…"

Arty gives her a dark look. "I've got it all worked out. We leave in a week to get ready."

Liria shifts in her seat, the pig-vinyl squealing. "When you say 'we'…"

"I mean you, too. You're an important part of this team."

Liria gapes. "But New York, Arty?"

"You're coming."

Liria leans forward, gripping the table, her eyes darting around the restaurant. "You spent six months telling me not to leave the house so that I wouldn't be in danger of being recognized. And now you want to go to New York? The place Peter Czetski lives? You're supposed to be dead, Arty, and I vouched that you were—"

"I told you," Arty cuts in, quiet and slow, "I've got it all worked out."

I think to myself that this is pretty exciting, actually. I've never met anyone who was supposed to be dead before.

Liria stomps and speaks quietly, though her angry words make explosions in the Dark Energy that are very visible. "Was it just bullshit all along, about needing to stay hidden? Were you just trying to control me?"

The waitress comes up with the coffee pot, regards the uncomfortable situation and the fact none of us have remembered to drink our coffee, and scurries off again like she's seeking shelter from a ticking bomb.

"It wasn't bullshit," Arty says. "But I have a plan."

They stare at one another. My heart pounds. The soundtrack to an action thriller movie plays in the Dark Energy.

10

Liria's eyes drop out of the staring contest. "I can't go anyway. I've got work. They'll never let me have more than couple days off."

"Quit your stupid job, then."

"Arty, I can't quit my job. We need the money."

"You're fucking going, Christina. I need you to keep…things…from going all crazy." She smiles sweetly at me before looking back at Liria, and I curl my hand around my coffee cup, because I may be what she calls a crazy thing, but I'm not mentally challenged enough to not know I'm the crazy thing to which she refers.

"Besides," Arty continues, "you don't need your job. I'm sure Justin won't mind paying rent for a while. After all, when all the deals are closed from last night, his take is going to be over thirty grand."

Liria blinks at me. I pour some cream into my coffee and stir it, watching it swirl. The notion of all that money buzzes around me like a fly, but I don't quite notice it.

"Thirty thousand?" Liria says.

"Yes, roughly," Arty says.

I look up from my coffee. Arty is watching Liria closely.

"A couple of them are still in bidding wars, so it may go higher," she says. "I'll let you see an accounting once it's all done."

I blink as that buzzing money-fly finally lands on my nose. I shake my head to dislodge it, but it returns. "Excuse me, did you just say I have thirty thousand dollars?"

"That's what she said," Liria says.

I look back at my coffee, squeezing the smooth

11

porcelain cup tight in my hand. "I'm going to lose my social security money, like Mom said." The thoughts of Mom and money and all these things happening right now start up a trailer trash fight in my head which is very hard to look away from. Mom throws a coffee cup at me and I half-duck before I realize I don't have to do that in the Physical World.

"It's going to be okay, Justin," Liria says. "You're going to make enough money that you won't need your social security."

Arty slurps her coffee and sets the mug down with a thump. "Let your attorney worry about the social security money. Speaking of which, we need to discuss the petition your fuckhead of a mother filed."

I twitch as something touches my thigh. It's Liria's hand. She's gazing at me with big, worried eyes. My shoulders are hunched and my face is scrunched up, like someone has tightened my spiritual drawstring. I sit up straighter, rolling my shoulders and imagining the mind-police hauling my trailer trash thoughts off to the drunk tank. "Mom is part of the trap, I think. Does the attorney you hired know about those sorts of traps?"

Arty gazes at me. Liria squeezes my thigh. The waitress brings our food, but no one seems to notice except Arty, who picks up her fork and spears a grape from her bowl of fruit.

"I spoke to Patty Harris this morning," Arty says, crunching the grape like a wolf gnawing a rabbit's head. "She's the lawyer, and she's really good. She says your mom doesn't have much of a chance of success as long as we play our cards right. Stewart and I will write declarations that you've entered into fair and legitimate business contracts with us and are running your affairs satisfactorily. Liria will say that you're her roommate, that you pay your share of rent and expenses, toss your dirty socks in the laundry basket, and always put the toilet seat down. All you have to do is keep it together in public." She raises her eyebrows at me. "And I mean, no breakdowns or any of that fainty bullshit you pulled when I showed up at my apartment. Actually, I'd appreciate it if you just kept your mouth shut as much as possible when we're around people. Can you do that?"

Liria huffs. "Arty…"

Arty's eyes don't leave my face. "Let him answer."

Liria crosses her arms and looks away. I look back at my coffee.

"Well?" Arty says.

"I don't know what this test is," I say to my coffee. "I don't know how to pass it, so I don't think I should say anything right now."

Arty sighs heavily. I imagine that it's my coffee sighing at me, because I don't want to look at Arty or remember about her at all.

"You're upsetting him!" Liria whisper-shouts, her fingers clenching my thigh.

"I'm just trying to do what's best for him and his career."

Liria snorts. "Good one. You're doing what's best for you."

Arty takes a breath to add to the growing pile of

angry words.

"Please don't argue," I say. "It's not appropriate for the restaurant atmosphere, or any atmosphere. I'm certain it's contributing to climate change at this point, actually."

Both of them go silent. I glance up to see Arty regarding me with the corners of her mouth twitching up. She and Liria both giggle. It's the first time I've seen them laugh together, and I suddenly remember they used to be girlfriends. It makes me feel like my heart is collapsing on itself.

Liria sighs. Under the table, her hand unclenches from my thigh, and her fingers creep over to interlock with mine. "I'm sorry, Justin." Her giggle is completely gone, and her big eyes squint up with tears. "I didn't mean to upset you."

I like the feeling of her hand in mine, though I worry Arty can somehow see through the table and know it's happening. I stroke Liria's thumb with mine. "Don't cry, Liria."

Liria wipes her eyes. Arty massages the skin between her eyebrows for a moment before she picks up her knife and smears cream cheese on her bagel with violent strokes. "I'm sorry too, Justin. I don't want to argue. Just, you know, try to keep it together. Please. If you feel like you're going to faint or…whatever…tell one of us, okay?"

Liria looks at me. Under the table, she puts her foot next to mine.

"I will try to do that, Arty," I say, because I'm not sure what else to say.

"Thank you, Justin." Arty munches her bagel, and Liria drops my hand, picks up a slice of bacon

14

and stirs it around in her pancake syrup as if it's the saddest thing she's ever done. I remember my oatmeal, and try to organize my mind around the idea of eating.

"By the way, Justin," Arty says. "Since all that bullshit happened at the opening and you weren't able to go out with Mina last night, I talked to her. She's still in town today. She's going to meet you for a little date at three o'clock."

Liria stops with her bacon halfway to her mouth, dripping syrup onto her plate. "What, Arty? No."

"What's your problem?" Arty says. "She's his girlfriend."

"Not anymore," Liria says. "That bitch dumped him, and now she wants to torture him by trying to get back together."

I wad myself up like a used tissue around my slimy snot feelings.

Arty gazes at Liria and stabs her poor fruit. "Fine. I'll call Mina and tell her you can't see her today."

"No, I think I should see her."

Liria huffs. "Justin…"

"I think the social dance says I have to see her, because there are wild emotions running around, and if we don't round them up they may trample us all to death."

Liria snickers, and look over to see her smiling. She is so beautiful. "You're right," she says. "But I just don't want her to hurt you."

"She can't hurt me any more than she already has. Those emotions are already galloping free."

Liria presses her lips together, and she nods.

"Okay. But just…just call me, if she upsets you, and I'll come get you, okay?"

"Okay, Liria."

Arty taps her fingers against her forearms, watching us from inside a cloud of churning, unreadable thoughts.

Chapter 2

There is a knock on our apartment door at almost exactly three o'clock, and I open it to find Mina there, wearing a new red dress that glides around all her curves. As nervous as I am to see her, I am still relieved she's here. I have spent the last two hours sitting on the hard floor of our empty apartment, discussing business with Arty in a very complicated emotional climate.

I glance back at Liria, who is huddled in a corner, alternately picking at her cuticles and tugging at her blue hair. I think that the climate in here is not good for her either, and she needs some sort of psychic rain jacket to protect her. But it is too late to change my mind and stay with her, and besides, I'm probably not very good protection against the emotional elements.

"Hello, Mina," I say.

"Hi, Justin."

"Have fun, you kids," Arty says.

Liria's last glance before I shut the door hollows my guts out.

Mina and I stand in the hallway looking at each other. I'm wondering about Liria, and wondering about Mina, and the Dark Energy fills with sadness.

"Where do you want to go?" she asks very quietly.

"Would you like some ice cream? I don't want any coffee right now. I've done enough twitching for the day and I don't need a beverage that will help me do more of it."

Mina giggles. "Sure, ice cream sounds good." We start down the hall. "Why are you so twitchy, though?"

I twist my shirt in my hands as we go down the stairs. I've had to change clothes four times today to find the ones that flow with the turbulence in my life right now, and I'm still not sure if I'm dressed correctly. "Arty is a very intense person," I say.

Mina squints at me. "She told me she bought your contract."

"That's correct."

"Isn't…isn't she the one who threatened to kill you?"

We head outside, and the sun is very warm in the cracks between the buildings' shadows. The roar of the City picks us up like an ocean wave. "She did threaten to kill us," I say. "This situation is very confusing, actually."

"Justin, I'm worried about all this."

I hear all the worry and muttering in the Dark Energy too. I step over the cracks in the sidewalk, because they are channels that carry the bad vibrations, like in that poem about breaking your mother's back. I don't need to bring Mom any further into this situation by breaking her back, I don't think. I wonder what sort of court petition she would throw at me that happened. I imagine the cops serving me with a big photograph of mom screaming her head off, and them telling me it's very important I respond within thirty days.

"What are you laughing about?" Mina asks, and I remember her being there.

"Nothing," I say. "I'm very worried too." I stop walking. "Right here is the ice cream place. I haven't been here yet but I'm sure it's good." I hold the door for her, and she watches me with a furrow between her dark eyebrows as she goes in.

Mina's lips pull sideways as we wait in line, and I know she's chewing on her cheek in the way she does when she's nervous. I stare down at the tubs of ice cream behind the glass, wondering which is the right one to pick.

"Justin," Mina says. "I think you should come home to Piedras."

I stare at the sweet cream lavender flavor, but lavender flowers are club-shaped and I think the taste of it would beat me over the head. "I can't go home to Piedras. Mom and David will put me in an institution."

"We won't let them. I'll help you get a lawyer."

"Arty already has a lawyer for me."

Mina opens her mouth to say something else, but the people in front of us leave with their cones and it's our turn to order. I get the sugar-free cheesecake, and Mina gets cookies and cream, like she always does. Mina tries to pay for it, but I stop her and hold a twenty out to the cashier. "Arty says

I made thirty thousand dollars last night, so I can afford your ice cream."

Mina goes very still and pale as the cashier gives me change. "Wait, what? Thirty thousand...whoa. So you...what are you going to do with the money?"

"I haven't met the money yet, so I don't know how we'll get along together. Arty just gave me some cash as an advance while the wheeling and dealing completes its cycle."

I have to remind Mina that the man is trying to hand her an ice cream cone. She takes it and we go to sit at a tiny, round table, on white chairs with backs the shape of hearts. We lean on them. I wait for the love in the hearts to surround me with pinky good feelings, but that doesn't happen.

Mina gazes at me and doesn't eat her ice cream. "That's a lot of money, Justin."

I stir my ice cream around in its cup. "Yes. I guess people liked my pictures. Arty wouldn't sell all of them, because we need some to take to New York."

"New York?"

"Yes. Arty has another show for me there. We leave in a couple weeks."

Mina's ice cream is dripping onto her hand. She quickly licks it off. "I...I mean, that's cool, about the money, and the other show...but...I worry Arty is taking advantage of you, is all."

"Arty is a powerful presence in the Dark Energy, and it's difficult to deal with. But it looks like it's what has to happen in my life."

"No, it's not what has to happen. You can get out

of that contract and come home."

I watch her. Our love for one another has melted into a sticky sweet sadness that drips all over me like Mina's ice cream cone drips on her. "I don't think I can do that, Mina."

"Why not? We can get legal help to take care of the contract and your mom's petition, and get you enough money so you can rent your own house in Piedras or Paso. I can help. There are lots of resources for people like you."

People Like You is what Mom always says about me, and I wonder what it is about me exactly that makes them call me crazy, that walls me off from People Like Them. I imagine all of the crazy people piled in a gigantic bucket labeled People Like You, and I imagine Mom picking it up and emptying it into the trash.

"The Dark Energy brought Arty into this situation," I say. "There's nothing I can do about it, but I'm hopeful that it is ultimately for the best, because of other signs I've seen."

Mina gives me a shiny-eyed pity look. It also reminds me a little of Mom, and it gives me anger prickles. "The Dark Energy didn't do this to you, with Arty," she says. "It's just a bad situation that you landed in, and you have to do something to get out of it. If you let people walk all over you because you think it's meant to happen, I'm worried you're going to end up…" Her eyes fill with tears. "I just care about you, Justin, and I want you to be happy. I don't think you're going to be happy with Arty and that…that…I mean, they're drug dealers! And Arty is violent!"

Her words cause a compression wave in the Dark Energy, which hits my eardrums with a whumph and makes them ring. I look around to see if anyone else has noticed, but it appears people are still involved in their normal ice cream activities.

I don't know what to say to Mina. My tongue weighs as much as a sandbag. "You don't know about the Dark Energy yet," I manage. "Mina, your cone is melting very badly."

Mina blinks and huffs. She tries to do damage control with her tongue, then just rolls her eyes, gets up, and throws the cone in the trash. She sits back down and starts wiping her sticky hands on napkins from the dispenser. Her eyes are full of tears, and she's not looking at me. "I think you need your medication adjusted again. It's not really working."

"I don't know what the medication is supposed to do besides what it's already doing."

Tears streak Mina's cheeks and she dabs at them with the sticky napkins, which is probably a bad idea. "This isn't fair. You don't deserve for your life to be like this."

"This is the current I'm caught in, though, and paddling against it would get me nowhere. If you work against the Dark Energy, everything you do twists around and you end up in the same place you would have been anyway. That's why you broke up with me. Because the Dark Energy didn't want us together."

Her expression crumples, dislodging more tears. She grabs a handful of clean napkins and dries her eyes. "I shouldn't have broken up with you. It was a mistake. If I hadn't, maybe you would listen to me now and come back to Piedras."

I stare down at my paper cup of ice cream, which is milky soup now. "It's complicated how the currents flow."

Mina sniffles. "I don't know what to do," she whispers.

I glance up at her, but it's hard for me to look at her right now. My gaze falls back down and I pick at a seam in the plastic table. "I'm too much trouble in your life, Mina."

"You won't give me another chance? You won't just try it my way? Getting out of the contract and coming back home?"

I run my finger up and down the table seam, trying to arrange my feelings along that straight line, but it won't happen; the tickling pressure on my fingertip doesn't vibrate strongly enough to attract the other feelings to it.

There aren't any words left for me to say, so I don't say anything.

Mina sniffs louder. "It's Christina, isn't it?" The words are a sharp slap, and I look back up at her. She is squeezing the wad of dirty napkins in her hands, her lips pressed together like vice grips. "I knew you two were together. I knew she'd suddenly turn straight when she realized you could make money and support her."

Her anger flows into the space between us, and into me too. "We're not together, but she's my friend and she's a very nice person, and you shouldn't say those things about her."

"If you're not together yet, it's just because you're so...because she doesn't..." Mina tosses the lump of napkins hard onto the table and looks away out the window with red eyes.

A jitter makes an earthquake in my nerves. "Please don't cry, Mina. Please don't yell and be angry." I want to say something to make this situation better, but I don't know how to fill the cracks and make our world whole again.

"I'm sorry, Justin," she says. "I'm really sorry. I just can't...I can't handle this. I love you, but you're too wrapped up in your Dark Energy, and you can't see...you'll never be able to see..." She squeezes her eyes shut and shakes her head. "I'm sorry, Justin," she says again. Then she stands up and runs out, and it's just me sitting at the table alone, with a pile of crumpled dirty napkins and a paper bowl of ice cream soup.

I sit there for a long time. I can feel people shooting me curious looks. I know they think I have done something horrible and ungentlemanly, and that is why Mina was angry. But I have to sit there withstanding their judgment because I can't find the strength to stand up and go home.

I wish I were smart enough to learn the lesson the Dark Energy is trying to teach me without having to go through all this torture, but I guess I'm not. I hope that I will figure it out soon.

After a while, I remember that I've left Liria alone with Arty and that it has to be bad drama for her. I throw away the garbage and rubble of the final destruction of my relationship with Mina and follow the sidewalks home, still stepping over the wandering cracks. I could just melt away into the City's vibrations, but I don't want to leave Liria behind.

When I get home, Liria is sitting alone on one of two brand new blue loveseats. She is watching Adventure Time on a mattress-sized television and eating a long rope of red licorice.

She jumps up and takes me in her arms, the licorice dangling from her lips. "You're back." She pulls away from me, and her eyes search my face. "You okay?"

"I'm sorting out the complicated frequencies, but I'm okay." I look around at the furniture. "Lots of things happened while I was gone. Where's Arty?"

"She left."

The heavy sharp-taloned vulture perched on my heart suddenly takes flight. "That is a wonderful thing."

Liria laughs and pulls off a bite of licorice. "Arty bought us some furniture because Stewart told her we didn't have any. It got delivered right after you left."

"That was very nice of her."

"Nice, or whatever. But come sit down and tell me how it went with Mina."

We flop down on one of the loveseats, and I clutch my elbows. "It was very distressful and neither of us even ate our ice cream, so the whole situation was just engineered toward failure."

Liria's face gets very serious. She pulls off another bite of licorice. "I'm sorry."

"I am too."

"What happened? I mean…"

I tell her about Mina trying to get me to move back to Piedras, while I pick at a seam in the new loveseat. It is an underwater color. I am sitting on a gigantic sea anemone.

Liria's brow furrows. "Things are pretty complicated now, but they'd be worse if you went back to Piedras. Your mom would mess with you, and Arty would probably sue you for breaking the contract."

"I believe that is a correct assessment."

We both jump as Liria's phone buzzes with a loud, hollow sound on the new coffee table. She scowls at it and picks it up. "Hello?" She listens. "What day?" She tugs at her hair. "Okay, but where…" She huffs. "Are you sure, Arty…okay, if you say so, but…okay, okay, Arty. Bye."

She hangs up, frowning. "She got our tickets for New York, leaving a week from today."

An unsettling note sounds in the Dark Energy, and I remember a thing that has been bugging me since breakfast. "Liria, what was all that stuff you were talking about regarding New York being dangerous?"

She frowns harder. "It's a long story."

"Does it have a dancing bear in it? Because I like those sorts of long stories."

She snorts, then breaks into giggles, which has beautiful harmonies so that the bad vibrations don't seem so scary.

"I would like to hear the long story, even if it doesn't have a dancing bear," I say. "Is this about those gangsters you told me about once? The ones whose money Arty stole?"

Her giggles die away. She crosses her legs, then swings the top one nervously. "Yeah, it's about

26

them." She drags her hands down her cheeks. "The people Arty stole from were her father, and her father's boss, who's one of the big guys. They both live in New York."

She bites off a chunk of licorice distractedly. "The big guy, he thinks Arty's dead. I vouched for her, to the big guy, that she was." She gives a little grimace. "I actually thought she was, at the time. But, anyway, this guy has spies everywhere, and if they spot Arty…and me…"

My ears ring. An electric current of fear runs through me. "That is very bad and dangerous."

"Yeah. Yeah, it is."

"Liria, I don't think we should go to New York. Maybe we're wrong about what the Dark Energy wants. Maybe it's a trick."

She stares at her knees for a while, picking at her cuticles. "If Arty says she's got it worked out, I think she means it. She's a bitch sometimes, but she's anything but stupid. I…I think it's okay for us to go."

"I don't want you to be in danger. If something happens to you, things will not go well for me."

"Shhh, Justin." She puts her arms around me and hugs me tight. "It's okay."

"If something happens to you, the Dark Energy will be furious at me. It will pull me in forever into the bad place that people call hell."

"No, Justin, hush."

"Liria—"

"Let's do this, Justin," she cuts in. "We'll see what Arty has worked out, and if it seems safe to us, then we'll go, okay? But if it still seems too dangerous, we'll find a way to back out."

I consider this as Liria rocks me back and forth in her arms. I take a deep breath, "Okay," I say.

"It's going to be okay. It maybe isn't going to be easy, but we'll get through it together. I feel like, as long as we're together, things are going to be all right. It seems like we were brought together for a reason, you know?"

I press my nose into her good-smelling hair and speak through it. "It seems like it. But sometimes it's hard to say what will happen."

I can feel the tension in her back muscles as she shifts slightly in her seat. "You've got that right."

Chapter 3

I am finishing up a painting when there is a knock on the door.

Liria is in the shower, singing a Miley Cyrus song along with the splash of water off her body.

Knocks on doors are often bad news for me. Will the bad news just go away if I don't answer? I think about it. The knock comes again, and I stare at the door. When the knock comes a third time, I think that's the answer to my question. I put down my brush and go over to answer it.

I open it quickly, like ripping off a Band-Aid. It is a woman with golden-brown hair cut close to her head. She watches me through large sunglasses. Thick makeup covers fading bruises on her high cheekbones and around her full lips, and I wonder if she's been in a fight.

My hand tightens on the doorknob and I resist the urge to slam it shut again. "Hello," I say.

"Hi, Justin."

The voice is familiar, and I twitch in confusion. "Arty?"

She smiles, and it is a slightly different smile than before, because her lips are different. She takes off her sunglasses, and her eyes are brown, not green. "They did a good job on me, right?"

I realize I'm staring, and stand aside to let her through. I shut the door, and I still am staring at her. "You had plastic surgery, I think."

"Darn tootin'. They tore me apart like a house of Legos, and put me back together in a different order."

I can't stop looking at her, even though it's a social dance violation. She's even dressed differently, in a navy blue pantsuit and black blouse. Her breasts seem much bigger. "I didn't know they made Legos out of human flesh," I say. The thought of that gets caught in the folds of my brain, and I have to tug it out, like when you accidentally vacuum up a sock and have to free it from the rotor. Arty is speaking again, and I force my mind back into the conversation.

"...think it will keep us out of trouble. I needed a complete overhaul, anyhow." She glances toward the bathroom. The water has stopped, but Liria is still singing in her squeaky, overzealous voice. Arty shoots me a wry grin. "She should enter one of those TV singing contests, right?"

"That would be unintentionally funny."

Liria comes out of the bathroom, still singing and drying her hair roughly with a towel. She goes abruptly quiet when she sees our visitor. Her forehead crumples, and her lips twist. "Arty?"

Arty does a little twirl. "How do you like it?"

Liria walks around her, inspecting her like she's

some sort of strange new contraption. "That's really weird."

Arty blows a raspberry then winces, her hand darting up to clutch her bruised jaw.

"Does it hurt?" Liria asks.

"Yeah, still hurts a little. But it's getting better. Do you think the goons will recognize me?"

Liria peers at her. "I…I don't think so. The only way I recognized you was by the way you looked at me, and the fact I didn't know who else would be here."

Arty gives her a strange look, but it is gone quickly and she smiles. "So, are you guys ready to go to New York tomorrow?"

My heart wiggles around in my chest as Liria and I exchange a long look. Things are beginning to fall into place in the Dark Energy. Liria nods slightly.

"Yes, Arty, we're ready," I say.

***

We are actually not very ready, though, because I've spent all week painting while Liria worked at the coffee shop and decorated the house with a strange assortment of items she found in thrift stores. So the rest of the day is us swarming around like busy ants, trying to get all our things together.

It turns out that taking paintings and drawings on an airplane is not an easy thing to do, because they have to be wrapped up a certain complicated origami way and packed into slots in special, padded boxes. Arty sits fretting and gently poking at my new painting, wondering if it is dry enough. I have painted it in watercolors like she asked, because oil paints take too long to dry, but by three in the afternoon it is still a little damp and she is considering blasting it with the hairdryer. I tell her that would probably be a bad idea, and Liria gets Stewart involved so that he comes over and rants and stomps at Arty about how she has less art sense than a wild gorilla. Luckily by the end of the day, the painting is dry enough that Stewart feels comfortable wrapping it in an even more special way involving wire frames and special paper and probably some quantum physics and voodoo. When I tell them to just leave that painting here and show it later, Arty stares at me from behind her brown contact lenses. "This is a huge show, Justin. I'm not missing any opportunities here."

Our flight leaves at six in the morning, and Arty stays the night in our apartment because we need to get up extremely early. She sleeps on the floor between Liria's and my pull-out loveseat beds, even though I offered to be the one on the floor.

I lie awake for a long time. Arty breathes loudly and dream-twitches in her rustly sleeping bag. Liria fidgets with her blanket and stares at the ceiling, and I can feel her nervousness in the Dark Energy. I wish we could talk to one another, but Arty would probably be grumpy about that.

Eventually, Liria and I fall into the peaceful grove of willow trees in the Other Place. Liria sits beside me with her head on my shoulder, plucking blades of long grass. The wind gusts across the long prairie, leaving its meandering belly-prints in the grass and whipping the tree branches into a gentle frenzy.

"Arty looks very different, but I'm still nervous about New York," I say. "What if the goons recognize you?"

Liria shrugs, weaving the grass between her fingers. "As long as they don't recognize Arty and figure out she's alive, I'm fine. The only thing they would have against me is that I'd lied about her being dead. Arty's plastic surgery is really good, and I think it's worth the risk for us to go. It's a really good thing for your career."

A butterfly flutters down out of the sky and alights in Liria's blue hair. Liria smiles, her gaze rolling upward as if she could see it through her skull. "Is that a butterfly in my hair?"

"Yes," I say. "It's very beautiful." Its velvety black wings writhe with moving neon swirls of indigo, the colors stark and deep and perfect. The scalloped edges are laced with delicate lines and dots of bright yellow. I put out my finger, and the butterfly crawls onto it.

I bring it up in front of my eyes and examine it from all angles. It folds and unfolds its wings, showing off for me I think, the patterns flashing like electric blue sunbeams off glass.

The neon swirls twine out of its wings and wraps around my mind, caressing it, probing it, and coaxing me toward something I don't understand.

I get a jolt of fear. I want the butterfly off of my finger now, but I can't seem to move. I can't look away.

The butterfly turns to face me with its over-large

eyes. It twitches its antennae in a predatory way, gripping my finger with its sticky legs.

Its alien features balloon monstrously, consuming my entire field of vision. Every hair swells as big as a tree trunk. Its deeply black scaly proboscis is as thick as a python. Steely light slides along it as it furls and unfurls slightly.

The butterfly's staring eyes flicker, and I see each octagonal facet is a television screen showing commercials: toothbrushes gliding over too-white teeth, smiling women in aprons posing with boxes of manufactured food, slogans and logos and mascots. I'm held transfixed by those images. They whisper and caress me and fill me up with lead.

The butterfly's tongue uncurls with lightning speed. It hits me with a crack, and my body ignites with a burst of horrible pain. It passes through my flesh like a honed knife through a tomato.

My meat and bones smoke and burst into flames, blistering, boiling and melting into a pool of sticky liquid. My mind screams in agony. The butterfly scuttles over, staring at me through its television eyes. The images on the screens flicker: a man in sunglasses driving a car, a mom watching her kids caper through a sprinkler, each picture a feeble ghost over the deep, all-consuming void behind them.

The butterfly positions itself with its creeping, hairy legs. It slowly unfurls its tongue again, licking at the puddle of my melted flesh. It probes deep and sucks me up like hot, thick soda through a straw. Empty, horrible dread mingles with the unbearable pain. I'm being sucked toward a hell of the worst kind. I don't know if I'll get out. I don't know if I'll survive.

"Justin."

I sit up with a gasp. "Wha?"

"Time to get up."

I blink. The pain is abruptly gone. My body feels light and dizzy and my lungs ache. Arty's surgically-altered face looms where the butterfly's had been, washed over by the streetlights shining through the warped windows.

"You awake?" she asks.

"Yes, Arty, here I am." My voice is hoarse. I'm still trying to remember how to breathe.

I look over and see Liria blinking at me blearily, her brow furrowed. I wonder if she saw what the butterfly did to me, but I don't have time to ask her.

Arty claps her hands. "Okay, up you two. Time to get cracking."

We pull clothes over our awkward, sleepy bodies, then start to haul our loads of boxes and baggage down to the street to our waiting cab. The poor driver hunches like a whipped dog under Arty's violent instructions as he helps us shove it all into the car. It takes up all the available space, and Liria and I have to wedge ourselves into the remaining nook in the backseat. Arty sits shotgun with another box on her lap, and we drive through the middle-of-the-night darkness to the airport.

I have never been on an airplane before, and so I have no idea how much of an ordeal it is. We unload all the paintings and haul them through the wandering crowds to the baggage check, where Arty jabs the clerk with pointy words, insisting they treat my paintings with supernatural gentleness. I imagine the poor lady being forced to call God and arrange for angels lift our luggage up to a soft, fluffy cloud where it can drift serenely alongside our airplane without being jostled. I'm happy when every box has been checked and we are relieved of that situation.

Going through security is not much more comfortable, though, with all the cop-looking people and their instrumentation, radiation seeping into my every private crevice and revealing things I didn't even know about myself, probably. The fluorescents drool unhealthy light over the whole scene, and it's too early in general. But the security personnel seem to decide we're not dangerous enough at the moment to necessitate further probing, so we pluck our shoes off of the conveyor belt and go purchase big cups of hot coffee to drink at our gate. We curl around them wordlessly, Liria and I trying to slurp up enough caffeine to make our vibrations resonate at an awake Physical World frequency. Arty drinks hers too, though I'm pretty sure she only ever vibrates at awake frequencies anyway. She is the most Physical World person I've ever met.

The Dark Energy in the airport is strange, because all the people here are on their way somewhere else. It is even stranger, bright and jumpy, once we board the plane a half hour later. Liria makes sure I have the window seat, and we crowd in, Liria beside me and Arty at the aisle.

My knees press up against the seat in front of me so that I feel like a folded-up baby outgrowing its womb. It smells like people in here the way that feed lots smell like cattle. There's not very much actual air, to tell you the truth.

I watch the airport employees scuttle around the tarmac outside. The stripes on their reflective vests glint in the early dawn light and remind me of the bright patterns on the butterfly's wings. It makes me even more uncomfortable. I squeeze my eyes closed. "I don't want to be sucked up in that butterfly's tongue. It's a horrible feeling, and I don't want to know what's inside that belly."

Liria takes my hand, and I jump in surprise at her touch, my eyes shooting open. She gazes at me, her face full of concern. "What are you whispering about? Are you okay?" She strokes my hand, runs her fingers up and down my arm, and I take a deep breath.

"I'm nervous about what the butterfly might do to me."

Arty hard-eyes me. My skin prickles like it does before a storm, because she is swelling up with lightning ready to strike. "Has he ever been on an airplane before?" she asks in an undertone.

"No," Liria says.

"He'd better not fucking freak out. If we get kicked off this plane…"

"He won't, Arty," Liria hisses. "Just *stop*. You're making him worse."

I take another deep breath. Liria strokes my arm, her fingers slow and soothing. My knee vibrates, making the seat in front of me tremble until the man sitting in it turns around and gives me the full force of his lizard-like glare. I try to stop, but my body can't stop being scared right now because of the serious fear in the Dark Energy.

"What is all the thumping that's happening under the plane?" I ask.

"They're just loading up the luggage," Liria says.

The intercom springs to life, which makes me twitch. A woman comes on and says that they're closing the doors, that we're being locked in this plastic womb filled with farts and bad breath, and that we'll be taking off soon into thin air. A flight attendant stands in the aisle and tells us all the ridiculous things we need to do when the plane crashes. I get a very vivid image of all our lifeless corpses dangling from the ceiling of the plane, held aloft by those little yellow oxygen masks. I wonder if that's why they put them there, so that the bodies are all lined up neatly like shirts in a closet and easier to collect after a crash. Or maybe they just fill the masks with poison gas when the plane is going down, to save people from having to experience their guts being splattered across three square miles of the earth's crust.

Liria leans closer to me, running her hand all the way from my shoulder to my fingertips now. "It's all right, Justin."

"I think something bad is going to happen."

"Nothing bad is going to happen," Liria says. "You're just scared because it's your first time on a plane."

"There is a lot of fear in the Dark Energy right now."

"I don't feel it." She presses her cheek into my shoulder. "The fear isn't in the Dark Energy, it's in you. Try to…try to let the fear go, okay?"

I take a deep breath of the animal-smelling air, and get a comforting whiff of Liria's sandalwood and cloves. "Letting the fear go sounds like an extremely good idea," I say.

The plane engine turns on with a sound like we're inside a huge vacuum. We jerk into motion and back out of our parking spot, just like a car.

We drive around the runway for a while, turning corners and going in circles as Liria holds me and strokes my skin. I keep taking deep breaths, but the plane just keeps turning around and around and it's annoying because I just want the plane to crash and get it over with. "Are we lost?" I ask. "Are we looking for the right road out of here?"

Liria giggles, but the man in front of me turns and glares at me again, sending spears of anger through the Dark Energy. I can feel the mutters and agitation all around me.

"The pilot knows the way out of here, don't worry," Liria says.

We stop. The engine whines, then all of the sudden we are hurtling forward with roaring, rushing speed. I'm pushed backward into my seat, and I try to see the giant, invisible hand that's doing it, but I can't.

The nose of the plane tips up. There's a weird floaty feeling, and the invisible hand withdraws. Outside the little plastic window, the ground retreats beneath us. Everything gets smaller and smaller, the tiny waves on the bay shrinking, the streets turning into lines on a grid filled in with bushy green trees and the square roofs of houses. Then wispy, damp cloud fingers caress my window, and we are up and through them, their white tops gleaming brightly in the morning sunshine.

It is hard to believe I am above the clouds. My heart thumps in my open chest. I have forgotten to be scared anymore. "This is very amazing," I say, and Liria smiles.

"I'm glad you like it," she says.

But the man in front of me is still not happy. I can feel his tight fury in the Dark Energy. My body is still and quiet now, but I think I jostled him too much already with my jitters. He pokes an orange button above him on the ceiling. It has a stick figure of a person on it, and I wonder if it's the humanity button. I wonder you become more of a person by pressing it, because it seems like that's what he needs right now. I gaze up at my own button, and I raise my finger toward it, because it would be interesting to know what that feels like.

Liria snatches my hand away and holds it. She sends me a sidewise glance that looks both frightened and like she wants to laugh. "Don't," she whispers.

The man in front is still sending scowling glances at me, and soon one of the flight attendant women comes down the aisle.

"Keep him quiet, Christina," Arty mutters, and Liria squeezes my hand. It looks like I have caused more trouble in everyone's lives again.

"Liria, can flight attendants call the police?" I whisper. "Am I going to be arrested?" I imagine a cop plane zooming up alongside us with its lights and sirens blaring. See the air cops hauling me out the window in handcuffs, and having to teeter over the wing and jump across the vast void below and into their plane. It is not something I want to have happen.

Liria smirks. "No, Justin, don't worry."

The flight attendant leans toward the angry man. "What can I help you with, sir?"

He cranes his neck around and his rheumy eyes fix on me, bleeding hatred. "I'd like a new seat. This guy keeps kicking me and screaming about how the plane's going to crash."

The attendant looks at me. Other people around us are looking at me as well, and I twist the hem of my shirt.

"He's not screaming about anything," Arty says in a calm voice. "And he's just tall. Every time he moves, it jostles the seat, but he can't help it."

I watch Arty, because she is very adept at controlling the Dark Energy, and it's fascinating, actually. The flight attendant glances at me before looking back at the angry man.

"He is quite tall, and I can see why that would be a problem. The flight is pretty full, I'm afraid. I'll try to cut a deal with one of the people in the bulkhead and see if I can get them to switch seats with him so he won't bother anyone."

The man's face blooms red. "Oh no. I don't want some mental defective like that sitting in the exit row. Give *me* the bulkhead seat."

The woman's face goes blank. "Sir, please calm down. I'm going to go see what I can do to get this situation resolved."

The elderly lady sitting next to the angry man

peers at me through the crack between the seats. "I don't mind switching seats with this gentleman next to me," she says. "It wouldn't bug me to be jostled a little. The young man can't help that he's tall."

"I don't want to sit in the middle seat," the angry man says.

The attendant's face goes even blanker so that I'm afraid it's going to create a vacuum of expression that could suck other people's faces in. "Let me see what I can do," she says, and stalks off toward the back.

"I'm a lot of trouble in people's lives," I say. I glance around me nervously. "I'm surrounded, Liria."

Liria runs her fingertips lightly up and down my arm again.

"You're less trouble than some people," Arty mutters, and the man whips around to face her.

"I heard that, honey. Hey, it's not my fault you're traveling with some oversized headcase. Why should I have to pay for it?" His eyes graze over my face, and all of the sudden I see him clearly. I feel a sick fear. It's taking me over, and I'm panicking. I can't breathe.

"Liria," I say. "This man has the sickness. He has the sickness, Liria."

Her eyes take me in, going wide. The man and Arty are saying more ugly things to each other, and the sound of it is like drinking a cup of vomit. "Look at me, Justin," Liria murmurs. "Look at me, and don't pay any attention to him."

But I can't help it. He's so loud, and his dirty vibrations are covering me. "Liria," I say, and she takes me in her arms, pressing my face into her soft neck.

"Hush, Justin."

"I need out of here."

"I've got you, you're safe," she says.

The sickness washes over me. I can feel it pulling at me, and I press my face harder into Liria's warm skin.

The flight attendant is back. "Sir," she says calmly. "We have a seat in the back that we're going to move you to now."

"Yes please," I mutter. "Yes, go away, please." Liria strokes my head. The man complains some more, making the Dark Energy writhe with his gross vibrations. It is going to take me. I am going to lose and it is going to be horrible. I can feel death around me. Death and failure with their clinging stench.

Liria starts whispering in my ear, drowning out the sick man's nauseating arguments. She talks about the tall grass and the gurgling stream in the Other Place meadow. She reminds me about the fish on wheels. I concentrate on her tickling, whispering voice, and my grip on my knees loosens, my neck muscles unravel. Her voice pushes back the vibrations of sickness. She talks about how one day the vulture businessmen will fly away and we'll be alone in that peaceful place.

The man in front of us starts demanding they upgrade him to first class. My stomach starts to knot again, his diseased aura pushing back, but Liria's breath in my ear washes me clean. She is my protection. She is the antidote for the sickness, and it can't touch me when she's around. I take a deep breath of her sandalwood and cloves, and let it out.

Another flight attendant comes over. They have to threaten the man with legal action before he agrees to switch seats. As he roughly grabs his carry-on and stalks back toward the rear, I finally can take a completely clean breath.

In fact, I feel a sigh of relief going up all around. There is even some applause, and the man across the aisle gives Arty a high-five. The sickness retreats, and the ripples in the Dark Energy gradually smooth out. I sit up and look at Liria.

"Are you okay?" she asks, her brown eyes full of concern.

"Liria," I say. "You are so wonderful."

Her cheeks turn a little pink.

The flight attendant comes back and smiles at me, but it isn't a happy smile. "I'm sorry about all the commotion," she says. "I understand that you're tall, and that's not your fault, but do try to minimize how much you impact the seat in front of you."

"I will certainly try," I say.

She nods, giving all three of us a furrowed-brow look, and bustles off toward the back.

I am exhausted now, and eventually, the hum of the airplane's engine soothes me into a doze.

I have muddled dreams about having to paint the entire inside of the airplane, crawling around in all its tight spaces to get every square inch. I have to paint it just right, or we'll lose cabin pressure and the oxygen masks will attack us, like a many-tentacled kraken. I work very quickly and carefully. I paint a hatchway underneath my seat, a wooden one with a carved handle, and as I finish it, it opens.

A man sticks his head out, glancing around the cabin of the airplane. It's Lee Harvey, Liria's friend that died. "What's going on up here?" he asks.

I am jerked awake by the crackle of the pilot coming onto the intercom. My heart startles into a dead run, but then I realize he is just announcing we're beginning our descent and not something more terrifying. My stomach drops out from under me, and it feels like I'm floating again.

Liria sits up, stretching and rubbing her nose, and I can see the layers of sleep peeling from her. Arty is working on her laptop. She doesn't spend very much time sleeping I don't think.

I'm sticky and rumpled, and I try to stretch my legs without disturbing the new person in front of me. The plane plunges through broken clouds, and I see rows and jumbles of tiny buildings stretching out for forever below us, the afternoon sun glinting off its millions of windows. It looks like a Zen garden; the streets are rake lines amongst the pebbles. Away in the distance, a thick forest of skyscrapers rises. Arty points out the Statue of Liberty standing in the shining harbor before our plane swoops down low and touches the ground with a bump.

The happiness of being back on solid earth again soaks up through my toes. We file out of the airplane like cows up the ramp to the slaughterhouse, though I hope our experience will actually end up being better than that. I keep my eyes on my flopping shoelaces so I don't see the man with the sickness again.

The sickness-man and the dreams about Lee Harvey and the butterfly have given me the jitters. I'm worried about what the Dark Energy has in store for us.

We escape into the bustling airport, where we gather up our complicated luggage again and pile all of it and us into a cab.

We drive for a while. Arty sits up front and argues with the cab driver about routes, because arguing is just the way she makes conversation, I think. I stare out the window at a city with neighborhoods that stretch on and on and on, bigger than ten San Franciscos put together.

We pull down a street lined with twisty-branched trees, and the driver pulls over. We are in front of a brick apartment building, six stories stacked up in layers of arched windows and topped with concrete filigree. We offload our luggage. It forms an immense pile on the sidewalk, and I stand staring at it. It has been harassing me for two days and I feel like it is my arch enemy. I'm not sure how to defeat it.

"Liria, stay down here with this stuff while Justin and I carry boxes up," Arty says.

"Where are we?" Liria asks, looking around her. "I thought we'd be in a hotel?"

"We're staying in one of my dad's empty rentals."

Liria gives her an incredulous scowl. "Your dad's…"

"It's perfectly safe. Come on, Justin."

I feel a prickle of fear about Arty's father, but I don't have time to think about it because Arty is staring at me. She and I pick up two of the big boxes of paintings, which hardly defeats the pile at all. She leads me into the front entrance of the apartments while Liria watches the pile in case it makes any sudden moves or tries to get bigger when we're not looking.

Two men are sitting on a red velvet sofa in the lobby, and they watch us as we go by. They are talking about a film festival, and the way they talk is a little strange. I realize I am much further from home than I've ever been.

We get in the elevator and take the boxes up to the third floor, lug them out into a dim, wood-floored hallway and down to a door at the end. Arty sets down the box and fishes a key out of her slacks. The knob is made of iron, and the lock clicks solidly when she opens it.

The apartment smells a little bit musty, but it is very nice. I set my box down and wander around the place. It is sort of like Liria's and mine back in San Francisco, with an open kitchen and wood floors, except this one has two bedrooms and a big clawfoot tub in the bathroom. It has furniture already in it, a big sectional sofa and a marble-topped coffee table, beds and dressers in the bedrooms.

We bring up the rest of the boxes and luggage, until we are sweaty and grumpy about it. Liria helps us with the last load. When she gets into the apartment she puts the suitcase down and stands looking around with crossed arms. I can tell she likes the place, but isn't about to say anything.

Arty sighs, shoving her hands in her pockets.

"I'm starving. Liria, let's go get some takeout while Justin gets started on a new painting."

Liria wrinkles her nose. "Jesus, let him rest, Arty. And you don't need my help getting takeout."

She raises her eyebrows. "I can't carry all that food. And you always get pissed at me if I get the wrong thing."

"I would like to paint right now," I say, "but I don't mind people being here while I paint."

Liria gives me a little smile. Arty raises her eyebrows. "What, you'd rather stare at him painting than take a walk with me? I'll be good. I swear."

Liria taps her foot rapidly on the wood floor, then sighs and rolls her eyes. "Okay, but I get to pick the place."

"That's the spirit," Arty says.

They go out, and I open the box with the blank canvases and select a three-by-four-foot one. My easel is in there too, and I set it up. I run my fingers over the blank face of the canvas.

I wonder if I will get to go to art school, like everyone keeps saying I should. Stewart says art school isn't really like regular school, so it might not be so scary for me. He says people who know a lot about painting and drawing would show me different ways to do it; that they would teach me more art magic so that my pictures have more presence in the Physical World. And they'd show me how to do things like stretch my own canvases.

I dig in my box of paints and decide to use both watercolors and acrylics, because the Dark Energy wants me to paint the butterfly from the Other Place. The background needs to be in watercolors, and the images in the television-screen eyes, too, but the outlines of the butterfly need to be in acrylics.

I am just getting started when there is a knock on the door.

My brush freezes over the canvas, my blood pounding through my veins. These knocks on the door are always ominous. I'm thinking it might be the goons Liria was talking about. In fact, I don't know who else it could possibly be. No one else probably knows we're here yet.

I grip the brush tightly, because I don't know what other types of demons could be in New York. What if it is the sickness-man from the plane? It's possible that the Dark Energy sent him here to finish me off.

There is the sound of a key in the lock, and the door pops open. My heart struggles in my chest. Footsteps clomp on the wood floors, coming toward me. I hold my brush up like a sword, but I don't think I could hurt anyone very badly with a paintbrush, even if I poked them very hard.

A man comes in, and stops when he sees me, looking surprised. He is short, with thinning brown hair brushed back from a wide forehead. He has very intelligent eyes, and they are a light green color. They are Arty's eyes, the way they looked before she started wearing the brown contact lenses. "You're Arty's father, I think," I say. My heart is still beating very fast, because apparently, this man is a mob boss. I don't know if he's going to put on his sunglasses, stick a toothpick between his teeth, then mow me down with a tommy gun.

He doesn't do that. "You must be the painter," he says. "What's your name again? Jeremy something?"

"Justin Flaherty."

"Justin. That's right. I'm Morton Kopanis." He looks me up and down, and his eyes fall on the paintbrush, which I still have raised in front of me. He grins. "Relax, kid, and put that thing away before someone gets hurt."

He goes in and flops down on the couch, sighing. I hesitate a moment, then put my brush down and stand there twisting the hem of my button-down shirt between my fingers. Morton jerks his chin toward one of the armchairs. "Sit down. You're making me nervous."

I settle into a blue linen wingchair and clutch the armrests while he gazes at me.

"Where're Arty and Liria?" he asks. "They on some romantic date?"

"No. They went to get some takeout."

"Speak up, kid, I can hardly hear you."

"No," I say, more loudly this time. "They went to—"

Morton cuts me off, waving a hand. "Naw, I heard you. But Jesus, for such a big, good-looking guy you're sure meek." He stares at me a moment, smirking. "That probably works out for you, though. Women love wimpy, dreamy-eyed creative types. I'll bet they flock around like pigeons. I'll bet guys like you can just sit back and let women do all your fighting for you."

I clutch the armrests harder. Morton reminds me a lot of his daughter. "I don't enjoy fighting, Mr.

Kopanis, and I don't try to get anyone to fight for me." But I am thinking of Mina and Rebekah, and Liria and Arty, and it occurs to me that they have all fought for me or about me in one way or another, and this makes my stomach hurt.

Morton smirks harder as if he's read that thought, and it makes me very nervous that maybe he has. "Sure, sure," he says. "I wouldn't break character if I were you, either. It's best to maintain the illusion at all costs."

"What illusion is happening?" I look around me, but everything seems like the normal Physical World to me. Morton's eyes go squinty and he gets a weird smile. I pick at a seam on the armrest, and am very happy to hear the door open, and hear Arty and Liria's voices, because this man is very strange.

Arty seems to be telling a story about trying to buy a scarf, which is somehow funny enough to make Liria laugh. I suddenly feel very strange and alone. Their voices wash in like an ocean wave, crashing against me, sparkling and playing, but I am just a rock stuck here staring at Morton Kopanis.

When they walk into the living room and see us, they fall abruptly silent. Liria goes very pale, and looks away from Morton, her lips tight. Arty fills up with anger too, because it seems like this man is an air pump of bad feelings.

Morton turns in his seat to look at Arty, and his eyebrows shoot up so fast I wonder if his nose exploded. "Jesus Christ. Nice tits, Fireball. How much to have those things installed? And did they just put the old ones in the Goodwill bargain bin, or what?"

"Hi Dad," Arty says. "Nice to see you." She goes into the kitchen and slams her bags of food on the breakfast bar. Liria follows her silently and starts getting plates out of the cupboards.

"I'm serious, you look great," he says, then glances over at me. "She looks great, right? Much better than before."

"I think she looked just fine before," I say, and Morton waves his hand at me again.

"Aw, keep it up, kid. I'm sure you'll get laid someday, although I think you're wasting your talents in this case."

Arty pounds her fists on the countertop, making the plates rattle. "Holy Jesus, Dad, do you ever, *ever* fuck off?"

Morton's mocking scowl melts off his face, and he blinks. "Settle down, Arty, I didn't mean anything by it."

"The fuck you don't mean anything by it. Insult me to my face, and then insult the poor kid when he stands up for me. Real fucking classy."

"I'm not trying to insult anybody. Just comes as a surprise, is all. I didn't know you'd gotten yourself renovated."

"What, you expected me to just strut into town, dropping calling cards at all my old friends' houses? Maybe invite Zuhzuh over for dinner?"

"With you, I never know. You've done stupider things."

"I wouldn't put Liria in danger like that," she says.

Morton and Arty have a staring contest, and Morton's eyebrows rise higher and higher until

Arty's gaze drops to her plate. She angrily slops food onto it, splattering it everywhere. My fingers burrow like moles into the armrests. I am really jealous of my chair, actually, because being an inanimate object sounds great right now.

"Why are you here, Dad?" Arty says.

"Thought I'd stop by, see how you were doing. Jeez, Fireball, you're my daughter. And I wanted to see what all the fuss was about." His eyes dart over to me, because I am the fuss-creating force in the room, apparently. I shift in my seat. If I have the power to create more fuss than this man, I probably should work hard at rearranging my vibrations.

Arty sighs heavily and stomps into the living room with her food. Liria frowns and slowly scoops food onto her own plate. "We got you some tofu and eggplant, Justin." Her voice is very small.

I want to say thank you, but I'm afraid to make any noise. I don't want to announce the fact that I exist right now and risk creating more turbulence. Arty flops cross-legged on the couch with the plate on her lap, and the tension in the room springs my body up out of the chair and into the kitchen.

I let out a breath when I am behind the dividing half-wall and out of sight of Arty and Morton. The seething silence coming from the living room is louder than if they were still fighting. Liria is taking a long time to serve herself, stirring food around in the containers, and I stand very close to her because it's comforting. "Liria," I say very quietly. "I think Morton Kopanis is crazy."

Liria stops stirring. Her lips twist up and she hides her face in her hands, stifling a snort. "That's

53

the truth." Her hands fall from her face and her smile melts away. She starts stirring the food again.

"Are you okay?" I ask.

"I'm okay." She tugs one of the food containers toward me. "This one's the tofu."

I spoon some up with some rice, and we go out into the living room, where Morton is staring at his daughter. She is eating her food and staring at her cellphone.

Liria and I sit down together on the sofa. Morton gazes at us thoughtfully, stroking his round chin. "This is interesting," he says. "Some real interesting romantic stuff going on here."

Liria and I look at each other and realize that our legs are touching. We jerk away from one another.

Arty lets out a sigh that sounds like it was mangled in transport. "Dad…"

"Is this the guy you've chosen to stud your babies? Because if so, I'd like to register my protest."

Liria goes very stiff and hunches over her plate. Arty stares at her father, clutching her fork in a way that makes me very scared that she is going to stab him with it. Violence is taking up all the room in here and crowding us all against the walls, and so it takes a while for what Morton has said to sink into my brain. When it does, I put down my fork. "You're misunderstanding what's going on here, Mr. Kopanis," I say. "It's certainly not anyone's intention for me to father any babies."

They are all staring at me now. Liria is still hunched over her plate, but she is looking sideways at me and hiding a smile. Arty has a very strange, wide-eyed look, and suddenly both she and her father start to laugh. The tension in the Dark Energy loosens a little.

"Jesus, kid, you're something else," Morton says.

"He's got a point, though," Arty says, her grin fading. "You're being a fuckass."

"I'm just asking," he says.

"Justin's here to paint, and he's really damn good at it. He's nobody's stunt cock, but even if he were, it'd be none of your fucking business."

Morton shrugs. "Just wondering."

"Yeah, I'm sure you were," Arty says. "I'm sure the rat in your brain is always running on his little wheel a mile a minute."

He rubs his eyes with his fingertips. "Can't blame a guy for being observant." Then he sighs and folds his hands in his lap. "I'm not here to fight with you, Fireball. I'd like to see the kid's paintings, when you're done eating."

Arty sets her plate down, although she's hardly eaten anything. "I'm done. They're in here, but we'll have to take them out of the boxes."

They go into the other room and I can hear them talking and rummaging, the crinkling of packing paper. The tension slowly drains out of the room. Liria stays with me on the couch. She's picking at her food and looking sad again. "This is an upsetting situation," I whisper. "I think it's upsetting for you also."

Her lips twist gently, and her gaze darts to mine. She presses closer against my side, and I put an arm around her.

"Will you tell me why you're upset?" I say.

"I'll tell you later," she murmurs.

"Justin, come in here," Arty calls.

Liria and I look at each other.

I get up and walk into the back room feeling like a man going to a very bad dentist appointment. I imagine being strapped to a dentist's chair while Arty and her father argue and angrily work on my teeth, and I realize I have stopped in the hallway and am twisting my shirt to pieces. I take a deep breath and go in.

Arty and her father are gazing at my big painting. He looks up at me when I walk in, and his expression is different than when he was looking at me before. "This is incredible," he says. "I mean, it's fucking weird as shit, but Jesus."

"Thank you," I say, because I'm fairly certain he was trying to give me a compliment.

He asks me to explain to him what it is exactly, and so I try to, though it's hard to explain this one without talking about the Dark Energy. I feel like Morton is one of those people who's probably very strict about that taboo, and he might react extremely badly if I broke it. So I just say all the art-people words like perspective and surrealism. He raises his eyebrows and nods, and I think I've passed the test.

I have to talk about the paintings for a long time as Arty pulls them out of the box one by one. When we get to the drawing of Liria that I did of her before we met up again, where she is on the floor of the Other Place house watching the ceiling movie, Morton gets very insistent that he's taking it home with him.

"Bidding on that one is currently at thirty-five hundred," Arty says. "I think I could get at least five for it here in New York, likely more after the show, but I'll be generous and let you have it for five."

"What, for a tiny fucking pencil drawing?"

"They're already writing him up in the *Times* and the goddamn *New Yorker*, Dad, and he's only had his work out in public a few fucking days."

They exchange a long look. Morton's eyes keep darting to me. "Jesus," he mutters.

They start to haggle about the painting. Their words are like bullets I have to duck to avoid. Eventually, I realize that they have forgotten I'm there, so I sneak back to the couch.

Liria's plate of cold food is sitting on the coffee table, and she's staring at the walls. I sit next to her and put my arms around her. I can feel her trembling, and I wonder what's wrong, but I don't ask again. I just hold her, rocking slightly back and forth like she does with me when I'm upset.

"I want to get high really bad, Justin," she says. Her voice shakes and I can feel her tears on my shoulder.

"Being high would make you feel better, is what you mean," I say, and she nods.

"Yeah. I just...I'm not doing very well right now."

"That heroin wasn't healthy for you and just made you hide all of the time in the Other Place and eat nothing but sugar. And it made you so sick when you didn't take it." I clutch her tighter. "I want to be able to make you feel better, so that you don't want it anymore."

She puts her arms around me and buries her face in my chest, taking deep breaths. "You do make me feel better."

I'm thinking that my powers of making her feel good apparently are sort of lacking right now when we hear the footsteps of Arty and her father in the hallway. Liria sits up, wiping her eyes, and I take my arms from around her.

Arty comes into the room and catches sight of her, with her red eyes and blotchy face. Her lips press together, and she turns to Morton. "Dad, we've got work to do here. Why don't you and I go out to dinner tomorrow or something?"

"All right, all right, Fireball."

She herds him out the door with more arguing, then comes and flops down into a chair, sighing. "I'm really sorry, Liria."

"It's not your fault," Liria says, drying her eyes on her shirt.

Arty grimaces. "I hate that fucking cuntbag."

Arty and Liria watch cartoons for the rest of the evening, because I think Arty knows that's a good way to cheer Liria up. I work on my painting of the butterfly, which is disturbing, but I know it is a thing I need to do because if I don't face him down, he might sneak up and attack me again. His huge eyes tower above me. The commercial images flash and flicker: women with long, lean legs; men smiling and patting dogs on the head; children scrambling through the kitchen to the breakfast table.

With a flash, that steely-thick coiled tongue lashes. I dodge aside, and it hits three inches from my feet with a deep, dead thump. I back up as the tongue worms along the ground, which is blank and white like porcelain. The tongue is searching for me, feeling its way along. The little black rubbery lips on the end nibble and taste the smooth surface. I realize the butterfly can't see me very well because of the images in its eyes.

I have to paint faster. I have to paint obstacles, or the butterfly will find me. And if it finds me, it will find Liria too.

I am startled back into the Physical World when Liria comes and says goodnight. She stands looking at the painting for a little while with a little open-mouthed smile, then wanders off to one of the bedrooms.

Arty is yawning as well. "You take the other bedroom," I tell her. "I'll sleep on the couch, because I want to stay up and paint."

She stands and stretches, then comes over to look at the canvas as well. She gazes at it, tapping her finger on her new, pouty lips. "That's fucking weird." She laughs. "Butterfly monster."

"Yes," I say.

"With stacks of televisions and…are those mayonnaise jars?"

"When I get all the labels done they'll be condiments of all kinds." I'm not sure how condiments can be an effective obstacle, but somehow they're appropriate. "What gives the obstacles their defensive power is this little valentine heart, though." I point with the tip of my brush at the little heart-shaped scrap of faded red construction paper lying on the ground at the butterfly's feet. I still can't find the memory of what it means in my brain.

I can feel Arty looking at me as I run the brush over the canvas. "It's amazing. You've been working on it for like six hours now, though. Don't stay up too late. We have a big day tomorrow."

I tell her I won't, and she goes off to bed.

I paint for another hour or so, then curl under the blankets on the couch.

I fall into the Other Place almost immediately, and find myself in a supermarket, its shelves piled high with gray lemons and odd-shaped pineapples and packages of products. The label on one box reads **"Blazing Innards,"** and another canister announces **"Orange You Glad."** Liria is pushing a cart down at the other end of the aisle. Beside her is that dead friend of hers, Lee Harvey.

Anger nibbles at my brain with its piranha teeth, because he is back again. He won't leave her alone. I stalk down the aisle toward them, and they turn to look at me as I approach. Lee Harvey smiles. He is wearing a cowboy hat and overalls. "Look who's here," he says.

Their cart is full of odd-shaped packages wrapped in white plastic. Their labels read things like "Superior great drugs" and "Blissful high."

Liria gazes vacantly at the shelves.

"You don't need this stuff," I say.

She blinks at me. I don't think she's seeing me correctly. I don't think she's all the way here. I put a hand on her shoulder. "Liria, look at me."

She looks over at my hand, and then at me, frowning. The haze dissolves from her eyes and she smiles a little bit. "Justin," she says.

Her gaze slides over to Lee Harvey, and her smile panics and flees. Lee Harvey's skin is shrinking over his bones. His eyes cloud over yellow and opaque, and his flesh fades to a dead blue. Thick, black blood drizzles slowly from a corner of his mouth.

Liria screams. I startle awake, and she is still screaming.

I jump up and untangle myself from the blanket, then go running into her room. She has stopped screaming and started crying.

I crawl into bed with her, and I wrap her in my arms. "It's okay, Liria."

"It was Morton," she says between sobs. "Arty's dad was the one who had Lee Harvey killed."

I hush her and stroke her hair and let her cry, all the while feeling the Dark Energy's net tightening around us.

Chapter 4

The sun washes over my eyelids and pulls me to the surface of my dreams. I open my eyes. The new surroundings shout in surprise until they remember who I am and why I'm here.

I roll over. The light falls across Liria's sleeping face. It is peaceful now, all its curves soft and graceful. I want to trace them with my finger. But I don't, because that's a social dance violation and would also wake her up.

Her hair has dark brown roots where it is growing out from the blue. I remember how it used to look when I first met her, thick and long and almost black, falling in waves to her shoulders. She was beautiful even then, even when she was pale and sick, shriveled and twisted from the drugs.

I've always wondered what exactly happened in that time between when I met her in the park and when we found each other again in San Francisco, and now I know that Morton had her friend Lee Harvey killed during that time. I wonder how complicated it must be to be in love with the daughter of your best friend's murderer.

My stomach churns like a cement mixer. Morton Kopanis is very bad news. He is pacing circles around us now, waiting for his chance to strike. I wonder that a man like that can walk around like a normal person. I start to wonder what it is like for the Dark Energy to make you kill someone, but I quickly build a brick wall so those thoughts smack into it and shatter. I can't think about it, because it's too horrible.

I hope the Dark Energy will not tell Morton to kill me, or Liria. This thought jitters me up so I can't lie here any longer. Arty is banging around in the kitchen and I smell coffee, which is a smell that fits into all the right places in my brain and so I know I need a cup of it right now. I slip out of the warm blankets.

My mind is so full of things to think about that it's not until I walk into the kitchen and get caught in Arty's dangerous look that I realize I am coming out of Liria's bedroom.

I freeze, my bare toes curling in fright against the cold, wooden floor. "She had a bad dream. She was screaming."

Arty clutches the coffee pot in one hand, a cup in the other, and I watch them closely so I can duck if she hurls them. That wouldn't be fatal I don't think, but it would hurt very badly.

She throws blunt words instead. "Are you fucking her, Flaherty?"

I press my toes into the floor. "No, Arty, I'm not doing that."

Her surgically-crafted nostrils flare, and she

flexes her fingers on the coffee pot handle. "But you love her."

I wrap my arms around myself. I wonder if this is one of those times when the Dark Energy wants me to tell a lie. But I realize that I can't, anyway. "Yes, Arty," I say.

She stands there with her lips pressed tight together. Her chest heaves, the movement of it amplified because of her plastic-stuffed breasts. The Dark Energy scampers into the nooks and crannies and peeks out with frightened eyes, wondering what she is going to do, but I don't move, because there is nowhere I can really run, actually. I am in this situation with Arty and there's nothing I can do about it.

She lets out a pained breath and slams the coffee pot and mug onto the counter. The contents slosh out and splatter the granite. She hides her face in her hands, and she is trembling just a little bit.

It takes me a moment to realize that I am probably not going to die right now. It takes me another moment to realize that I am actually feeling sorry for Arty.

"Arty, are you okay?" I ask.

She makes a noise like a frog falling into a pot of mashed potatoes. I'm not sure what that means.

"I don't want to fight with you about Liria," I say. "It's a pointless fight for us to have. She loves you, but you've hurt her very badly. She loves me, I think, but not in that way, because I'm a man. Us fighting with each other won't change any of that and will just upset everyone."

After a while, she takes her hands away from her

face. Her contacts are out, and her eyes are green again. They are clear and don't have tears in them, but I can see feelings hiding in there. I think even Arty's own feelings are too scared of her to come out. Her mouth quirks slightly. "How are you…how can you even…?" She shakes her head and blows a breath out her nose. "I used to think this Gandhi Jesus thing you have going on was an act, but it's not, is it? You just…you're just never angry about anything."

"That's not true," I say. "But I try to keep it behind the wall as much as possible. Anger makes the Dark Energy horrible and doesn't accomplish anything."

She stands studying me. A tiny, wry smile creeps into her lips. "That's it, right? It's because you're a fucking nutjob. Anger makes you pass out or whatever, so you avoid it at all costs." She examines my face and winces. "I'm sorry, Justin. I'm acting like my fucking dad."

I shuffle my feet. "I'm extremely used to people calling me crazy, but I don't know why not wanting to be angry makes me crazy."

"You're right, you know." She opens the cupboard above her head, gets down another cup and pours it full of coffee. "Have some coffee with me. We have to go meet these New York art creatures in a few hours."

I take my coffee and follow her into the sunny living room. We settle onto the couch. Arty sits cross-legged with her long, freckled feet showing under the hems of her baggy pajama bottoms. It is strange to be sitting like this with Arty. It feels a little like sitting down for coffee with a case of nitroglycerine. I keep very still so she doesn't suddenly explode.

"Let me tell you about this woman who owns the gallery where you're going to have your show," she says. "She's about as different from Stewart as you can get. It's like she auditioned for the part of some bizarre, intense New York art gallery owner, and got it, even though she overacts a little."

"That sounds slightly frightening," I say, and Arty snorts into her mug.

"Don't let her scare you. She's really interested in your art—she had to compete with three other galleries to get this show—so you have the upper hand." Arty taps her short, raspberry-painted fingernails against her coffee mug, and I wonder if the flavor they give off makes her coffee taste like raspberries. "I've never seen word about anything spread so fast in my life as I have about your art. It's crazy."

"Maybe it's because my own crazy transmitted its vibrations into the Dark Energy and boosted the signal," I say.

Arty's lips twitch. Liria's bed squeaks, and Arty looks over her shoulder as Lira pads out of the bedroom.

Liria stops in the mouth of the hallway and looks back and forth between the two of us, a slight crease between her brows. "Hey." A faint question mark flavors the word.

"Good morning," Arty says, sipping her coffee.

"Morning," Liria says, her gaze lingering on me.

"I'm sorry you had nightmares last night," Arty

says, then she slaps herself on the knees. "We should all get dressed and go have breakfast so we can get today's living nightmare started."

***

It is around noon by the time we get my pictures packed back in their boxes and catch a cab down to the gallery. It is on the ground floor of a tall building of weathered brick, across from a little park rioting with orange-and-yellow flowers. There are lots of people on the sidewalks, clustered around in little groups or alone. More people sit at tables in the open-air cafes. It is a little like San Francisco, but the vibrations are different.

We lug our boxes inside. The gallery is much bigger than Stewart's. It has huge windows facing the park. The ceilings are high and edged in plaster molding, and the walls are white-painted brick. There is a maze of inner walls here too, like at Stewart's gallery, only more elaborate and extensive.

The space feels huge and warm, and has a good smell like old wood and hidden dust. I think the walls and floor have been together so long that the barely have to whisper their secrets to each other anymore, and can nestle together in companionable silence.

As we carry in the last boxes, a middle-aged woman in slacks and a sleeveless blouse strides toward us. Her sleek brown hair has a streak of gray in the front, and billows behind her as if caught in the great gale of her forceful energy.

A handful of other people scurry after her. She somehow makes them look small, even though a couple of them are taller and bigger than she is. Her astute eyes take us all in, and she smiles at Arty. "You must be Iris Pierson," she says, and it takes me a moment to figure out that this must be Arty's fake name. I am the only one without a fake name now, apparently.

Arty puts down the box she's carrying and clasps the woman's hand. "It's nice to finally meet you as well, Ms. Corinth," she says in a softer voice than normal. She gestures toward me in a graceful un-Arty-like way. "Let me introduce the artist, Justin Flaherty, and his friend Christina Guzman. Justin, Christina, this is Deborah Corinth, the gallery owner."

Even Arty's posture is different, more languid, and Liria and I exchange a glance. It is like we are suddenly traveling with a different person.

Ms. Corinth's gaze falls on me, her colorless lips forming a little "o" of surprise. Both Liria and I put down our boxes and shake her hand. One of Ms. Corinth's entourage, a young man with very black hair, steps forward. "Let us take those for you." He and all but three of the others scuttle away with them toward the back, then return for the ones we have piled up by the door.

One of the people who doesn't help is a short, bald man in a sport coat, who I recognize as the man from the *New York Times* I spoke with at my opening. The other two are young women in expensive-looking suits.

Ms. Corinth's eyes never leave mine. "You're

not at all what I expected, Justin." She keeps my hand after she finishes shaking it, enfolding it in both of hers.

"Thank you for having my paintings in your gallery, Ms. Corinth," I say, shifting on my feet. She gives a little start, then breaks into a grin, turning to look at the bald man.

He squints at me with a little smile. "How was I remiss in my description, Deborah?"

She laughs. "Well, I can't expect you to have an eye for a handsome and genteel young man, Dickon." She introduces the man as Dickon Rond, and I'm glad, because his name hadn't decided to stay in my head. She says the two well-dressed women beside him are Michelle Lalty and Tianna Tajo, who work for the *New Yorker*.

Ms. Corinth pats my hand. "I'm anxious to see these paintings of yours in person, Justin. Let's go take a look."

We follow her swaying hips toward the back of the gallery. She throws her hands around as if tossing rice at a wedding. "We're setting up your show in the best part of the gallery, over here." We stop in a section where the walls are bare, the delicate white paint glowing in the light from lamps hidden in the overhang.

"It will be very nice to see my pictures up here," I say.

"Yes," she says.

Three of the box-carriers, young men dressed in jeans and t-shirts, are unpacking the boxes now. Their vibrations are very art-student, which is a frequency I have learned to identify by hanging out with Stewart's employees. They lean my pictures against the wall and gaze at them, talking to each other in quiet voices, sending me little glances.

"Let me see," Ms. Corinth says.

Her minions obediently step back. She stands there, staring. They have laid out the big painting, the painting of Liria's struggles, and several of my drawings.

Dickon Rond comes to stand beside Ms. Corinth, wearing a faint grin as he glances between her and the paintings.

Finally, she lets out an elaborate sigh with musical notes in it, and Dickon chuckles.

"I may have neglected the handsome part but, as you can see, I didn't steer you wrong with regard to his work."

"I want to see more," she says.

Her minions resume unpacking the boxes, and Ms. Corinth swoops over and puts her arm around me, steering me over. I feel like I am a leaf being blown around by her hurricane. She wants me to "explain" all of the pictures, and how I painted or drew them, and so I get out the toolbox of art words I've learned lately and hammer them into long sentences that don't make much sense to me but seem to make sense to others. Ms. Corinth nods forcefully as she listens, as if my rambling is very important.

When I'm done saying all my words, her gaze falls on Liria.

"And you're the subject of this," she says, gesturing toward the painting of Liria's struggles.

Liria's cheeks tinge pink, and I think she's

remembering when I painted it, when she was horribly sick from quitting drugs. "Yes," she says.

"You're in several more of them as well," Dickon adds, raising his eyebrows.

"Are you two married?" Ms. Corinth asks.

I shift on my feet. "No. We're…"

"Roommates," Liria says hesitantly. "Best friends."

"Justin's single," Arty adds, her lips curling into a lazy tiger grin. "He and his girlfriend just broke up."

This statement makes me feel empty inside, and I wonder what sort of game Arty is playing with the Dark Energy, saying things like that in this atmosphere. I feel eyes on me, and look over to see they belong to the woman from the *New Yorker* named Tianna. They are so dark you can barely see the pupils, and ringed by long, thick lashes. She smiles at me, and I smile back.

Liria is watching me too. Her arms are crossed and she has a strange expression.

Chapter 5

Ms. Corinth stands watching two of her art student minions hang my butterfly painting on the wall. It is framed now, and looks very professional. Arty is excited about the idea of someone paying lots of money for it.

I can feel the money changing hands all around me. I can feel people watching and waiting for me to figure out what the Dark Energy is trying to communicate with all this. But I can't quite grasp the lesson. It just seems bizarre, that the Dark Energy would turn itself into a commodity, and so I'm frightened I'm going to fail this test.

"Okay, that's it," Ms. Corinth says as the painting aligns with perfect straightness. The minions step away, and she stands gazing at the picture for a long time. My show begins tomorrow and, unlike Stewart, Ms. Corinth's vibrations seem to smooth out the closer it gets. Her minions, however, are beginning to pop like popcorn.

"It's very beautiful," Tianna says, nodding toward the painting. I like her voice. It would be cozy for her to read me bedtime stories.

"Thank you," I say.

She regards me out of the corners of her dark eyes. "We've all been wondering whether you've considered going to art school."

"I'd like to, but it's very expensive," I say.

She grins but immediately sees I don't get whatever the joke is, and it fades. "I think you'd get a scholarship. But I'm not sure they could teach you anything you don't already know."

"That's not true," Michelle, the other woman from the *New Yorker,* says. "I'm sure there are things even Justin doesn't know." They smile at each other and stifle little giggles behind their hands.

Girls are always talking in their secret language, communicating things different from what they're saying. Sometimes I wonder if they have their own version of the Dark Energy, no boys allowed.

I stare at my feet and pick at the callous on my finger. "I don't even know how to stretch canvases or clean my brushes the right way." Their giggles die down, and I'm glad. "I have almost everything to learn about painting."

"I can teach you how to stretch canvases," Minion Annette says, smiling at me as she stands on a ladder positioning another hanger.

"That would be very nice," I say.

Liria is watching me, but looks away when I catch her at it. She has been drifting around lately on a cloud of her sad feelings, and she won't really let me join her there to talk about it. It is upsetting, but Arty has hoarded away all my time and only doles it out for sleep and art activities, so I haven't had much to use for talking to Liria. I'm worried she's angry with me for some reason, but maybe she's just stuck in a bad bubble of memories about Lee Harvey and Morton Kopanis.

I've finished another painting besides the butterfly this week, and also two drawings, because of how Arty has been keeping me caged up like a trick artist monkey. It's been a tense ordeal to make sure those are framed correctly and on time, because Ms. Corinth thinks there are so many different colors and styles of frame that go with them so very wonderfully, and so she keeps changing her mind about which she wants. When the frames are finally the correct ones the pictures are hung in their places, but then Ms. Corinth wants to see them hung in different places because of the beautiful lighting and something about them creating a narrative arc with other drawings. I think for a moment that she's going to build a boat with them like Noah did in the Bible, but that isn't apparently what that means because people are just hanging them on the walls like normal.

I am very tired now, but the butterfly painting is the last one that needs hung. We all watch as Ms. Corinth gazes at it, her lips moving silently along with the conversation she's having in her head. Everyone waits, and the Dark Energy is tough and buzzy with their furious hoping that she will finally be happy with things the way they are.

Ms. Corinth breaks into a grin. "Perfect. We've done it. We're ready for the show."

There is an explosion of breaths being let out,

and people clap and laugh about the relief they are feeling. Several people pat me on the back and shake my hand.

Tianna raises an eyebrow at me. Her eyebrows are very fascinating because of how perfect they are, like cartoon eyebrows. "Are you ready for our interview?"

I'm still picking at my callous, and I squeeze my hands together so I'll stop. "Yes." I glance over at Liria, who is staring at the butterfly painting but I can tell from her expression that she's not seeing it. "Can Christina come with me? I like having her there."

Liria blinks at the sound of her fake name, because I've called her back into the Physical World. She smiles at me, which makes me feel warm. She hasn't been smiling much lately.

But Arty raises her chin. "Actually, Christina, I need your help with something."

Liria's smile melts away. She lifts an eyebrow at Arty, and Arty stares back like a stone statue that you can't convince of anything. Liria's shoulders hunch, and she nods. An agitated creature made of frustration wallows in my chest. I am beginning to see that Arty is trying to keep Liria and me apart, and I wonder if it is the Dark Energy that wants it that way, or if it is just what Arty wants. Either way, I am not strong enough to paddle against that current and I'm not sure Liria even wants me to.

I follow Tianna and Michelle into an office in the back of the gallery. I feel like a balloon that has been released into the sky. Liria used to hold my string, but now I'm pushed around by the wind without anything to ground me. Everything is so strange here in New York, with all these art people and things going on.

Michelle and Tianna have me sit down behind a desk while they face me from the other side. It is a strange feeling, as if I am the boss of this situation, though I am very much not. The chair is the type that spins and has wheels, though, which is good.

"You're from San Francisco, right?" Tianna says. "But I believe I read in the *Chronicle* that you just moved there."

I push the chair back and forth in a half spin, which is relaxing. "Yes. I've only lived in San Francisco for a few weeks. I was in a small town called Piedras, in central California, before."

"Never heard of it," Tianna says.

"No," I say. "It is not a place one hears of."

She and Michelle laugh. "What shows did you have before the one in Stewart Califax's gallery in San Francisco?" Michelle asks.

"The one at Stewart's place was the first one I had ever."

Their eyebrows go up, and they exchange a glance. "Really?" Tianna says. "Wow, the *Chronicle* article said you were an unknown, but I didn't think they were being that literal. How did you get the show at Califax's then?"

The chair wheels squeak as my feet jitter on the floor. "My ex-girlfriend Mina's uncle knew Stewart, and she sent him photographs of my drawings." Hurt pangs through me when I say Mina's name.

Both women study me closely. "I've never

known anyone to get so popular so fast," Tianna says. "But, then again, I've never seen art like yours."

A little smirk curls Michelle's lips. Tianna glances at her, her eyes widening and her lips drawing tight. Michelle keeps smirking. There is a lot of girl social dance going on in this conversation, and I understand it even less than the regular social dance. "People seem to really like my pictures," is all I can think to say. The words hobble feebly out into the conversation, not sure they can keep up with Michelle and Tianna's silent communication, but the women seem to notice my words and take pity on them. They straighten up and become more serious.

They ask me questions about my education, and I have to tell them I don't even have my GED yet. Then the questions start to stray into Mom territory. They want to know more about my childhood because of the ridiculous things that Liria snuck into Paul Legrange's article. I start to wish even more that Liria were here, because she is comforting in these sorts of situations, but then again she would probably tell more stories that portray me as a little boy with a sad clown face. I twist in my chair.

"My childhood is more uneventful than Mr. Legrange would have you believe. I lived with Mom or Grandma in various places mostly in California. They didn't beat me or lock me in closets or anything."

"But your mom kicked you out of the house," Michelle says, leaning forward over her knees.

"Mom is a complicated person," I say.

"What about your dad? Where is he?" Michelle persists.

I have to stop myself picking a hole in the nice new slacks Arty bought me. "I never knew my father. He jumped in front of a train is what Mom says. That was when I was just a couple years old."

Michelle sits up again. Both the women are looking at me with faces full of pity even though I never knew my father and so I'm not any sadder about him dying than I would be about any other stranger. It is difficult to have the capacity to be upset about every person in the world who dies. I spin in my chair some more.

"I don't think we need to bug him about this," Tianna says. "We have enough for a good article."

"You're right," Michelle says.

Tianna smiles brightly. "We'll make sure lots of people come to your show, Justin."

"Thank you, that's very nice of you," I say.

Stewart has arrived at the gallery during the interview, and I am very happy to see him when I come out. There are so many new people, so it is nice to have someone else I know to try to catch my balloon-string. He gives me a huge smile, and clasps me into a warm hug. "Justin," he says, patting me on the back enthusiastically. "I saw the article about you in the *New York Times.*"

"It was a very nice article," I say. "Dickon is an extremely nice person. And he mentioned you in there too."

Stewart smiles a little embarrassed smile. I can tell he's really happy. "Dickon Rond isn't always an extremely nice person. You're just an extremely talented person."

"Everyone keeps saying that," I say.

Ms. Corinth declares that she's taking all of us out for Chinese food to celebrate, and I think that's a good thing because her employees need to be fed and appreciated so they don't start screaming like frustrated infants. She calls ahead to make a reservation, and then we all strut down the sidewalk in a chattering crowd because the place is just a few blocks down. I walk close to Liria. These art people make me slightly agitated. I want to take her hand, but she's got them stuffed in her pockets and it seems like she's not looking at me on purpose. Then Arty calls her over because she and Ms. Corinth want to ask her something, and the frustration creature in me kicks and twitches. I don't know what I did to make Liria mad, but I'll never get a chance to ask if Arty keeps yanking her away from me.

I wonder if Liria and Arty are getting back together. I wonder if that's what this is all about. That notion kicks me hard in the throat.

Tianna speaks at my elbow and I jump slightly because I hadn't noticed her there. "How do you like New York?"

"It's very big," I say when I catch my breath and find some words to say.

She laughs. She has a good, happy laugh. Her hair is black and bushy and hardly stirs in the hot breeze. I really want to touch it because it looks like it would feel very interesting.

"I came here from Chicago, but New York still seems big to me," she says. "It was a little overwhelming when I first came here."

Her smile makes me want to smile back. "New things overwhelm you with waves of strangeness sometimes, but there are always nice people you can grab onto so you don't get swept away."

Tianna's eyes crinkle up, and she throws her head back and laughs again, throwing happy notes into the Dark Energy. "Even the way you talk is art," she says.

We are at the restaurant now, and we crowd through the front door into an almost warehouse-sized room that smells of garlic and spices. There is shiny red-and-black-lacquered everything. The intense sizzling and pan-clanking and conversation almost completely covers the jazz music on the stereo.

There are fifteen of us, and they've had to push three tables together in the middle of the dining room to fit us all. There is a great deal of noise and jostling as we all find places. I want to grab Liria's hand to make sure she sits by me, but she is over at the other end of the crowd, still looking sullen. At the last second, she sees me looking at her, and jumps through the crowd confusion just in time to get the chair next to me before Annette does, which makes me feel very good.

We settle into our seats. "Christina, what's wrong?" I ask. Liria gives me a long look, shiny-eyed and almost scared. She shakes her head.

"I'm all right," she says. "It's nothing."

I know it's not nothing, and I wonder why she doesn't want to tell me. Fear dribbles through me like ice water. Maybe she wants to tell me she's back with Arty, even though she said she wouldn't ever be, and so she's embarrassed to say it. That would make me very upset, even though I have no right to feel that way.

Tianna sits on my other side. Stewart, Arty, and Ms. Corinth sit across from us. Ms. Corinth is talking loudly and laughing a lot. Arty and Stewart keep exchanging amused glances that they think no one notices.

Banter and discussion ensue about what we should order, because we're going to eat family-style. Arty tells everyone I'm vegetarian, which causes a commotion of teasing comments. I have to insist that I don't want to force-feed everyone tofu and that I'll be responsible for my own dish. There is more arguing and upheaval but finally, we've ordered our food and it's all taken care of, which is a relief.

"I'm not used to traveling in a herd like this," I say. "It is very noisy and difficult to find your direction without causing an accidental stampede."

Liria snorts, and Tianna chuckles.

"I didn't know you were vegetarian," Tianna says. "I used to be, but I just couldn't keep it up. Meat is just too good. Pot roast, and shredded chicken tacos, and grilled steak."

"I have never liked meat," I say, and she gives me a disbelieving grin.

"That's crazy," she says.

"Yes, that's what I'm told." I shift in my chair. I want to take Liria's hand, but she has them clutched in her lap.

"I was thinking," Tianna says. "I know how to

stretch and prime canvases too, probably better than Annette." She smirks in Annette's direction. Annette has lost the game of musical chairs so badly that she is stuck next to Peyton, the most intense and disconcerting of Ms. Corinth's minions. Her ignore levels are turned up so high she doesn't notice Tianna's smirk.

"I could teach you," Tianna continues. "It's not hard, really. I can even show you how to make the stretcher bars if you want."

"Do you paint also?" I ask.

She wrinkles her cute, upturned nose. "Not as much as I'd like. I have an MFA, but I can't make money painting like you do. That's why I have the job at the *New Yorker*."

"It's a very good job," I say.

"Yeah, it pays the bills."

"The business of trading paintings and drawings for money is very confusing," I say. "Your job at the *New Yorker* might be better than making money from art. The art job seems like something that I'm not that much a part of, actually. I'm just the caged monkey that paints and waves to the zoo patrons sometimes, and the money is something that happens at me, and not because of me."

Her face melts into that pity-look again. "Yeah, I can see how it would feel like that for you. I think part of that is because it's happening so fast. You'll get used to it, I think."

I pick at a chip in the table's black lacquer. "I would very much like to know how to stretch my own canvases. It's something I should learn."

She grins again, and I'm glad, because the pity-look pushes wrong shapes at me.

"How long are you going to be here?" she asks.

"We're staying for two days after the opening tomorrow."

"Could you come to my apartment on Sunday?"

I glance at Arty; Ms. Corinth is leaning forward talking to her, and Arty looks frightened that she might become a casualty of the other woman's flailing gesticulations.

"I'm fairly sure that would be okay," I say. "It seems like one of those things that Iris thinks is the right shape to fit into my schedule."

Tianna smiles in a way that gives off its own light. "It's a date."

***

We catch an Uber home after dinner. Arty sits in the passenger seat and talks about all sorts of business things regarding who will be at the opening tomorrow and what I should say to them. I try to cram all of it into my head, but it's not easy, especially because I'm distracted by Liria huddled against the door at the other end of the backseat. She's staring out the window with her arms crossed.

"Justin, are you listening?" Arty asks.

"Yes, Ms. Pierson," I say. "You were telling me not to do violations of the social dance if the guy from the Museum of Modern Art shows up."

She gives me a bland look. Now that she is not busy being the flighty and breathy-voiced Iris Pierson, she is back to being Arty, the woman who might hurt me physically if I make her angry. "I just want to make sure we're on the same page here," she says.

"I'll be good. I will not fart or say cuss words or talk about the Dark Energy." I run the crease of my slacks between my fingers, feeling her eyes singeing my skin, because I have just now done a violation of the social dance in front of the driver. I glance over at Liria, who is looking at me for once, but she doesn't seem angry. I can't tell what she's thinking.

"Just, if you start to feel weird or anything, tell me or Christina," Arty says.

"Yes, Ms. Pierson," I say.

When we get back to the apartment, Liria goes to her bedroom and shuts the door. Arty sits on the couch, chewing on her lip as her fingers tickety-click over her laptop keyboard. I'm left standing there with a stomach full of jitters.

The Liria situation is like a whirlpool in the Dark Energy, threatening to suck me down screaming. I don't feel like painting right now. I feel like running. I slip on my shoes and go out before Arty can protest.

The neighborhood is mostly older apartment buildings with little shops on the ground floors. I run around and around it, dodging other joggers and people on evening walks with their dogs. The sun goes down as I traverse the grid of streets. I'm afraid to go too far because I don't know anything about the neighborhoods beyond this one. They may be dangerous, full of sneaky people waiting to drag you into uncomfortable games of the Dark Energy.

I get back to the apartment just as the last light is

seeping out of the world. The Dark Energy has mostly smoothed out, and I feel much better. The situation in the apartment is still twisty, though.

Arty glances up from the couch as I come in. She is now watching some serious drama on the television about people who will do anything to make money. I think she may be extracting pointers from it.

"You have a good jog?" she asks.

"Yes, Arty." I stand waiting for her to complain about my behavior, but she goes back to her show. Liria is not on the couch. Her bedroom door is still shut.

I take a shower, and then I get out a blank canvas and start another painting. The picture pulls me into a peaceful scene in the Other Place, a ledge on a cliff overlooking a river gorge. Above me, the vulture businessmen glide in circles on the updrafts, the breasts of their suit jackets extended like wings. Behind me is a cave and inside it, Lee Harvey is playing dice with a bony, hollow-cheeked woman in a neon pink sundress.

The dice are huge, lopsided and multi-faceted. They clank like soup kettles tumbling down the stairs when they're thrown. As they bang and rattle to a stop, Lee Harvey throws up his arms. "Yay! I got the triple-cross super taco!"

I'm jolted back into the Physical World when Arty tells me she's going to bed. Her contacts are out, her green eyes fixed on me with something like fascination. "You really check out when you're painting," she says. "Your brain wanders off to la-la land."

"Painting and drawing take me to the Other Place while I'm awake, much more easily than the other way," I say.

A crease grows between her brows, and she opens her mouth to say something. She seems to think better of it, and shakes her head. She was going to yell at me for my bad moves in the social dance, I think.

"Don't stay up too late, Flaherty." She goes off to bed, and the apartment seems much calmer. The walls and plumbing and appliances whisper along with the cars outside.

I am very tired, so I clean my brushes, put them away and curl up on the couch under my soft quilt.

I have just fallen into one of those normal brain-housekeeping dreams when the couch cushions move and I come awake with a gasp.

My heart thumps because I don't know what's going on. Then the shadows resolve into a crossed-armed figure sitting beside me.

"Liria," I say. Happiness fills me, and sudden hope that maybe she is ready to stop being angry at me for whatever it is I did. "What's wrong?"

She pries her arms apart and picks at her cuticles, staring at the floor. "Justin, will you…will you come sleep in my bed with me?"

My guts do complicated things. "Of course. Did you have another bad Other Place dream?"

"No. I just can't sleep. I can't…I can't stop thinking about Lee Harvey."

"He won't leave you alone. It makes me angry."

She grimaces and gets up. Her sad expression is illuminated by the orange streetlights. I follow her into her room, and she closes the door very quietly.

I crawl under her covers. Her bed is more comfortable than the couch, and when she climbs in and scooches over to nestle against me, it is very much more comfortable and perfect. It feels like it's where I belong.

I put my arms around her, and she puts her arms around me. My heart is going very fast. "I don't know what I did to make you angry, but whatever it is I'm very sorry."

"I'm not angry at you." The bed shivers as her foot waggles. She doesn't say anything else for a long while.

I break into her silence, hoping I'm not committing criminal trespass. "I would like to know what's bothering you, even if it's not something I did. I want to make you feel better. We're in the Dark Energy together and so when we feel certain ways it affects the other one of us like that."

"I…" she says, and her foot wiggles harder. She holds me tighter, trembling. "I don't want to lose you, Justin. I need you." Her voice is thick.

I hold her tightly, stroke her hair and hush her, the way she does with me when I'm upset. I let her sadness take me over. It doesn't hurt. It feels good, because of how we're together with our feelings. "You won't ever lose me," I say. I want to say more. I want to tell her how I feel like we're one person in the Dark Energy, and how she makes everything right and beautiful. I want her to know how every thought of her sends up colorful sparks in my brain, and how she is the only person I will ever love like this. But I'm afraid she would be angry if she knew how I really feel.

She sniffs and wipes her nose. "I've never really had anyone before. I've always been alone. I had Lee Harvey, but it wasn't really...it wasn't the same."

I press my nose gently into her coconut-smelling hair. "I know what you mean, because the other people I've had in my life weren't really there. I could only see them from the outside. I thought that was just the way it worked, that we were all kept separate, with different lives and different missions. But with you...I'm very glad that we've found each other in the Physical World."

She presses closer, and starts shaking with sobs. "I'm so scared. I'm so scared, and confused, Justin."

Her feelings wash through me again, and borne on their crest is the muttering ooze of her thoughts, her memories. I close my eyes tightly as their patterns grate against my own. Pictures and ideas burst like pustules in my mind. The things Liria has gone through. The violence and the twisted bad sexual things, which worm their way up my spine. I grit my teeth so I can bear it, because I want to take it away from her so she doesn't have to carry it any longer.

"I'm sorry, Liria," I say, and I'm crying too, now. "I'm sorry and I want you to have nothing but good feelings. I don't want to ever give you bad feelings like that."

She shakes her head quickly against my chest. "You don't. You never give me bad feelings."

"But you're worried I might." I realize this has

been her problem all along, and that she is not with Arty again. It is almost worse than her being with Arty, though. I want so badly for her to not feel that way about me, but I don't know what to do about it.

She takes a shuddering breath and holds herself stiff like a steel mannequin. "You're not like other people, Justin. You're not like other men at all. I…I love you, Justin."

The words melt into my soul, but it isn't enough to push out the sadness. "I love you too. But you're worried about feeling that way about me because of what might happen. You're scared of the bad feelings that won't leave you alone, and you don't want to open the feelings-door so that they can come in."

She takes another shuddering breath. I can hear a small giggle playing through it, which is surprising. She nods. "Kind of like that, I guess."

I press her against me. "I don't want you to have to feel bad like that. I want to make you happy."

"I'm too screwed up. I'm going to end up pushing you away because of how screwed up I am."

"No, Liria. You're not pushing me away, and you're not screwed up. Having a sludge of bad feelings and memories collected in you is not something wrong with you, that's just the way it works with people."

She is silent for a long time again. She has stopped crying and is not so tense anymore, but I can feel her picking at her cuticles behind my back. The ugly thoughts start to wander off. They're not filling the Dark Energy with their gross smells anymore, and I take a deep breath of relief, breathing in Liria's good scent of sandalwood and cloves. Our thoughts whisper small half-formed questions at one another, trying to figure each other out and find their places.

"What are you whispering about?" Liria asks, and I jump slightly because she hasn't spoken aloud in so long.

"What? Oh, nothing," I say. "Nothing. It was the thoughts whispering and not me."

Liria laughs and presses her cheek against my chest. "You were whispering along with them."

"I guess I was. I guess I didn't realize."

Liria giggles again, but then the brightness of her laughter drains out and it's just the turbulence of her worry again. "Justin. I'm worried that you...I..." She huffs. "I'm not being fair because I'm...because it bugs me that you have a date with Tianna." She says the last part really quickly and tenses up again.

There's a loose thread in the neck seam of Liria's nightgown, and I run my thumbnail along it. I have to fight the urge to press my lips to the soft skin of her neck. "I don't have a date with Tianna. She just wants to teach me to stretch my own canvases."

"She called it a date."

Her words bite, but I can tell she isn't angry, really. I feel her sadness swell again, and her thoughts about men who were only ever interested in having sex with her. Men who didn't have any room in them for caring about her. "You're worried that I'll abandon you and be together with another woman." It's a surprising thing.

She begins to tremble again, and nods. Her voice is tight with crying. "You'd be happier with someone else. I'm too messed up to be with you…I want to, but I'm too messed up."

I'm confused for a moment that she wants to be with me girlfriend-style, because I'm a man, but I can see the pathways in her thoughts. She likes people who don't scare her and men usually scare her.

It is extremely nice to not scare someone. My vibrations seem to jitter fear into people a lot for some reason.

I slide my other arm under her shoulders and wrap her all the way up in my embrace, because I want to make a shell for her that the horrible things can't break through. "We're together in the Dark Energy, Liria. You're the only person I've ever seen there. We're together like that forever, because that's the way it is for us. You don't have to worry about me being with other women. I wouldn't be with other women even if you didn't like me that way, because there's no room for other women. You fill that place up."

"Really?"

"Really. And I don't want to do anything with you that would produce bad feelings, because that would completely defeat the purpose."

She nestles closer against me, drawing little circles on my back with a fingertip. "I don't think it would be bad feelings with you. I'm…I'm just not ready yet."

I stroke her hair. "That's okay, Liria."

She sighs a relaxed sigh and settles comfortably

in my arms. One of her bare feet wiggles in between my calves, and she intertwines her legs with mine. "I don't care if I'm crazy, as long as we're crazy together," she says.

I smile. Her body settles in with mine. A sweet note plays in the Dark Energy, and I realize I will never be unhappy again. I realize that everything will be okay forever as long as I have Liria. "If this is what crazy is, then being called crazy is a compliment."

She giggles again. I hold her, and pretty soon the tension leaves her completely and she falls asleep.

Even though I am in a strange place with lots of confusing things happening all around me, I know I'm where I'm meant to be, and that is the best feeling there is.

Before long, I fall asleep too.

Chapter 6

We dream that night of sitting on the rock ledge above the river valley. Behind us in the cave, Lee Harvey is playing blackjack with a couple of the vulture businessmen. The television-eyes butterfly is dealing, his fascinating neon wings sticking out from the back of his suit jacket. They're folded and draped down his segmented back like a Technicolor cape. Every so often he unfolds and flutters them with a noise like radio static.

Liria purses her lips. "What is that butterfly thing, anyway?"

"I don't know, but he makes me uneasy," I say.

The butterfly stops dealing. His wings tremble. Slowly, his ugly head turns, and he fixes us with his giant, segmented stare.

Liria gasps. I want to take her hand, but the butterfly's commercial-eyes have turned me to stone again.

He picks up a thick, disturbingly-fleshy red firehose which lays curled at his feet. It pulsates like a gross worm. Written near the dark, gaping nozzle

93

is the word **"FAME!"**

He turns it toward us. The butterfly's hairy mandibles twitch, and my heart stops. Vulture businessmen stand like sentries on either side of him, and I realize they both look a lot like Arty's father.

Lee Harvey reaches behind him and twirls the handle of a faucet. A blast of electric color explodes from the nozzle into Liria's and my faces.

Liria and I come awake at the same moment, the coffee grinder's buzz slicing us from the womb of the Other Place like an obstetrician's scalpel. It takes me a moment to realize that I have been safely delivered out of that horrible situation and into a very good one. Liria and I are snuggled together very close, our arms around one another. Our hearts pound together as we blink the Other Place from our minds. Liria smiles, and I smile back.

The coffee grinder whirs again in the kitchen, grating the smiles from our faces, and fear grows in me.

"Liria, I think Arty is going to murder me for being in your room."

Liria shrugs. "She's not going to murder you. She has better ways of messing with people. But don't worry, Justin. She'll never admit it, but she needs you. You're her meal ticket right now, and she's not going to screw that up by murdering you or anything."

I let my brain sort this into piles, and some of the fear fades from me. "You really think so?"

"Yes. I mean, she's not going to be sunshine and rainbows, but she never is about anything."

"There aren't many rainbows in Arty, it's true."

Liria laughs and rolls out of my arms and out of bed, which makes me feel like half a person for a moment. Her blue hair sticks out in all directions. She takes off her pajama top, revealing the smooth, golden skin of her back. She has a pretty little mole over one shoulder.

"Besides," she says, looking over her shoulder as she hooks her bra, "you stayed in my room before, and she didn't murder you." She pulls on a t-shirt, and she isn't naked anymore, which is disappointing.

"I suppose…" I clear my throat. "I suppose that's true."

She tugs a comb through her tangled hair and checks her reflection in the oval mirror over the dresser. I pull myself out of bed.

We go out the door. Despite Liria's assurances, my shoulders hunch around my ears. I wish I could pull my head inside my neck and hide from Arty like a turtle.

Arty is in the kitchen, setting out the cream and sugar. Her eyes fall on us, as emotionless as an alligator's. A jolt of fear spikes through me. It gets sharper when that look disappears behind a bright smile. "Good morning," she says. "You guys ready for the opening today?"

I watch her warily. "Yes, Arty."

"Can't wait, it's going to be awesome," Liria says. She pours two cups of coffee, and hands me one. "Drink up, Justin. You've got a big day ahead of you."

"Yes, I know." Liria and I look at each other, her

lips pursed against a smirk. She is having more fun than I am, I think.

Arty settles onto a stool at the breakfast bar, stirring a spoon around in her mug and watching us. I think she's going to say something. I'm sure she's going to ask questions about why I was in Liria's room. But she doesn't. She turns her gaze from us to the walls and starts outlining the many plans and the complicated schedule for that day. Liria and I drink our coffee. I'm not sure what to do about this situation, but at least Arty doesn't seem like she's going to kill me just at the moment. Maybe she wants me to do a certain number of paintings first.

When I've slurped down my coffee, Arty orders me to take a shower and get dressed in the nice clothes she bought me. "We need to get down there early to head off Deborah Corinth's destructive bouts of ADHD," she says. "She'll start moving walls around and suspending your paintings from the ceiling if we don't stop her."

So I climb into the shower. I get out, put on my boxers and socks. Then I see the clothes Arty has laid out on Liria's bed, and I get a sick feeling. "Arty," I call, "these clothes are at cross-purposes with today's situation."

"What's that, Justin?"

I close my eyes tightly, but the clothes' wrong vibrations seep through the cracks in my eyelids. "I can't wear these clothes at all. I think they have toxins, actually. I don't know if they'll ever be the right clothes for any situation."

"They don't have toxins, they're clean," Arty drawls from the doorway. I turn toward her with my back to the clothes and experiment with opening one eye.

"They have toxins woven into the fabric, I think."

Her green eyes flash. "Don't pull this bullshit on me, Flaherty. I bought you some perfectly nice clothes. I need to trim your hair, and we have a million other fucking things to do, and we're going to be late if you don't get dressed."

I wrap my arms around my bare, wet torso and close my eyes again. I'm getting motion sickness from all the turbulence. I wonder if Arty poisoned the clothes with her bad intentions, because she's angry with me for sleeping in Liria's bed.

I hear Liria's footsteps come down the hallway. "What's going on?"

"He's being a goddamn baby because he doesn't like the clothes."

"They're very poisonous," I say. "It makes me extremely nervous that maybe you're trying to poison me, Arty. You really don't need to do that."

"I'm not fucking poisoning you, Justin. Jesus!"

Liria starts arguing with her. I hug myself tighter, my pores prickling because of all the bad fumes in the air.

"Fine," Arty says. "If you want to enable this bullshit, Liria, you deal with it. Go buy him some new clothes. There's a whole slew of boutiques down the street." She digs in her pocket for her wallet and flings a credit card at Liria. "Use the business card."

Arty stomps into the living room, cursing under her breath, leaving Liria standing in the bedroom doorway. She reaches for the clothes, but I grab her arm.

"Don't touch them! You'd have to take a million showers if you did, and then we'd really be late. I think we should wash that quilt too, because they touched it."

Liria slowly draws her hand away from the clothes and waggles the credit card between her fingers. "What kind of clothes should I get you?"

"The slacks need to be a darker brown like earth, instead of…" Bile rises up in my throat and I can't even talk about the color of the slacks Arty got me. "And the shirt, it should be white with thin brown vertical stripes."

Liria chews on her cheek and nods. "Okay, I'll try to find those."

"Thank you, Liria."

She smiles, ducking her head.

"Don't take too fucking long!" Arty yells as Liria heads out the apartment door.

I get a broom from the closet and carefully pick up the clothes with the handle, trying not to look at them. I balance them on the handle with my face turned away as I walk to the kitchen. I slip them into the trash under the sink and quickly close the cupboard door.

Arty comes in and leans on the counter. "Are you throwing those *away*?"

"Yes, Arty." I go into the bedroom and get the quilt, picking it up by a corner and folding it over the place where the clothes touched. Arty follows me, scowling.

"I could have at least taken them back!"

I carry the quilt to the little laundry room and carefully stuff it in the washer. "It's not a good idea for anyone to touch those clothes. I can still smell them on this quilt, actually, and I hope this soap is pure enough to nullify their badness."

Arty's fists clench and her eyes squeeze shut as I pour in soap and start the washer. She sighs. "Come on, Flaherty. Let's cut your fucking hair."

She goes into the living room. I wash my hands thoroughly just in case I got some of the clothes poison on me before going out for my haircut.

Arty's standing in front of a straight-backed chair, holding a towel. "Sit," she commands.

"Yes, Arty." I do. She drapes a towel over my bare shoulders. She comes at me wielding the scissors, and I have a moment of intense panic. But she doesn't stab me with them; she just snips a half inch off the front so that it's out of my eyes.

"The haircuts-be-damned look is cool, but I think you've let it go too far," she grumbles. She seems less angry now, but I still sit very still with my eyes squeezed shut as the scissors click and the clippings tickle my cheeks.

"I didn't know you could cut hair, Arty," I say. There is a slight tremble in my voice because I'm having a hard time not picturing the scissors stuck in my head like a knife in a cheese log.

"Sure. I cut my own hair too."

"You do a very good job."

"Thanks." She finishes up, blows the clippings off my face, and removes the towel. I go into Liria's bedroom and look at myself in the mirror. My hair is still long, but not as shaggy. "It looks very nice,

Arty, thank you."

She comes and leans against the doorjamb, tapping the scissors against her thigh, and I catch her with that alligator look again before she smiles. "Don't mention it." She turns to go back into the kitchen, and I watch her go. I don't know what she is thinking, and I wish I did. Arty has all sorts of thoughts that are like large, hungry sharks circling just under the surface of the Dark Energy, and it feels dangerous to take your eyes off them.

I wonder if she was trying to poison me with those clothes. I decide I will have to be more careful and keep a closer eye on her.

***

Liria gets back with forty-five minutes to spare. Arty is extremely agitated about the time situation. "What took you so damn long?"

Liria scowls. "I couldn't find the right shirt." She takes it out of the bag, gazing at me with big eyes like a frightened kitten. "It has brown plaid stripes instead of vertical ones. I looked everywhere…"

I examine the shirt. It smiles at me with its vibrations. "That is the right shirt. Thank you, Liria."

She smiles.

The pants are the right ones too. I pull them on and I feel a lot better, even though Arty is approaching screaming volume with her commands to hurry up. Then I remember something, and dig in my suitcase.

I find the hat Mina gave me. It is a good luck hat.

The blue of it is like a shield, and I need that right now. I put it on over my bouncy new haircut. When I meet Arty and Liria at the door, Liria hides her mouth with her hand and Arty builds up pressure like a teakettle about to whistle. I take a step back.

"*No,* Flaherty," Arty says.

I think she must mean my hat. I adjust the bill to make it straighter. "Is that better?"

Arty's anger steams out of her ears and mouth and I take another step back, putting my arms up to defend myself. "No hat at all," she says. "Take it off."

"I can't take it off, Arty. It's an extremely vital part of this outfit. I think the atmosphere might get infectious if I don't wear it."

"What's the problem?" Liria says. "Let him wear the hat. It's cute."

Arty closes her eyes and has a private conversation with her angry feelings about my hat. She opens her eyes again, mutters some bad words about being late, and flings herself out the door.

Liria and I follow.

We get to the gallery in time, which is a gigantic relief. Ms. Corinth is standing in the entry talking to some very wide-eyed caterers. "It would be nice to have the canapés arranged to sort of mirror the concepts presented…oh, Justin, there you are." She breezes over to give me a small hug, and the caterers scuttle off like mice escaping a distracted cat. "Are you ready for the big day?" Her gaze lingers on my hat a moment, but its vibrations don't seem to be as agitating for her as they are for Arty.

"I'm very much looking forward to it," I say,

because it seems like a thing one should say.

She fusses with my hair, brushing it back from my forehead. "Yes, it's going to be beautiful. You're just, just a *genius*, Justin. You're going to *explode* into the art world."

"I hope I don't cause any damage," I say. Behind me, Liria snorts. Ms. Corinth rolls her eyes, smirking, then pulls me off to look at some things she's changed in the setup.

The morning passes very quickly, because the nervous energy is speeding up time. Before I know it, people are starting to arrive, and Ms. Corinth is gathering them in small flocks around me for introductions. There is a man from the Museum of Modern Art, like they said, and several people that just like to look at and buy paintings for something to do. Some people are kind and curious, but others have a look that I am very used to. As one man is walking away, he mutters to his wife, "He's like an overgrown eight-year-old. I doubt he can hold his brush straight. Dickon Rond must have had a stroke."

Later, the same man and his wife come over to me; the man stands back frowning and not looking at me while the wife tugs at my elbow, dragging me over so I can tell her the story of the butterfly painting.

All the people want to know what is in my mind. Arty has tried to arrange my thoughts in attractive patterns for display, going over and over what I should say when people ask about my paintings, giving me little scripts to recite from so that I can talk about the Dark Energy without actually talking about the Dark Energy. If the questions are a test, I think this is a good way to pass it. I'm glad Arty is sharing some of her expertise on controlling the Dark Energy, even though it is difficult for me to trust her motives.

Tianna shows up at around five, and waits on the edge of the crowd for her chance to shake my hand. "Looks like it's going pretty well," she says, once she's able to push her way through.

Over the heads of the others around me, I see Liria clutching her elbows, watching us without looking at us the way girls are so good at. "Yes, there are a lot of people here," I say.

"You're going to be big, Justin," Tianna says.

"I'm already very tall," I say. "If I swell up bigger, I'll explode like Ms. Corinth says."

She scrunches up her nose and laughs. Liria nudges her way through the swarm of people and comes to my side, taking my hand. When her skin touches mine, a tension I hadn't realized was in me begins to dissipate.

"Hi, Tianna," she says, smiling in the way girls do when they don't like one another.

Tianna's gaze falls briefly to our clasped hands, then she smiles back at Liria in the same way. "Hello, Liria, you look gorgeous. I love how your hair goes with that purple dress."

Liria thanks her, and they smile at each other for too long. Then I feel a ripple in the Dark Energy, and I forget about it.

Liria and Tianna feel it too, and we look around. The ripples are coming from a man who just walked in. He is shaking Ms. Corinth's hand in a familiar way, and she throws back her head to laugh at something he says. He doesn't look like much in the Physical World, just a middle-aged man with glasses and receding brown hair, but the power emanating from him makes people's eyes dart in his direction and changes the sound of the conversation around us. When he shakes Arty's hand, she does a little curtsy and smiles demurely with her altered lips, seeming so unlike herself that it makes me a little bit dizzy. I worry that this man maybe has the power to completely erase people's brains and make them into something they're not.

I twitch when Ms. Corinth points at me. The man's eyes lock on mine. Liria squeezes my hand and smiles. "Must be some big shot."

"That's Harold Plath," Tianna mutters, and even though I don't know who Harold Plath is, I know by the way Tianna says his name that Liria is right.

Ms. Corinth and the man come toward us. The crowd parts to let them through as if pushed back by the force field of the man's eminence. I try to breathe out my nervousness, and to not inhale any of this man's brain-erasing vibrations.

Ms. Corinth smiles at me. It's bright and glittering like diamonds I cannot afford, and so I figure someone else must have paid for it. "Justin," she sings, "This is Harold Plath, who owns an empire of glorious galleries spanning this country and Europe. Mr. Plath, this is Justin Flaherty."

He clasps my hand firmly, peering at me with curious, gray eyes. "Hello, Mr. Flaherty. I've heard so much about you in the past couple of weeks. I thought I ought to come get a look."

"Mr. Plath, it's an honor," I say, because Arty has made me rehearse the social dance with regard to important personages. Around us, everyone has gone silent and is watching as if we're putting on a play.

"Well, let's show you what everyone is so excited about, Mr. Plath," Ms. Corinth says.

Ms. Corinth's shoes clomp on the wood floors, loud in the silence, broken now only by soft strains of jazz music from the hidden speakers. I hear the softer and more tentative patter of everyone else's shoes as they herd along behind us. Liria takes my hand again and we exchange a nervous glance.

We go first to the uncomfortable painting, where it hangs on the front wall in a splash of warm spotlight.

"He calls this the *Uncomfortable Painting*," Ms. Corinth says, her voice hushed as if the picture were a sleeping baby.

I watch Mr. Plath's face as he approaches it, how the crease eases its way out of his forehead, his gaze skittering over the canvas. His thick fingers reach out as if he'd like to touch it, but he doesn't. Instead, his hand draws back to push his glasses up his nose then splay out over his mouth. He sits regarding the painting for a long time. The furrow slowly creeps back into his brow.

He glances at me, and he has that look that tells me he's heard all about me in the Dark Energy now. "This one," he says, "is it about you trying to capture the images out of, out of the air, out of your imagination, and the world trying to get in the way?"

I smile, because the Dark Energy has told him about the uncomfortable painting. He has described it almost exactly the way Arty told me to. "Yes," I say.

His fingers creep toward it again and make little swiping motions, as if he's mimicking my brush strokes. "You didn't go to art school," he states.

"No, not yet," I say.

"I think I'm glad you didn't go to art school," he says, and I hear several people behind me chuckle; I think one of them is Tianna but I don't turn to look. He draws himself up straight. "I want to see the other ones."

So Ms. Corinth leads us on a meandering path around my show. Liria, Arty, and Stewart come with us, and some of the herd keeps with us, as well; others stay behind in the main showroom, and I can hear their low, excited conversation start up again.

Mr. Plath wants to talk for a long time about every single picture, and the glow of sunlight starts to fade from the far-above ceiling by the time we're done. My feet are starting to hurt, and I want to sit down, so I'm glad when we get to the last picture. After we talk about that one, Mr. Plath looks at me very seriously. "I'd like to take you to dinner, Justin."

"Thank you," I say. "I'm very hungry."

Ms. Corinth's laugh traces an airy arc above us. Mr. Plath gives me a little smile, then blinks at Arty and Stewart. "You two are his representatives, correct?"

"Yes, we hold a contract on his work," Arty

says. Stewart squints at Mr. Plath in an odd way and taps his fingers on his forearms.

"Will you come as well, then?" Mr. Plath says. "And you, Deborah?" He grins at her, then at Liria. "And of course the muse."

They all agree, so we head for the door. Liria squeezes my hand. Something important is going on. I think I might be getting another show, which is nice. I hope it will be in San Francisco, so that Liria and I can go back home.

More people have showed up, and are mingling in the main gallery. It's starting to sound like a party. The guests watch us as we walk through. A couple people come over to talk with Mr. Plath, and Ms. Corinth whispers in one of her minion's ears while the minion nods and glances in our direction. Finally, we escape and gain the sidewalk.

There are two shiny, black cars with tinted windows waiting for us in front of the gallery, and the driver holds the door of one of them open for me. Liria and I slide into the backseat, and Mr. Plath takes the passenger seat. Arty, Stewart, and Ms. Corinth get into the other car.

As we pull out from the curb, Liria and I glance at each other. Her eyes shine in the dim interior. We are both thinking that Mr. Plath seems to have a large amount of money.

He turns slightly in his seat, studying me. "Mr. Flaherty, you're a very talented artist."

"Thank you, Mr. Plath," I say.

"Not only that, but you're a compelling person, it seems. I read Mr. Legrange's article about you. It sounds like you've had to overcome a lot of obstacles in your life."

I look away from him. Liria is smirking, and that just makes it worse. "I think Mr. Legrange's article makes a big deal out of little things," I say.

"Don't minimize your struggles. People want to hear about them." He turns further in his seat until he's almost backwards. His hands gesture between the seats as he talks. "What a lot of people don't realize is that you can't just sell art anymore, you have to sell the artist. The artist's life, their triumphs and failures, their exploits and romances," he raises his eyebrows at Liria, "are every bit as valuable as their work—more so, in some cases. People want larger-than-life celebrities, but they also want to see their humanity in its sometimes horrific glory. They want a window into the famous person's life. They want to be entertained."

I squirm, and Liria takes my hand. "My life isn't really that interesting, and I'm not a famous person," I say.

He smiles. "Not yet, but you will be. What's the term of your contract with Ms. Pierson and Mr. Califax?"

"Six months. It's up in January."

The car pulls up to the curb again, and we get out. Liria smooths her dress over her knees. We are in front of what must be a restaurant. A painted wooden sign hangs from the awning; it says **"Camille's"** and nothing else, as if that explains the place entirely. You can see through the tall front windows. The people inside are dressed very nicely, candlelight glinting off their wineglasses and jewelry.

Arty, Stewart, and Ms. Corinth get out of the other car, which has parked behind ours. Both vehicles pull away as Mr. Plath holds the door of the restaurant open for us.

The hostess looks up from her podium as we walk in, and she smiles, her teeth golden ivory in the low light from an art deco chandelier. "Mr. Plath, we have your table all ready." She leads us through the maze of tables and to our place by the window. Mr. Plath orders two bottles of wine as we all settle into our places.

Liria sits next to me, and I take her hand underneath the green linen tablecloth. She looks at me with a small smile, and I am so glad that she is here. I wonder if she will let me sleep in her bed again tonight.

I tear my gaze from her because I realize the waiters are pouring wine in Liria's and my glasses. I open my mouth to say something, but the waiter is already wending through the tables back toward the kitchen, and so my words escape tardily.

"It's not legal for me to drink alcohol."

"Me, either," Liria says. She's staring at her glass with her nose wrinkled.

"Me either, probably," Arty says before downing half her glass.

Ms. Corinth laughs. Stewart snickers, his eyes crinkling at Liria.

"That's right," Mr. Plath says, squinting at me. "You're how old?"

"Eighteen," Arty says, gazing at me over the rim of her wineglass. Despite the brown contacts, it is a very Arty-like look that slices through me, and I wonder why her thoughts are so sharp.

"So young, that's incredible," Mr. Plath mutters. "Well, raise your water glass, or just drink your wine if you want, we won't tell." He grins and raises his glass in a toast, as do the others. Liria and I glance at each other and pick up our waters.

"To art," he says.

"To *art,*" Ms. Corinth says.

Everyone drinks. I see Stewart exchange a long glance with Arty. There is so much social dance going on at this table that I'm certain I'm going to trip over someone's feet.

"Justin," Mr. Plath says, setting down his glass. "I think you are a spectacular talent. A phenomenon."

"Thank you," I say, clutching my water glass.

"I would like to promote your work," he says. "I want to become involved."

There is a silence at the table. Arty and Stewart look very agitated now, and I realize this must have something to do with the contract.

"What does that mean, exactly, that you want to become involved?" Arty asks. She has resumed the mantle of Iris Pierson. She smiles with sweet politeness and slowly twirls her almost empty wineglass.

Mr. Plath leans toward her, folding his hands on the table. "I could arrange for a tour of my galleries, and for many other interesting opportunities. I think I could make it worthwhile for all of you."

The Dark Energy hums. Arty crosses her arms underneath her gigantic boobs. "Your interest in Justin is quite flattering, though not surprising. But please know that it's not just the money for us, Mr. Plath. We like to be, as you say, *involved,* as well. Being a part of Justin's career is part of the payoff for us. So, if you're suggesting you want to buy his contract, there's no amount of money that would make it worthwhile for us." Stewart leans back in his seat and crosses his arms as well, frowning at Mr. Plath.

"Of course, of course," Mr. Plath says. "I would want you to stay involved, as you've been so integral to his career up to this point. I'd want you to be on the tour with him, in fact. I'd have to buy out the contract, of course, but I would like you two to stay on, either with some sort of profit-sharing agreement, or on the payroll as consultants or some such. These would all be details we could hash out with the lawyers. It's the art I care about. Let the money take care of itself. I just want to know if it's potentially possible." He's looking at Arty, not me, but I break in.

"I want Christina with me," I say. "It would be very nice to be on a tour, Mr. Plath, but not unless I can have her there."

Liria squeezes my hand under the table.

Mr. Plath fixes his gaze on me, and for a split second, I see something strange in his eyes. I'm not quite sure what it is, but it reminds me of Arty's alligator look. He smiles. "Of course," he says. "Wouldn't dream of leaving her behind."

I stare back at him. He shifts slightly, and the screen from the television behind the bar reflects in his glasses, showing a commercial for antacid medication.

Fear stiffens my spine, and sweat pops up on the back of my neck. "On second thought, I don't think getting the butterfly involved in this is a good idea," I say.

The stares of everyone around the table pierce me like syringes full of poison. "Justin..." Liria says.

"I think Justin needs to take a walk to process this," Arty says, with a hardness in her voice that pushes at me. "Christina, why don't you go with him?"

"This is a very complicated test," I say. "I'm not sure I'm ready to pass it. The butterfly is a really frightening character and I guess I didn't put up enough obstacles. That tongue is really unpleasant."

Liria puts her arm around me and tugs at me gently, but I can't move because the butterfly has me hypnotized again. Mr. Plath's mouth has fallen open and I wait for the tongue to dart out. I can't see his eyes behind those television images.

"Justin," Liria says, tugging again. Her voice is soothing, but there's an urgency in it. "Let's go on a walk, okay? Please."

Her voice wiggles through the binding vibrations of the hypnotism and lays soothing fingers on me. I take a deep breath and force my neck to twist out of the butterfly's gaze. Liria's eyes are wide and scared. "Justin, please," she whispers.

"I think you're right," I say. "I think getting out of here is an excellent idea."

I get up so fast my chair tips over. Ms. Corinth lets out a little yelp of surprise, but I'm out the door already.

Liria's footsteps trot behind me on the sidewalk, trying to keep up. The headlights and street lights and illumination from the windows flood the night with brightness. The stars are dim and forgotten, part of another world. The sidewalks are crowded with people dressed very nicely and smelling of perfumes, but they have an underlying metallic stench and their clothes are just costumes. They are all part of the butterfly's army. They wear his uniform of money and class. They are trying to push me back toward him, trying to stifle my breath, but I shoulder through. A woman cries out as I push past, and a man yells something angry at me. They will rise up and drag me back to the butterfly kicking and screaming if I'm not careful.

"Justin, wait," Liria says. She's panting trying to keep up.

"We've got to get out of here," I say. "The gangster vulture businessmen have made an alliance with a whole new army. I don't know how they surrounded us so quickly, but this is a big and scary trap."

I jump as a hand catches my arm. "Justin, slow down."

It's just Liria. I keep pushing forward, dragging her along with me. "We can't slow down. It's too dangerous here."

"Justin…" She tugs hard on my arm, and I stumble off course, down an emptier side street. The suffocating press of soldiers slowly releases me from its grip. My footsteps slow. The cool night breeze cools my sweat, and I take a deep breath. "You were right, Liria. I should have listened to you. They can't find us down here. It's off their flight path."

She takes my hand and leads me into a small park. Coreopsis blossoms glow bright orange in the light from a streetlamp.

We sit on a bench. Liria wraps her arms around me and presses her nose into my chest. "It's okay, Justin."

I take her into my arms. "What do we do? How do we get away? Arty has all the money and I think she was part of this trap all along. I don't think she'd give us money for flights back to San Francisco, and that's a very long walk."

"It's okay, Justin. Calm down. Let's think about this."

"Maybe we could run away and get jobs and apartments here in New York, but I'm worried our enemies would find us again if we stay here. They're all over the place."

Liria snuggles up closer. "We don't need to do that, Justin. Hush. It's going to be all right."

I sit holding her, feeling her hands on my back. The night breeze rustles in the leaves and through the flowers, bringing their scent intertwined with exhaust and food. It's soothing. Even if the gangster vultures and butterfly army are after me, there is a whole big world out there for me to disappear into. The trap the Dark Energy has laid for me doesn't seem so big anymore.

Liria looks up at me, resting her chin on my chest. "Do you feel better?"

"A little."

"Good. You don't have to worry, Justin. I don't

see the butterfly army. I think you're just getting scared because of all the stuff happening, and you're imagining things."

These words jostle me as they find their places in my brain. "Really? But, Liria, there are so many of them, how could you not see?"

"They're just people, Justin. Not an army. Just regular people, and you were imagining that they were part of an army."

Coldness inches up my spine. "How can you say that, Liria? You're in the Dark Energy too, and you see them, just like I do. If you're not seeing them, there's something wrong."

Her brow furrows. The streetlight reflects in her eyes, a bright veneer over dark, unfathomable pits. Suddenly her hands on me feel horrible, like spiny, creeping insect legs, and I scoot away from her, to the other end of the bench. "How could you be part of the trap, too? How could this be happening? Nothing is real, and that isn't fair. We were together in the Dark Energy and that's too low of a trick."

Fear crawls all over me with buggy feet. Liria's eyes spring wide, darting around the streets. "Don't yell, Justin, please. I'm not part of the trap, I swear it."

I wrap my arms around myself, trying to scrape the fear-bugs from my skin with my fingernails. "I can't handle this. It's too much. I don't want enlightenment. I'd rather die. I'd rather die!"

"No, Justin. I love you, Justin, please."

"Everything okay over here?"

My head jerks up. Two uniformed police officers stroll into the glow cast by the streetlamp. Their belts are full of guns and sticks and all sorts of ways to hurt me. They stare at me with their deadly serious cop faces and I feel like I'm going to throw up my whole self until I'm nothing but a puddle of vomit.

"Oh no, the police," I say. I rock back and forth because if I stay still I'll fall into a dark and horrible place. "Mom and Rebekah are part of this too. It's too big of a trap, and there's no way out."

"Everything's fine," Liria says to the police. "My friend is upset, but I've got it under control."

"Sounded pretty upset," one of the cops says. "Heard him all the way down the block." He turns on an extremely bright flashlight, blasting us so hard with its white glare that I'm thrown against the back of the bench.

Liria sits up straight too. "He's…he has a mental illness. He's not dangerous at all, he just gets really scared sometimes."

My heart pounds, and I swallow down bile. Liria and I are encased in a blinding bubble of flashlight beam, and I can't see anything outside of it. "This is something that really needs to happen, I guess," I say. "You can't fight against the Dark Energy."

"Mental illness, huh?" Flashlight Cop says, his voice drifting through the walls of the bubble. "What's your name, sir?"

"You don't need to play that game," I say. "You already know my name. I know you're with the butterfly army. Please, I can't play this game anymore."

"I assure you, we're not playing games and we're not part of any butterfly's army," the other cop says. "We're going to need your name, sir."

Liria scoots over next to me, her movements tentative. I'm still rocking back and forth. I wish they would just take me and get it over with, because I hate the torturing part. "Liria, I'm frightened and I don't want you to be part of the trap," I say. "I don't think it's fair that I don't get one real thing for myself. I don't think enlightenment is worth it."

"I'm not part of the trap," she says quietly, her voice tight with tears. "We're going to figure this out. Right now, you need to tell them your name."

A sob twists its way up my throat. I press my forehead into my knees. I'm shivering very hard. "I want so badly to believe you. I'm so scared, Liria." Everything is swirling around me in a rush of sickening light and color. There are so many voices in the Dark Energy and they are all saying different things so I don't know which one is the truth. I try to cling to the idea that Liria isn't part of the trap so that I don't get spun off into nothingness. I've been wrong before about people being part of the trap when they weren't. The Dark Energy can be tricky sometimes.

Liria's arms go around me, and they're not bug arms anymore.

"The butterfly is trying to trick me into thinking you aren't real," I say. "I hate it, Liria, and I don't want to believe it."

"Shhh, Justin. Don't believe it, because it's not true. I love you Justin, and I'm here for you. I'm on your side and no one else's."

The cops' radios blast out a hissy message, and I

jump.

"Sir, we need you to calm down and tell us your name, please," Flashlight Cop says again. His words drop like live grenades into my thoughts. There is no niceness in his voice at all.

Liria rocks along with me. I take a deep breath. "Liria, I can't say my name."

"You can do it, Justin," she whispers. "I love you. It's going to be okay."

"Nothing is okay right now."

"But it will pass. Think back to the way it always passes. Remember how things always calm down and are okay again."

I think about it. I cling to that thought as hard as I cling to the one about Liria being on my side, and the world swirls more slowly. I take another deep breath. "Justin Flaherty," I say. "My name is Justin Flaherty." I squeeze my eyes closed and keep rocking, concentrating on the small point of stability in the universe, which is Liria being on my side and no one else's, and the idea that everything will be okay again at some point.

"Spell it," the cop demands. I do. I give him my date of birth and my address, even though it is very hard to push the words out of my throat. Liria holds me, and her tears soak through my shirt and wet my shoulder.

"He's an artist, a painter, here for a show at the Corinthian," Liria says. "He has an illness that makes him scared sometimes, but he's not dangerous at all. He'll be okay in a minute."

"Can I see identification for both of you?" Flashlight Cop asks.

Liria fishes her wallet out of her pants, and helps me get mine out as well, which is hard because my body is hunched over and won't un-hunch. She hands Flashlight Cop our IDs. His beam slides sideways as he hands them to the other cop, and I blink the blindness out of my eyes. The other cop retreats, reading our information to someone over the radio. Flashlight Cop stays, and points his beam at us again. I'm cold, and sweating, but the world isn't swirling so fast anymore, because Liria is here and she's not part of the trap.

"You're an artist, huh?" the cop says. "The Corinthian, isn't that the place up by the Park?"

"Yeah," Liria says. "Justin is a really good artist. He was written up in *The New York Times* and everything."

"No kidding?" the cop says. His voice creeps over me, sarcastic and inhuman.

"You don't believe me, look it up," Liria says.

The cop doesn't say anything. He just stands there, shriveling me up with the radioactive beam of his flashlight while his friend talks on the radio. My skin sears and I squirm, sucking in air between my teeth. I'm fairly sure this is how ants feel when someone burns them with a magnifying glass. I was an ant once, when the Dark Energy was giving me a lesson, so I understand how they feel. That's probably why the butterfly chose this way to torture me.

Liria wraps me up tighter in her arms, shielding me from the light, and the searing feeling eases. I stop squirming. She whispers in my ear, reminding me about the cliff ledge overlooking the river valley in the Other Place, and how beautiful it is there. She tells me the butterfly is dealing the cards, but says that we'll beat him at his own game eventually.

I take another deep breath. "Do you really think so?"

"Yes," she says. "That's why we were brought together, so that we can be strong, and defeat the butterfly and vulture businessmen, and have a good life."

I cuddle closer to her. The brightness of the cop's flashlight doesn't burn so badly now. The Dark Energy is starting to smooth out again, and there is a peacefulness in the breeze. "I'm so glad we were brought together, Liria."

"Me too."

"I'm so happy you're not a trap."

She kisses me gently on the forehead. "I'll never be a trap, Justin. I promise. You're the most important person to me, and I'll never betray you."

I don't know how long we sit there waiting, but I feel a lot better by the time the other cop comes back and hands our IDs to us. "Okay, folks, it looks like you're good to go," he says. "Looks like things have calmed down a bit here."

"I told you he'd be fine," Liria says as she slides her wallet back into her pocket. I sit staring at my picture on my ID card, which looks strange in the bright light.

"Just checking up, ma'am," the cop says. "Sounded like there may have been a problem, and we were just doing our jobs. If you think he needs to go to the hospital, they could help him out there—"

"Definitely not," Liria says. "He's fine. Right, Justin?"

"I'm feeling much better now," I say. My smile on my ID picture is silly, and I smile back at it.

"Okay then," the cop says. "You two have a nice evening."

The flashlight cocoon abruptly disappears, bobbing back out toward the street, and I sit blinking as the outside world reasserts itself around us. I'm warmer now.

Liria gazes at me with wide, worried eyes. "You better?"

"Yes, Liria. The Dark Energy is still a little bit squishy, but it's not trying to tear me apart anymore."

Her cheeks puff as she blows out a hard breath. "That was freaking scary."

"It was extremely frightening, and I'm glad we won that battle. I don't like being arrested at all." I put my ID back in my wallet and pocket it again. "Thank you for fighting on my side, Liria."

She smiles and brushes a lock of hair from my forehead. "We're a team."

"I still don't know what we're going to do about the butterfly and the gangsters, but I feel a lot better about my chances now that I know you're on my side."

Liria's smile fades. She sits quietly, gazing out over the park and chewing on her lip. "I don't trust Mr. Plath either," she says, "but I think this is something that's meant to happen. You know what I mean?"

I think about it, a sick feeling churning up my

stomach. "I think you're right, unfortunately. I think we're meant to battle the butterfly in his own game, like you say."

She takes my hand. "I think you should let Mr. Plath have your contract. I think it's a really good opportunity, as long as you're careful. It will turn out okay in the end. The Dark Energy will help us."

I stroke her thumb with mine. She is so beautiful, and she has been very good at figuring out the patterns in the Dark Energy before. I nod. "Okay Liria. I think you're right."

"You feeling up to going back to the restaurant?"

Food doesn't seem like it exists on the same plane as my stomach right now, but I nod.

We walk back the way we came. The butterfly's army isn't menacing anymore, because we're not fighting against them now: we're going with the flow. But, when the time is right, we'll strike. I hope Liria is correct, that we'll eventually be successful in beating the butterfly at his own game, but there's no way of knowing with these kinds of tests. We'll just have to do our best.

When we get back to the restaurant, the others look up at us in surprise. I don't know how long we've been gone, but it's been a while because there are half-eaten salads and appetizers on the table, and new bottles of wine.

Stewart passes a hand over his face, Arty glares at both of us very angrily, and Mr. Plath studies me carefully.

Ms. Corinth smiles. "Oh, here you are," she cries. She stands and gives my shoulder a squeeze as I sit down. She has an expression like a worried grandmother. "I hope you had a productive discussion. We took the liberty of ordering you the porcini mushroom steak. I hope that's okay."

"That sounds very good, thank you," I say.

"Are you all right?" Stewart asks, frowning. He glances at Liria.

"He's fine," Liria says, scooting her chair closer to me. "This was just a lot to think about, you know?"

I clutch my hands in my lap, looking around at all of them. I wince when my eyes fall on Mr. Plath, and look away quickly. I'm not strong enough to battle him alone, so I'm very glad Liria is here. "I'm very sorry that I'm so much trouble. It's just hard to know how to do the right things sometimes."

Arty's burning glare slides out the windows. She takes a furious bite of her salad, looking like she wishes the lettuce were my face. Mr. Plath leans forward, resting his elbows on the table and propping his chin on his folded hands. I lean back a little and glance at him from the corner of my eye. He's squinting at me, and I can see that he's having a lot of thoughts about me right now.

"Mister Flaherty, you've been diagnosed with schizophrenia, is that correct?"

The Dark Energy tugs and pulls. Arty shoots Stewart a nasty look, but it hits the side of his face because he's looking at me and not her. I think that look means that Arty isn't happy Stewart gave Mr. Plath this information about me.

"That's what they say about me," I say very carefully. "That I have schizophrenia."

Mr. Plath does a little nod and leans back in his

chair, tugging his button-down shirt straight. "That wouldn't be an impediment to having a contract with me."

A cloud of tension-steam releases from Arty, Stewart, and Ms. Corinth's auras as they all relax into their chairs. I'm a little confused. Do they actually want me to have a contract with Mr. Plath? Are they part of his army too?

"I've worked with disabled people before," Mr. Plath continues. "They're some of my most talented artists, in fact. Are you on medication, Mr. Flaherty?"

I stare at him, because I trying to figure out what he means by saying he's worked with disabled people. I think for a moment that it's one of those completely unrelated sentences that sneak into conversations just to disorient everyone, but then I realize that maybe he thinks I'm disabled because of my schizophrenia. I'm picturing my brain rolling around in a wheelchair, and it's not until Liria squeezes my hand that I remember I need to answer Mr. Plath's question. "Yes, I'm on medication."

He nods again. "Good. I have a psychiatrist on staff who works with my artists. The contract would specify that you have regular visits with him, and stay compliant with medical orders. I believe that's in your best interests anyway, in order to stay healthy and happy, and it's yet another benefit of being part of Plath Arts." He smiles in a way that makes my body squirm, because it's difficult to align myself with the shape of it.

Liria clutches my hand tighter. "Wait, so Justin would be contractually obligated to take whatever pills you say?"

Arty sends Liria a look so explosive that I'm surprised it doesn't blow her off her chair.

Mr. Plath keeps smiling. "It wouldn't be me prescribing the medication, and I can assure you Doctor Schlopper is highly qualified and experienced. However, there is a second opinion clause in the case of disputes, if that eases your worries."

Liria glances at me uncertainly. "It does, a little."

"I would ask, though," Mr. Plath says, "that nobody discuss this diagnosis with anyone, especially the media, without talking to me about it first. We want to make sure this information is handled carefully and correctly, so as not to cause misunderstanding or concern."

Arty and Stewart nod. Liria scowls slightly, but nods as well. Mr. Plath raises his eyebrows at me. "That okay with you too, Justin?"

"That's okay with me," I say, because there's really nothing else I can say.

A group of waiters prances up. Half of them clear away our used plates and the other half slide new plates of food in front of us. The rising steam lifts the shroud of our mood like hot air inflating a balloon, and we all can move a bit easier.

Mr. Plath rubs his hands together, grinning. "There will be enough time to talk business after you and your attorneys have had a chance to review my contract. For now, let's just celebrate that fate and the muses have brought us together for a spectacular meeting of artistic minds."

"Hear, hear," Ms. Corinth says, raising her glass.

Stewart and Arty glance at each other. Liria and I glance at one another. We all raise our glasses, stepping in time with this complicated social dance. I'm dancing straight into a trap that will be very difficult to disentangle myself from, and I can only hope that Liria is right: that the Dark Energy will help us in the end.

"To fate," Mr. Plath says.

"To fate," the rest of us say.

And we all drink.

Chapter 7

Liria is crammed into the middle of the backseat on the ride back to our apartment after dinner. She keeps sending me little glances, and I know exactly how she feels. On her other side, Stewart slumps against the door of Mr. Plath's tinted-window sedan as if he is too distraught to maintain his posture. Arty is in front, shooting off sparks like a robot built by inept amateurs.

"This is *exactly* what I was talking about, Justin," she spits. "That little stunt of yours almost cost us a multimillion-dollar contract. And who knows what the deal will look like when he sends it over? He might think he can just walk all over us in exchange for his little shrink's babysitting services." She sends the driver a suspicious glance, but he is pretending none of us exist.

"*Stop it,*" Liria says. "He couldn't help it. This is really stressful."

Arty clutches her fist in her hair. "Stressful is fucking right. I *knew* he'd try to fuck this up somehow…"

"Lay off him, Iris," Stewart says. "It turned out okay, so what are you worried about? And Justin didn't *try* to fuck anything up." Arty fixes Stewart with her alligator look. It's strange to see her using it on someone else. Stewart returns it with a raised eyebrow, a corner of his mouth twitching up. He is obviously not as disturbed by it as I am. "I'm sorry, but you're being a bitch," he says. Arty's alligator look hardens and gets hungrier-looking, and Stewart snickers. "Am I wrong? Did I somehow misinterpret your totally polite and rational behavior?"

Arty scowls and turns to face front, muttering bad words.

Stewart rolls his eyes. "I know it's tough working with people who have mental health issues, but we'll all get used to Iris's craziness sooner or later."

Liria snorts. Arty shakes her head and sighs. I stare at my hands in my lap. The New York streetlights wash them in an undulating tie-die of glowing orange and white. I'm always so much trouble for people. I don't think I'm ever going to figure out how others deal with menacing situations like the one I'm in with the gangsters and butterfly army without doing wrong steps like rushing out of restaurant meetings.

We are silent for the rest of the ride. Arty scrolls through emails on her phone. Stewart gazes out the window at the faraway screen on which his thoughts are projected. The blue sludge of sadness and fatigue seeps through the cracks in the Dark Energy and leeches out my life force.

"That rich bitch had better offer a hell of a contract, is all I've got to say," Arty growls once we're out of the car and taking the elevator up. "Swishing his little bubble butt in and thinking he can just take over. I'm sure he'll want to keep ninety percent of the money, and leave all the dirty work to us." Her eyes dart to me when she says "dirty work," as if I am a pile of dishes in the sink.

Stewart leans against the wall of the elevator with crossed arms. "I'm sure he'll make us an offer we can't refuse." The door opens, and we all file into the hallway.

"'It's the art I care about, let the money look after itself,'" Arty mocks, a snort erupting from her carefully-crafted nostrils. She fishes the apartment key from her purse and fits it into the lock, the lobster-shaped fob swinging wildly. "He lets the money look after itself, all right. Didn't he make Forbes' list?"

"Number one hundred thirteen," Stewart says. "I looked it up during dinner."

The door pops open and Arty clacks through on her heels, tossing her purse onto the kitchen counter and whipping open a cabinet door. She fishes out a bottle of bourbon and stomps into the living room, flinging herself into a chair and taking a drink straight from the bottle. She passes it to Stewart as he settles into an adjacent chair with a sigh.

"We need to keep a profit-sharing status," Arty says. She grabs the bottle back from Stewart before he can even pull it from his lips. "And we need to make sure the term of the contract is limited to no more than six months." She takes another drink.

"He'll never agree to six months," Stewart says. He kicks off his saddle shoes and curls up against the armrest, reaching for the bottle again. "I think we'd be lucky to get him agree to a year. He's a long-term, whole-package sort of guy. He probably has some sort of intellectual property and noncompete language in his contracts. He wants to own Justin's brain for all eternity." Arty relinquishes her grip on the bottle and Stewart upends it, taking a short drink. I want to get them shot glasses for sanitary reasons, but I think they will have finished the whole bottle by the time I find them.

"No one seems to be asking Justin what he thinks," Liria cuts in.

Stewart swallows his whiskey. He and Arty look at us as we have just appeared out of thin air. Liria is leaning against me on the couch, holding my hand. Arty's eyes dart to it, and she grabs the bottle back from Stewart, taking a long drink.

"I don't think this has anything to do with me, actually," I say. "I just make the pictures. I don't know about business."

Arty puts the whiskey bottle down on the coffee table with a crack. It's more than half gone. "Exactly. Leave the business to us. That's what we're here for."

"If you're so worried about what Mr. Plath is going to do if he has the contract, don't sell it to him," Liria says.

Stewart barks with laughter. Arty gives Liria a wide-eyed look, uncomprehending and slightly frightened, as if Liria had bleated like a goat instead of saying actual words. "He'll find some way to edge us out entirely if we don't cooperate. Besides, this is undoubtedly good for Justin's career. We just have to figure out a way to maintain some vestige of control."

Liria's lips press together, and her fingers tighten around mine. "Whatever. You guys stay up and work it out, but Justin and I are tired. He can sleep in my bed again."

Arty freezes, and the angry Dark Energy wells up behind her blank expression. I get ready to duck and cover, even though I'm not sure I have the energy to do battle again right now. But instead of exploding, she shrugs. "Don't let the bedbugs bite."

Liria gets up, pulling me by the hand, and I rise uncertainly. Stewart is looking back and forth between the two of us, smirking. Then his eyes fall on Arty and he scoots away from her instinctively.

"Goodnight," Liria says.

"Goodnight," I say. I turn and follow Liria into her bedroom, leaving a ringing silence behind us.

Liria shuts the door, then strips off her dress and peels off her tights, tossing them angrily into the corner. "You need to stand up for yourself, Justin."

I stand very still, hoping somehow she won't notice that she's getting naked in front of me. "I don't have anything to stand up against. Obviously the Dark Energy will do what it wants with regard to the business issues, since it has the gangsters and butterfly army poised to attack if I try to escape that situation. As long as we have a place to live and enough to eat, then it's okay."

She unhooks her bra, letting her heavy, round

breasts free. I do notice that she's frowning at me, but I'm spending a lot of time noticing other things too. "If you don't care about that stuff, they're just going to walk all over you," she says.

"If they're walking all over me, I can't tell." I try to keep my eyes on her face, but she is so beautiful, with smooth curves and big rose-chocolate nipples and a perfect little belly button I really want to kiss. "I have everything I want right here, so they can have the rest."

The tension goes out of her shoulders. Her cheeks go pink and she grins, but she can't quite look at me, and I think she's finally realized she's almost naked, except for her underwear. She stands awkwardly, tracing a small scar on her hip with her fingertip, then reaches over and grabs the big shirt of mine she's been using as pajamas and shimmies into it.

She comes over and puts her arms around me, all those parts of her that she's just let me see pressing up against me. I put my arms around her too, and lean my cheek against the top of her head. I close my eyes, and see all sorts of pictures of her naked in my mind, but I think that's okay. I don't think Liria minds that it's happening.

"Liria, I love you," I say.

"I love you too," she says. "I think you're right. I think it's going to turn out okay."

"That's what you already told me earlier, I thought."

She snorts. "Yeah, but it's a complicated issue." She stands quietly, tracing my spine with her fingertips. "You really want me with you if you go on tour?"

"Yes. I need you with me. It's the only thing that the Dark Energy wants that makes sense right now."

We hold each other for a long time like that, then Liria turns off the light and we curl up together in bed. I want Liria extremely badly, but I eventually succeed at kicking that thought out of my mind. I fall asleep in Liria's arms as Arty and Stewart's voices drift down the hallway, still arguing about money.

***

In the Other Place that night, Liria and I sit at the blackjack table with Lee Harvey and a group of vulture businessmen. The television-eyes butterfly deals me a card face down on the table. He furls and unfurls his proboscis, fluttering his wings with a horrible grating static sound that threatens to short my brain out. I press my fingers between my eyebrows to reset my mind button, then lift the corner of the card to peek at it. It depicts a serious-looking man with his huge, fleshy, blood-red lips forming an "o". He holds up two fingers of his right hand beside his face. The caption at the bottom reads, "The Sucker."

I look at Liria. She is stretched out in her chair wearing a long, sequined gown. She glances at the card and wrinkles her nose.

I lay the card back down and look at the butterfly. "Hit me," I say.

Lee Harvey gasps, holding his hand to his mouth, and there is a burst of chittering from the vulture businessmen.

I don't know how I can tell, but I think the butterfly is grinning. One of his thin, black legs bends at the joint, and he pulls a card from the top of the pack with one of his hairy, black, two-fingered hands. He lays it face-up on the table. It shows a woman with slicked-back hair and a cunning, lopsided grin, flipping the bird. In the other hand, she holds up the little construction paper valentine. The card reads, **"The Last Word."**

I turn the other card over and raise my eyebrows at the butterfly.

One of the vulture businessmen leans over to look at them and croaks out a "graaak" noise. He gets up so suddenly that his chair wobbles like a spun penny, then scuttles out of the room with hunched shoulders. The rest of them rustle their suits and scamper after him.

The butterfly goes very still, raising its shining, cut-jewel eyes to stare at me. The only movement in the room is the flickering of the images in their depths: a woman in a bikini lounging on the hood of a car; an old man gripping his back with a pained expression as he leans over to pet the dog.

The butterfly's wings begin to vibrate. A low hum rises up in the Dark Energy. The noise is faint at first, just on the edge of my consciousness, but it grows and grows as its wings vibrate faster and faster. The sound of it eats me like battery acid, searing my brain. I grab Liria's hand and jump up. "Let's go."

***

We wake up with a start in bed.

The hum diminishes from my ears, replaced by the sound of rain hitting the windows. Grey, early dawn light floods the room.

Liria blinks at me. "Your dreams are fucked."

"They're not really dreams, and they're not mine. Though I would agree with you, that sometimes they're fucked."

She frowns, propping her head on her hand. "I still don't understand this. If those aren't dreams, what are they?"

I fiddle with a crease in the quilt. Liria's big brown eyes are still hazy with sleep. She's confusing sometimes, but she is wonderful. "You're in the Dark Energy with me. What don't you understand?"

She smiles, showing her slightly crooked teeth, and scoots against me, putting her cheek on my chest. "You're the one who knows about the Dark Energy. I didn't even know what it was until I met you."

"Really?"

"Yes."

I lie there, feeling her breathing, her fingertips tickling my back. "I didn't know that. I thought you knew all about it."

"Nope. I thought they were just dreams, until that day we met again in San Francisco."

"That's surprising," I say. I stare over her shoulder at the watery morning light reflected in the dresser mirror. I enjoy her tickly fingers. "The Other Place is just as real as the Physical World," I say.

"What does it mean? The...whatever? The stuff that happens there?"

"You mean the card games with the butterfly?"

"Yeah, that. And the vulture businessmen, and all of it."

I think about it. "There's a lesson in it, but I don't know what it is, exactly. The Other Place dreams that happen when you're asleep aren't as easy to decipher as when the angry Dark Energy pulls you there. It's a difference in level of vibration, I think."

"It has to be something about Harold Plath and his contract, though."

"That's an astute guess, yes." I roll the images this way and that in my mind. "That valentine reminds me of something, but I can't remember hard enough to make it solid." It's something that makes me sick and sad, like I lost something important. We lie there for a while, listening to the sound of the rain outside.

Liria wiggles out of my arms. It is disappointing, though it was inevitable. "Get up," she says. "Have some coffee with me."

The apartment is quiet and dim; Arty is still sleeping. It is cozy with the sound of the rain and the cars on the wet pavement outside. We make coffee and then Liria teaches me how to make French toast, mixing up eggs and milk and cinnamon, dipping in thick slices of bread we got at a bakery down the street. The egg mixture glops off in translucent sheets, and we have to gently knead it into the bread's spongy crevices.

Liria giggles as I flip my sizzling slice in the

pan. "Is that…did you burn Michael Jackson's face into it?" She snorts and points at a pattern of brown swirls in the golden, eggy toast. "Oh, my God. You did. That has to mean something."

For a moment, the Dark Energy presses on me with heavy, dark melancholy, because I remember once making pancakes with Mina like this. But then I look at Liria's beautiful face, and everything settles back into shape again. I will never be unhappy that I'm with her. It is meant to be.

I smile. "I hope it doesn't mean that Billy Jean is at my door."

She laughs. "I know. That bitch better step off." She squeezes my waist and slides the toast onto my plate with the spatula.

We hear Arty's door open, and Liria twitches slightly, taking her arm from around my waist. She flops another wet slice of toast into the pan, the smile gone from her face.

Arty comes into the kitchen with a tired scowl, rubbing a hand over her golden-brown, bobbed hair. It's starting to grow out red at the roots, and I wonder if she'll dye it again. Liria and I step out of her way as she heads for the coffee pot.

"Hungover?" Liria asks. Her eyes dart to mine, and she is smirking slightly. I try to smirk back, though I'm not sure if I'm doing it correctly.

Arty grunts. "Give me more credit than that, sweet cheeks. I've been drinking since before you were born. I'm an expert."

"What, you've been drinking since you were like eleven?" Liria asks.

"Just about." Arty dumps cream in her coffee

and shuts the refrigerator door a little too forcefully, making the condiment jars rattle in surprise. She slumps out into the living room.

Liria and I exchange a glance, less smirky this time. "You want some French toast?" Liria calls after her.

"Naw, not yet."

There is no syrup, so Liria and I put butter on our toast and go sit in the living room. Liria sits cross-legged next to me on the couch, and her bare foot touches my knee. We stare out at the rain.

"When is Stewart coming over today?" Liria asks.

Arty gulps her coffee. "Actually, he's here still. Didn't feel like trying to get a cab to his hotel last night."

Liria's eyes widen and she gives Arty an open-mouthed, lopsided smile. "You mean he's asleep in your *bed*?" She laughs. "Ohmygod, Arty."

"What? Don't be juvenile, Liria. We're just *friends*...like you two, right?"

Arty shoots her laser-beam eyes at us over her coffee cup. I feel squirmy about it, but Liria just shrugs and munches her French toast. "You two figure out what you're going to do about Mr. Plath?" she asks.

Arty's lips twist. "We did, and we talked to him already last night. He's drawing up a year contract, with Stewart and me as profit-sharing partners. We have to go back to California in a few days for that stupid fucking hearing on Justin's mom's petition, but then we're coming back here to New York. Harold is arranging for another apartment for us here in Manhattan while the show at Deborah's studio is running, since my dad needs this place. Then we're leaving for London, I think."

At the mention of Mom, the room goes dark like my bedroom closet when I was a kid. "When is the hearing, Arty?" I ask. My ears ring, and the sweet smell of Play-Doh in my toy box mingled with the bad sourness of my shoes washes over me, that horrible smell that meant I was having to hide with the darkness and monsters because the monsters outside were worse. But they always found me, like the policemen and the other soldiers always find me now. "Never mind, I don't want to know, I don't want to know when the hearing is."

Liria gazes at me wide-eyed. "Justin...it's okay, Justin."

The Dark Energy is sucking me through the butterfly's proboscis like I'm a thick and chunky milkshake. It wants to tell me something now, but I don't want to hear it. My intestines have turned into electric eels. This is too much, and I'm so tired. So tired of this.

"Justin..." Liria says. I realize that I'm clutching my plate of French toast so tightly that it's in danger of snapping in pieces.

"I have to run," I say, pulling the words out of my far-away throat in the Physical World. "I don't want a lesson right now. I want to run away from it."

"Justin, don't, Justin, it's raining," Liria says.

My breakfast plate clatters to the floor as I stand up. I dart into the bedroom, pull on my shoes. Liria comes in and says something, but I'm full up with fear and everything is closet-dark and crowded with evil things.

"I have to run," I say, and I dodge past her out the door of the apartment.

I clomp quickly down the stairs. The Dark Energy is tugging hard at me and the monsters are calling out to me with drunken man-voices. I burst through the front entrance and the cold rain engulfs me, dragging its chill, wet fingers across my skin. I splash through the puddles in the cracked sidewalks, breathing in the moist air and exhaust. The rain soaks my hair and runs in little trickling, meandering streams down my back. By the time it makes it to the waistband of my pajama pants, it's almost warm.

For a moment, the cold pushes back against the clutching Dark Energy and brings me into the Physical World. I try to think about Liria, and how good it feels to be in her arms. "I don't need a lesson," I say. "I'm not fighting the army and Arty's lawyer is taking care of the monsters. I have Liria and that's enough. I'm safe and I'm doing everything I'm supposed to do." A woman gives me an angry look and snatches her umbrella out of my path as I jog by. She's reminding me that it's not up to me to decide what the Dark Energy wants. I clutch my head. "But I'm doing everything I'm supposed to do! What else can I do?"

The fear and darkness ooze their way past the wall I'm trying to build with the cold and my pounding heart and thoughts of Liria. It makes my stomach sick, makes my feet stumble. I put my hands over my head. "No, no, no, no," I say, as if I can ward it off, as if it will listen to me. Two more soldiers, a couple of men in sporty rain jackets, watch me go by and their slimy, poisonous thoughts digest me. The butterfly slurps, dragging me further down toward his belly, which smells of shoes and Play-Doh and blood and pee.

My legs won't keep running, because I'm dissolving. My cheek splashes into an oil-sheened puddle as it hits the pavement, and the sludge of my melting body mingles with it in a hot-pungent soup. I have no walls any longer. I can't hide anywhere.

The butterfly stands above me, and I don't know why I didn't smell his sick whiskey-smell before and see how he was always there, working with Mom, and that he would always find me wherever I was. "There you are, you stupid little retard," he buzzes. His proboscis uncurls and hits me like a fist, and I hear someone scream. I think it's me. The butterfly slurps and slurps until he's slurped up my last molecule with a gurgling noise. The Physical World is swallowed by darkness, the frightening rumble of the butterfly's belly echoing in the cavernous space, and I'm crying and alone, locked in here.

Then rows and rows of lights click on, killing the darkness. They blink from every direction in a confusion of brightness. Words flash in a headachy yellow on a big screen above me: "*You're going to love it!*" it reads. Somewhere beyond the brightness, a studio audience claps and cheers.

"*Are you ready?*" the sign flashes.

"Yes! We! Are!" the crowd chants.

"No, I'm not," I say, but my words are

swallowed by the churning bile of noise and light in this butterfly's stomach.

"MAKEOVER TIME!" the sign announces.

Dread mangles my senses. I feel my body jerk, and look down. I'm solid again, and I'm standing on a conveyor belt which has begun to move. I try to jump off, but my feet are glued to it. It's carrying me under the huge screen, into the gaping mouth of a dark closet where the blinding lights don't reach, into the dark closet of the butterfly's intestines, and I know what is in there, I know what's in there now and I don't like it.

The crowd cheers wildly. I can't move. Fear burns me. The mirrored sliding door of the closet hangs off its rail, and I know I won't be able to shut myself in. I know they'll be able to find me in there. Tears wet my cheeks. There's nothing I can do, because the Dark Energy will do what it wants. The conveyor belt carries me through the door and into the swallowing blackness.

But the blackness isn't blackness, and it's not a closet: it's a car wash, with nozzles and rotating brushes that pound and punch the air, whirring with table saw noises. Everything is grotesque, neon circus colors that taste like puked-up pizza and ice cream, and I clutch my arms around myself, trying to curl into a pill-bug ball, trying to be someone who doesn't exist and can't be digested in the first place, but I know there's nowhere I can hide in here because they always find me.

The nozzles turn on, blasting me with a shower of Day-Glo green acid. My flesh melts again and again and it's always happening again, my screams drowned out by the roaring of the crowd. The conveyor belt pulls me onward toward the rotating brushes, and their metal teeth scrape and tear my melting skin away. The pain and stench of whiskey and shoes and blood and piss is all I know, it is the only thing I've ever known. It never began, and it will never end. It lasts forever, because there is no time, they've always found me and always will find me and always are finding me.

The crowd applauds. The butterfly's angry drunk voice screeches at me to get the fuck up, but I can't. A heavy steel roller plunges out of the ceiling and squishes me onto the conveyor belt. It rolls back and forth, crushing what's left of my bones. "Ooooooh!" the audience gasps. "Get! The fuck! Up! You little shit!" the butterfly screams.

But I don't exist anymore, finally. A blast of fiery air hisses from the nozzles, whipping up the dust of my former body into a gritty cloud, which swirls off into nothingness. The noise of the crowd and the butterfly fade, along with the pain.

It is just darkness now. I exist in blissful relief. The Dark Energy undulates in thick waves, and I am part of it, without a body of my own.

Like I always do, I wonder if I will stay here forever this time. It is not so bad, to be one with the Dark Energy like this, to not be or need anything, and not have to worry about pain any longer. But there is Liria. I hope I get to go back, because enlightenment is worthless if I can't be with her.

The waves in the Dark Energy start to form a pattern, lapping and sloshing into shapes. They congeal slowly into legs, and arms, and a torso. I have a body again. It's made of the vibrations but it separates from them as it ripens, because the waves can only slosh against the solid walls of matter and they can't vibrate perfectly together anymore.

The Dark Energy bleeds and twangs and glimmers. The chaos of it comes into focus, it freezes, and is not chaos any longer. I'm encased in a strange network, a machine made of golden wires, pulleys and cogs. It surrounds me in an intricate web.

I sit on a golden throne, dressed in a heavy raiment of white linen and silk. Gold bolts dimple the fabric of my rich robes up and down my limbs and torso, going straight through to my skin, but it doesn't hurt. The bolts are part of me, and a delicate wire runs from each bolt, connecting me to the machine.

I pull back my elbow, my muscles straining against the resistance of the wires. The wires slip against the pulleys, grinding the machine's cogs into motion with a slow whir and clickety-clank and ping. I pull harder, moving my elbow in a circle at my side. Those wires tug more wires, more pulleys and cogs, and set off a chain reaction. Soon, the whole machine is starting to work, the clickety-clank ping getting faster, more complicated, ratcheting up to a swelling symphony. My vision melts to a larger focus, and I realize the machine is huge, layers and layers of wires and connections melting off into the impossible distance. It all grinds into motion, each wire pulling at another and another, all of it set off by the movement of my little elbow. It's like watching the entire ocean on the day it was born, watching it come alive with its first wave and caress the earth for the first time.

The machine clicks and clanks with a beautiful wash of sound. The moving wires tug at the bolts on my arms and legs and belly, pulling me out of my throne. The rhythm of their movement makes my body dance. The machine I set in motion is now setting me in motion in turn, and this makes me laugh.

As I move my head back and forth with the rhythm, I notice shadowy figures amidst the shining network of the machine. I squint at them, and realize they are other people, attached to the wires like I am, caught in the machine's web.

I dance so hard that my consciousness detaches from my body, plucked from it like an autumn leaf carried away by the wind. I drift through the machine's clanging, ringing, moving parts. I am one with its music now, my soul resonating with its tones. I drift up and up, through so many layers. I lose sight of my body and keep going. Every so often, I drift by another one of the people caught in the network, all of them dancing, pulling at the machine and being pulled. I wonder who they are. They're all dressed the same as I was, and I can't focus on their faces.

I don't know how long I float. It seems like eternity, and like a split second. I am borne up on a surging wave of sound, and all of the sudden the wires and pulleys end. I am free of the machine.

I hover in thin air. The machine stretches out below me forever in all directions. The spider-silk-thin golden wires seem to meld into a solid, gleaming mass as I rise. At this distance, the motion of it is nothing more than a glimmer, and the music fades into a faint suggestion of melody and rhythm, like ocean waves rolling pebbles over the beach. I gaze down at the sprawling greatness of it and wonder, was it my movement that set it all in motion, or was it someone else's? Did we all move at once, or did the machine move us?

Movement catches my eye. A construction paper valentine flutters and swoops past me on the air currents. It the only other thing up here with me in the vast emptiness.

The heart drifts toward the machine like an autumn leaf. I suddenly think about Mom. I wonder where she is in that vast network below, and whether she is moving the machine, or it is moving her. Sadness engulfs me, but I'm not sure why.

Understanding tickles at the edges of my mind, my thoughts almost resonating at the correct frequency. Excitement makes my heart beat faster. Am I going to be enlightened now? Is this torture finally over?

***

I am jolted back to the Physical World as if I've been hit with a bat. The gigantic machine disappears abruptly, and its faint, cloying melody is replaced by the ripping blat of a car horn, the hiss of raindrops and tires on wet pavement.

I am very cold and wet. Liria's voice is speaking, every word a sharp handclap in my brain, demanding my attention. "He's my friend, and he's sick. I just need to take him home."

"What did he take?" a man's voice says. I can tell he's a cop, and the memory of the army and Mom jolts into my brain. It is disappointing, to be back in this battle. I almost want to give up, because I'm so tired.

"He didn't take anything, he has an illness," Liria says. "It makes him pass out sometimes." There are tears in her voice. I remember her arms around me, and her saying that she loves me, and I struggle against the immobilizing hands of the Dark Energy.

I find my body again, and figure out how to make it move. I open my eyes. There are tiny pebbles embedded in concrete of the sidewalk, each one a little island in a thin, rippling puddle reflecting the gray sky. Beyond it, the soaked and muddy hems of Liria's pajama pants hang limply around her sneakers, and a pair of solid, deadly cop boots watch me with their eyelet holes, ready to jump and stomp on my face if I don't do the right thing.

I sit up as quickly as I can. I'm dizzy. "I'm okay. No more cops, please. I don't need the cops again. I'm doing what I'm supposed to do."

"Justin!" Liria says. Her knees splash in the puddle as she kneels beside me. She squeezes me into her arms. She is very wet, also, but her skin is warm and feels good against mine. "Justin," she whispers, and her body shakes with crying.

I put my arms around her too. "It's okay, Liria. They can't hurt us because we're doing what we're supposed to."

I stroke Liria's damp back. The cop peers at me, reading all my thoughts, and I open my mind, let him see that I'm in compliance with the butterfly's orders. He is an older man with hair that is greying around his ears. Rain is dripping off his hat. Behind him, his car is pulled up to the curb, lights flashing. He looks familiar, somehow, but maybe it is just this situation that is becoming familiar.

"Good morning, sir," he says. "Can you tell me what's happening here?"

I will play his game, because that is what I'm supposed to do. "I have an illness that makes me lose consciousness sometimes. I was running, and that's what happened." Liria pulls out of my arms and stands up, and I try to push myself up off the wet pavement. It takes me a couple of tries, because I'm dizzy, and Liria has to help me, tugging at my armpit.

"Do you need to go to the hospital?" he says. "I can get an ambulance here."

I stand, blood pounding in my ears. Liria and I look at each other, and I see the fear in her. "No, I'm okay," I say. "I just want to go home and lie down."

The cop stares at me a bit longer, and he nods. He looks at Liria. "Get him home. Don't let him pass out in the streets like that, something bad could happen to him."

"Yes, Officer, I'm really sorry," Liria says.

The cop says something into his radio, and someone says something back to him, their voice tinny and wreathed in static. Liria puts her arm around me and guides me down the sidewalk, back toward the apartment. The noise of the cop's radio fades behind us, replaced by the staccato drumming and pinging of the rain on roofs and cars and garbage cans.

"Justin, are you okay?" Liria asks. There are still tears in her voice.

"Yes, Liria. I'm sorry I had to run off. I'm sorry I'm so much trouble."

"Shhh, Justin, no." She squeezes me tighter against her. "I love you, Justin."

"I love you too, Liria. Very much." I stare at my feet. I'm so cold that my skin is numb. I shiver violently every time a new rivulet of rainwater finds its way down my back.

"You're freezing," Liria says. "You need a hot bath and some tea and soup."

"That sounds very nice."

"There you fucking are."

My neck snaps up at the voice. Arty is stomping toward us, wearing a bright red raincoat with the hood up. Her eyes are like burning, angry coals that don't give off warmth.

"Where did you find him?" she demands.

"Let's talk about it when we get home," Liria says. "He's freezing." She tugs me onward, and Arty falls into step beside us.

"This is fucking bullshit, Justin," Arty mutters. "If Plath catches you flipping out again like this, he'll pull his contract offer so fast—"

"Leave him alone," Liria cuts in. "He can't help it."

"He'd better fucking learn to help it, or his career will be toast. He needs his medication adjusted like right fucking now. Stewart has a call into his friend for a new prescription."

Liria stomps in a puddle, spraying my legs with cold, gritty water. "Drugging him into a coma isn't the answer, Arty. Maybe if you would stop doing and saying shit that stressed him out so much—"

"Please, no fighting," I say, my teeth chattering. "It's really difficult for me to stay solid right now and the fighting is going to make me melt again."

Liria lets out a shuddering gasp and hugs me tighter to her side. Arty snorts and rolls her eyes, but doesn't say anything else.

It doesn't take long to get back to the building, because I didn't run that far before the Dark Energy took me. Liria holds me tightly as we go up in the elevator, but I can't even feel her warmth anymore.

She pulls me into the bathroom as soon as we're inside the apartment. Arty watches like a statue of a vindictive hell-goddess as Liria shuts the door.

Liria starts water going in the tub and helps me peel off my sopping clothes. I'm vibrating with cold and my muscles are very tight, so it's not easy. Then she helps me into the hot water, which burns for a moment before my skin gets used to it.

I ease myself down into the tub. It feels very good. Liria strips off her wet clothes as well and climbs in with me, turning off the water. She uses my special no-toxin soap to scrub me down, which feels nice. Slowly, the shivers ease out of my bones, and my thoughts come out of the places they were hiding from the cold and from the Dark Energy.

The air is full of steam, which undulates and billows with the peaceful air currents. I imagine each, tiny droplet of water to be a star or planet, pushed along by the galactic forces in the same way people are caught in eddies of Dark Energy. I am starting to breathe easier again.

"You okay?" Liria murmurs.

"I'm feeling much better, thank you." I blink at her. I almost wish some of my thoughts had stayed hidden because now that they're here, they're very interested in Liria's naked body.

She puts the soap down and begins spooning water over me with her cupped hands. "What happened? Why did you have to run? Was it because Arty talked about the hearing on your mom's petition?"

"That was upsetting, but the reason I ran is because the Dark Energy needed to tell me something, and I didn't want it to because it hurts and is frightening when it takes me like that."

Liria studies me, dribbling hot water over my shoulders. "What did it tell you? The Dark Energy?"

"I'm not even sure." I think of the golden machine. "I guess that I'm not the center of the universe, but I already knew that."

She chews on her lip. "You're the center of a lot of things right now."

"We all are," I say. "We're all kings of our own little kingdoms."

She smiles. She is kneeling between my legs in the hot water, and she looks very nice doing it. Her breasts are very fascinating, golden-brown with big nipples, and the skin is so soft it has a pearly sheen. I think they would feel extremely nice under my fingers, like velvety flower petals that taste like honey and sunshine. I wonder what she would do if I touched them. But then I remember about the bad feelings other men have given her, and I don't want to risk that happening. Letting those bad feelings into the Dark Energy right now would be like pouring rotten garbage onto a beautiful meadow.

"I think the Dark Energy is also trying to tell me something about Mom," I say. "I don't know what it is, though. It's a thing I can't quite catch."

"You'll figure it out," she says, letting water trickle down my bare chest. "I don't understand why you have these visions or whatever they are, though."

I take a deep breath, let it out. "Lots of people do, you're just not supposed to talk about it." I'm trying to pay attention, but Liria is very distracting.

"I don't know anyone else who has visions." She frowns with faraway eyes as she sloshes warm water on me. She's not paying much attention, either, and her fingertips graze my bare skin.

"I'm surprised you don't get lessons like I do, since we're in the Dark Energy together," I say.

Her thoughts run back from the distant places they've been wandering, and her gaze snaps to my face. "I want to tell you to take the medication Arty wants to give you so that what happened today doesn't happen again, because it's so horrible and scary for you. But it's just so…weird…because that place you go to is real, I know it is…"

A very uncomfortable feeling jolts through me. I clutch my elbows. "I can't keep the Dark Energy from giving me lessons, Liria. That would be horrible. I don't like the lessons but that's because I'm a coward. I need to be able to have the lessons."

It's easy for me to say this now that the lesson is over, but part of me knows that, when it is happening, I'd swallow all the medication in the world to get it to stop. I'm frightened, hoping the Dark Energy didn't hear that thought.

Liria's wide brown eyes shine. She stops putting water on me. "You're not a coward, Justin. Those lessons sound really scary."

My heart is beating fast. I stare at her, kneeling there naked in the tub, the steam plastering her blue hair to her skull. "Promise me you really aren't a trick or a trap," I say. "I love you, Liria, and the Dark Energy wants us to be together."

"Shhh, Justin, of course I'm not a trick or trap." She carefully eases down next to me, slipping her naked body into the small space between me and the side of the tub. Her soft breasts are smooshed against me. She pushes my wet hair out of my face with gentle fingers. "I promise I'm not trying to trick or trap you. I would never." Her eyes fill with tears. "Please believe me."

"I didn't think Mina was a trick when she asked me to get on medication, but I think the Dark Energy was just using her to get me out of Piedras." I'm clutching my elbows very hard now, and Liria presses her forehead into my shoulder. "I think there's a trick or a lesson in the medication she made me take. I don't know what it is. I don't know if I should keep taking it at all. There's so many cogs and wires in the machine that I can't hardly know what's going on and I'm so tired of having to guess."

Liria puts her arm around me, runs her hand along my wet back. "The medication doesn't stop you from getting lessons now, does it? It doesn't stop you from knowing about the Dark Energy?"

My hands unclutch from my elbows. I put my arms around her too, and it feels too good for it to be a trick or a trap. "No."

"I think the medication just makes it a little bit easier. It's not a trick, Justin. Mina was trying to help you, and so am I."

"How can I know that? I can't know that until I'm enlightened, and it's so scary not to know, because of the feelings you have when you care about people, how sour they can turn. It's like having a bunch of very good cheese where your heart is but it can go really, really bad if it spoils."

Liria laughs a little bit.

"But, Liria," I say.

"It's okay, Justin." She glances up at me. "I don't think the chest-cheese feelings you give me will ever go bad."

I look into her brown eyes. Every part of her is pressed up against every part of me, and it feels very comfortable and warm and right and really, really good, and she is in the Dark Energy with me. "I can't figure it out," I say. "It's scary because I can't understand all of the ways that the machine moves, or all the things that are happening."

"Either can I," she says very quietly.

My hands wander over the flower-petal skin of her back. "But I guess I can't care about whether you're part of some trick because I love you and we're supposed to be together with one another, and I'm glad about that, and I can't help any of it anyway."

She smiles, and she is so beautiful. "I'm really glad we're supposed to be together, too. You took care of me when I was kicking dope, and when Arty kicked me out. I...you just make me so happy, Justin, just because of the way you are. I'll never leave you."

Her eyes taste like rich coffee and the really good chocolate you only get on special occasions. My hands will never get tired of touching her. It's like touching the marble statues at the museum that you're not supposed to touch but can't help it. "I'm not too much trouble for you, Liria?"

She smiles, but tears are leaking out of her eyes. She shakes her head. "No. You're not too much trouble at all. Am I...am I too much trouble for you?"

The question is confusing. "Of course not. No, Liria. You're the thing that makes the most sense in my life. You're the opposite of trouble."

"I love you, Justin," she whispers.

Liria presses up against me. She pulls me closer with her hands on my shoulders. Then her lips are against mine and she is kissing me. All our feelings for one another and our slippery naked skin, the smell of her and of soap, is the sweetest thing. There are no bad feelings anywhere in the world right now. Her hands touch me, and I finally get to feel her round, warm breasts. I touch her nipples and feel her shiver. My other hand finds the perfect curves of her waist. Liria slips her slightly rough heel in between my calves, intertwining her legs with mine, and suddenly I want her in a way that is frightening, in a way that makes men pound their chests and roar and get violent in order to protect the thing that is the most beautiful and important and perfect in their lives. A moan escapes my mouth because of how good she feels, and Liria draws a breath, her lips still against mine.

And although we are cramped in the tub and Arty is in the other room probably plotting my murder, Liria puts her leg over my hip and slips me inside her, and I forget all about every trick of the Dark Energy.

Chapter 8

Liria snatches my hand away so that I don't pull the button off of my brand-new suit jacket. I'm facing down my lawyer, Patricia Harris, across a table in a back room of the San Luis Obispo County Courthouse. She's wearing an expression I associate with an Easter Island head. Getting her to smile would probably require a chisel and hammer.

"Are you ready for this hearing, Mr. Flaherty?" she says. "Do you have any more questions before we go in?"

"No, Ms. Harris," I say. "You did a very good job of preparing me yesterday." I rub the back of my neck. We spent hours going over how to talk to the judge and how to respond to questions, and my head is so full of words and situations that my neck is stiff from carrying it all around.

The lawyer stares at me. Her hands are flat on the table in front of her, and no part of her moves. "Well, like I told you, the worst that will likely happen at this stage is that the judge will order your evaluation by a psychiatric expert. I just found out

157

that we're going in front of Judge Hall, so it's unlikely our motion to dismiss your mother's petition will be granted today. I'm confident we'll win ultimately, however." Her eyes slide over to Liria and Arty. "Iris and Christina's declarations were very supportive, as were Stewart Califax's and Dr. Mingle's."

Arty picks at her fake nails, as if her true self is unconsciously trying to peel off the Iris Pierson costume. "I'm concerned that you're presenting Dr. Mingle's declaration. It doesn't seem supportive to me at all. She discloses his diagnosis and doesn't even specify that his medication dosage has been increased. I think you should have a declaration from Dr. Schlopper, who is his treating psychiatrist now."

Dr. Schlopper is a man with a wide frog mouth and only one very serious, earnest expression for his face. He wrote me a new prescription, which makes my aura a little more wooden, but it's not too bad so far.

Patricia's gold wedding band clicks against the wood table. "I think Dr. Mingle's declaration is better, since she's been treating him longer. The levels of medication aren't important. Dr. Mingle specifies that he's compliant with her medical orders, and that's what matters. By all accounts, Justin is competent and in control of his affairs. However," her yellowed eyes twitch slightly, "if this case is allowed to go through the discovery phase, I do worry this new contract with Mr. Plath might gum up the works."

Arty sits straighter. "How so? Justin's a highly

successful artist, with what looks to be a stellar career ahead of him, and he's entering into reasonable contracts to further it." The contract subject stirs up Arty's vibrations in a big way lately. She is extremely worried that I am going to explode with craziness and blow up my chances of having the contract with Mr. Plath before it's signed.

Ms. Harris' sharply-carved lips pull back, but it is not really a smile; it is actually very intimidating. "Well, the contract is technical enough that everyone will have to hire experts to analyze it. It will be easy enough for them to find problems…or to suggest that Mr. Flaherty isn't competent to enter into such a complicated business deal." She stands up, still staring down at Arty. "We should get into the courtroom. The hearing is about to start."

I stand on numb legs. A jitter tickles my spine, and my stomach is full of anxious tadpoles, but Dr. Mingle's new medication has dried out my soul and scabbed it over on the outside so I have a shell like a crab. It is difficult for many feelings to survive in such an arid environment.

We walk down the hallway past little groups of mismatched people—the lawyers in suits and their clients in stained t-shirts or cheap dresses. One lady is in sweat pants with **"Hottie"** written in sequins on the butt, which is not an outfit that harmonizes with the courthouse vibrations very well, I don't think.

I twitch as Patricia touches my arm. She slows her steps until we fall behind Arty and Liria, and puts her lips very close to my ear. "I'd like to remind you, Mr. Flaherty, that I represent *you*, not

Ms. Iris Pierson." She enunciates Arty's fake name carefully in a way that makes me think she knows it's a fake name.

"I understand, Ms. Harris," I mutter back. "Ms. Pierson is a very crafty person but I believe the way in which she crafts things is probably the shape that things need to be in for me."

My lawyer examines me, her eyes like polished jade-green stones, though the whites look tarnished. She gives a little shrug and a faint smile that is more in her eyes than her lips. "Just be careful and be sure to tell me if any of the contract language or anything anyone does makes you nervous."

I nod.

Arty and Liria wait for us at the door to the courtroom, and we walk in. It is a long, narrow, windowless room that smells like nervous people, bad coffee, and cheap hairspray. A wooden barrier separates us from a couple of podiums, some rows of chairs, and a large many-tiered judge's bench. Hard, official vibrations jab me with brutal angles.

Patricia leads us down a row of chairs on our side of the wooden barrier. We squeeze past the knees of a young man who is sprawled in his seat with a surly look, and an older man with extremely slicked-back hair who is sitting up very straight and wide-eyed. We settle into a group of empty chairs by the wall. They are like movie-theater chairs that fold down when you sit on them, except there are no cup holders and no aura of fun things that are going to happen.

Arty rolls her eyes away as Liria takes my hand. I'm certain that Arty has seen in the Dark Energy that Liria and I are having sex with one another, but she has not said anything. This makes me very nervous, because she is a creature that stalks silently.

A jittery current hits me from a different direction. Mom is sitting in the front row near the opposite wall, and her squinted-up, twisted-frowny expression bashes me like a gong-hammer before she sees me looking and faces forward again. She's wearing her best church dress with the red buttons like shiny, perfect ladybugs without spots. I always got in trouble when I was younger because I always had to sneak into Mom's closet and feel those buttons against my lips, because the shape and color of them just works that way.

Beside her, David shoots me a brief glance over his shoulder before leaning in and muttering something to a man beside him in a blue suit. I think it must be the lawyer they hired when they found out I had Patricia.

I wonder why my money is so important to Mom. She obviously still has David to help take care of her. But then I think about how her relationships always disintegrate into sad chunks and ashes, and how scared and screechy she gets when that happens. I wonder if she's just worried she'll have no one to screech at and take money from in between boyfriends. The thought makes me laugh a little bit. "Mom is weird."

I fall silent quickly because Liria gives me a look.

I wonder if I'm actually like Mom, and if my relationship with Liria will fall into debris like

Mina's and mine did. I shudder and clutch my elbows and tell myself it can't be true, because we're in the Dark Energy together.

A bailiff comes in and tells us to please rise. The crowd gets to its feet, shuffling and coughing and shoving cell phones into their pockets. A woman emerges from a door behind the huge desk. She has close-cropped, curly, dark hair, and is so tiny that she is engulfed in her judge's robes like a child in her mother's nightgown. I wonder if she is big enough to carry the weight of the justice she dispenses.

We sit again as the judge settles in behind her bench. I sit very straight, because the Dark Energy is very stiff and formal right now. My heart is bouncing back and forth off my ribcage and spine like a paddle ball.

Judge Hall shuffles her paperwork and raises her little chin to gaze out across the courtroom. "First case today looks like it's Mallone versus Cadwalleger." Her voice is strong; it's like a squirrel opening its mouth and letting out a bull bellow. Four people—two attorney-client sets—stand up and make their way to the podiums in front of the judge's desk. The clients are a man and a woman, and they shoot each other hurtful looks, squeezing bitterness into the Dark Energy like rancid lemons.

"The family law cases go first," Patricia whispers in my ear. "We have a while to wait."

We sit while case after case is called and people stand in front of the judge barking and bleating about marriages and restraining orders. The smell of their bad relationships turns the Dark Energy humid and yellow-brown. My knee jitters, trying to block that bad disease from infecting my relationship with Liria. Mom and David don't look at me again, but their thoughts pound into my brain like nails and I can see the vibrations of them deliberately not looking at me. I think Mom wants Liria and me to catch that bad-feelings disease so we will break up and I will come home. I squeeze my eyes shut and cover my mouth with my hand so it won't be able to get in. I take deep breaths through my nose, trying to let my nostril hairs filter out the bad-smelling poisons.

Liria squeezes my hand, and I open my eyes and see her beautiful face. She smiles at me, and I take my hand from my mouth and smile back. I relax into my chair. Our good feelings for one another are like a vaccine against the horribleness. I don't really know what I was worried about.

Eventually, the judge calls my case. "Flaherty versus Flaherty."

Liria squeezes my hand to give me one last dose of vaccine before I have to let it go. Patricia and I stand up, as do Mom and her lawyer. The judge peers at us with interest as we approach her podium. Mom's eyes land on my face and then dart away, over and over again, like an annoying fly. I try to ignore her. I can feel David's eyes on me too, but looking back at him would be a very bad idea.

Mom's lawyer rocks back and forth on his brown saddle shoes and tells their side of the story first. He reminds me a little of a pigeon, and his voice sounds like cooing because of how it's shaped by his meaty throat. A bead of sweat trickles down my back as he talks about how the doctors say I'm schizophrenic. He says Mom is worried that the art people will take advantage of me and take all my money, so she thinks it's a good idea if she takes advantage of me and takes all my money, instead.

The judge reads through the paperwork as she listens to him, and snips his narrative short with the slice of a sharp glance when it seems it will never be over. "Your client attempted to have the respondent taken into custody on a 5150 psychiatric hold, at his art opening in San Francisco, but law enforcement declined to do so, saying they didn't perceive a threat to self or others, correct?"

Mom's lawyer stops rocking on his heels and stands very straight. His eyes are glassy behind his thick, round spectacles. "Correct. However, our assertion during these proceedings isn't that Mr. Flaherty is a threat, but rather that he lacks the capacity to adequately run his affairs."

"Well, the petitioner doesn't seem to be helping him to run them adequately," the judge says. "Why did she interfere in his business practices by sending police to his opening to arrest him?"

"My client was worried about his wellbeing," Mom's lawyer says. "He'd left home and taken off without notice to San Francisco, and she didn't know where he was living. The only place she knew to locate him was at his opening."

Patricia stands with her hands folded in front of her, as peaceful as a tree in still air. The judge flips through more paperwork. "Yes, he ran off to the city to become an artist," the judge says. "Unlike most people who do that, though, he had a very successful reception." She turns her gaze on me. They are dark brown, small, and glitter like water bugs. "I've heard about you, Mr. Flaherty, believe it or not. They had an article about you in the local paper. I take it the opening in San Francisco went well?"

I grab one of my hands with the other so I don't fidget. "It went very well, Your Honor," I say. "There was a lot of interest in my work. All of the pieces got bids, although we turned some down because I'm currently participating in another show in Manhattan."

Her eyebrows shoot up. "Yes, I'd say that's doing well." She leans toward me over her bench. "I know you're a legal adult, but you were living with your mother before, correct?"

"Yes, Your Honor." This situation is very jittery. I try to put down roots to suck some of the deep, calm tree energy like my lawyer.

"So why did you run off without notice to the City? Why didn't you at least tell her where you were going?"

"Mom kicked me out of the house. I didn't talk to her after that because it was uncomfortable." Ms. Harris tells me to not bring up the Rebekah incident if I don't have to, so I leave that part out. Behind me, I hear a "Boof," and I know it's David who is boofing because of the nauseating, grating gray colors it blasts into the Dark Energy.

"My client didn't kick her son out of the house," Mom's lawyer says. "It was an unfortunate misunderstanding between them."

Patricia finally speaks up with a very pleasant voice. "We have several declarations supporting my client's testimony in this matter: one from a sheriff's deputy whom Petitioner told Justin was no longer welcome in the house, and another from a man in Piedras with whom Justin was living before he went to San Francisco."

Judge Hall's eyes dart to Mom. My eyes look over at her too, even though I don't want them to. The sight of her punches me in the guts. She has her lips all scrunched up and is looking at her attorney. I tense up, waiting to see what will happen. I'm worried the judge will ask more about the declaration from Detective Bickman and why the police were involved. Patricia said she didn't think Mom's lawyer would bring up the Rebekah incident, either, because of how the police knew Rebekah was lying and so it would look bad for them, but she isn't sure.

A moment passes, and then another, and Mom's lawyer is silent, and the judge doesn't ask any more questions about the police. Some of the tension goes out of my shoulders, but my back is sweating so much that I hope I don't end up filling up the courtroom with a huge wave of perspiration and drowning everyone.

Judge Hall shuffles through the paperwork for a long time. We all stand silently as she reads. The only sound is the ventilation system and the quiet muttering and shifting of the remaining crowd in their seats.

I stare at the San Luis Obispo County insignia on the plaque behind the Judge's bench. I wonder what it means, and why the county needs an insignia, like a gang. I imagine the judge with the county's seal tattooed above her butt like a tramp stamp, and I giggle.

Patricia lays a hand briefly on my sweaty back, and I am very embarrassed, because I shouldn't giggle in court.

The judge looks back up at me. "Mr. Flaherty, you've been diagnosed with schizophrenia."

I squeeze my fingers together. "Yes," I say, because this is what Patricia taught me to say.

"You're on medication?" the judge asks.

"Yes."

"You see your psychiatrist regularly?"

"Yes, Your Honor."

She looks at Mom's lawyer. "I've read through this contract that he has with, uh," she glances down, "Mr. Califax and Ms. Pierson, and it looks more than fair, counsel. I'm not sure what your concerns are."

"We're concerned that the parties may not be sticking to the contract," Mom's lawyer says. "Mr. Flaherty doesn't have the business experience to know when he's being taken advantage of."

"Very few eighteen-year-olds do," Judge Hall says. "Nor do I, for that matter. In fact, just last week, I got talked into purchasing an extended warranty on a laptop computer without reading the contract language. Turns out I got taken for a ride. Perhaps I should have a guardian to take care of my affairs too."

Patricia smiles, but Mom's lawyer doesn't.

Judge Hall's gaze falls back to the paperwork. A

sharp crease forms between her thin, dark eyebrows, and she looks up at me. "I have to confess, Mr. Flaherty, I don't blame your mother for being worried. You're entering into a pretty big venture. It appears to me that you're an extremely talented young man, and there are always people who will try to take advantage of someone like you. You seem competent enough to me, standing here politely in my courtroom and looking very handsome in your suit, but you are *young* and therefore inexperienced, and even if you're compliant with your treatment, you're definitely struggling under the weight of a serious disability that has the capacity to impair your judgment."

Her eyes glitter, and I don't say anything, because Patricia has taught me not to talk to the judge unless I'm asked a direct question. If she thinks my brain is shriveled up or entirely amputated and won't hold my weight, she's going to let Mom's brain be in charge of my life again. Mom's brain bounces around like a rubber ball, breaking things and creating bad situations. It really shouldn't be in charge of anything.

The judge sits up straight, and I flinch slightly. "However," she continues, "I think your mother might not have the capacity and expertise to run your affairs, either. I see she receives disability payments for a psychiatric diagnosis herself..."

"Mrs. Flaherty's mental health conditions don't limit the cognitive and reasoning abilities," Mom's lawyer cuts in, but Judge Hall gives him an arch look.

"I'm not sure that's true. These are some serious

diagnoses, and I have to admit her behavior in kicking her son out of the house and then trying to have him taken into police custody at his art opening doesn't particularly inspire confidence. But it would take an expert to tell us about her cognitive abilities, and we don't have one here."

Mom's lawyer falls silent, and the judge frowns down at the paperwork, flipping through it some more. Patricia watches her carefully, as if her x-ray lawyer vision allows her to see into her mind.

Finally, Judge Hall looks back up at me. "Mister Flaherty, you are entering into a very exciting period in your life. It appears I have a very talented man standing in front of me, from what I've read, and it seems probable that you'll be dealing with a lot of complicated contracts and perhaps a significant amount of money." She smiles at me, and I smile back, although my heart is pounding and I have a sick feeling.

Her smile disappears. "I agree with the petitioner in this case that you need someone to assist you with all these things," she continues, and I taste rotten bananas in my mouth. "It has got to be daunting, dealing with all these contracts and offers on your artwork and other things. Even if you weren't at the tender age of eighteen and suffering from schizophrenia, the opportunities for you to be taken advantage of would be legion. I would hate to see your spectacular talent and potential turned into an opportunity for someone else to make money. And that is why," she looks over at Mom, "I am granting respondent's motion and *dismissing* your mother's petition. Justin needs someone to help him with his affairs—anyone in his position would—but he doesn't need a guardian. The necessary elements for appointing one have not been proven in the least, and I'm afraid I have suspicions the petitioner's reasons for bringing this case are not completely altruistic." She gives me a fierce and proud look as air finally pours uninhibited into my lungs. "So, summary judgment granted in favor of Respondent. The case is dismissed with prejudice, and, Mister Flaherty, I wish you the best of luck. If you have a show here in SLO, I will be sure to be there."

The judge shuffles the papers and calls the next case. Back in the gallery, Liria squeals, "*Yes!*"

Mom stomps, her eyes full of tears, her mouth open like she wants to say something else. Her lawyer quickly puts his arm around her shoulders and leads her away. In the audience, David glares at me as if he's trying to shoot lightning bolts out of his eyes, but I'm not worried, because he doesn't have that superpower, I don't think, or he would have used it on me a long time ago.

Patricia beams as if someone's sprinkled fairy dust on her and made her suddenly human instead of a statue. "Thank you, Ms. Harris," I say, smiling back.

"I'm so glad." She squeezes my shoulder.

We head back through the gate in the wooden barrier, crowding around the people called for the next case as they come in. Mom and David and their lawyer are huddled by the wall in a dark cloud of anger, speaking to each other in hushed voices, and we ignore them as we walk by.

I smile at Liria, who is gathering up our things along with Arty. Patricia puts her hand on my back and guides me out the door, not waiting for them.

Her face finds its normal etched position as we go out into the hallway. She pulls me off to the side and stops, examining me. "Justin, I do agree with the judge that you should have someone look after your affairs, because all these contracts would be confusing to anyone who isn't trained in contract law. I hope you will let me review the contract with Mr. Plath before you sign it."

It is starting to seem like the gangsters and butterfly army are moving in on my money in earnest, even though I still don't have any actual money yet. I don't know if Patricia is one of them, or what the Dark Energy is making her do, but she really seems like an honest person. "I'll think about it," I say.

She nods. "Call me to talk about it after it's drafted. I'll give you a phone consultation to discuss my further involvement, free of charge."

I blink at her, because she doesn't seem like a person that's ever free of charge.

The courtroom door opens again and Arty and Lira come out, grinning.

Liria bounces and throws her arms around me. "Oh, my God, *yes*!"

I hold her, stroking her back. Her happiness makes me even happier. Arty glances at us with eyes like cold, brown marbles before smiling at Patricia and shaking her hand.

"You kicked ass in there, Ms. Harris. Thank you."

"Glad I could help. They could definitely appeal this, though, so we're not out of the woods yet."

"They wouldn't dare appeal," Arty says. "They haven't got a chance."

The courtroom doors open once more and Mom, David, and their lawyer come out. Mom has tears running down her cheeks. Her lawyer is talking to her in a low voice, but he clams up when he sees us and tightens his grip on Mom's shoulder, leading her away. My heart runs around in awkward circles as they hurry by, Mom and David eyeing us like we're a group of murderous cannibals. Their ugly vibrations fade down the hallway behind my back.

"Those assholes better not try some bullshit appeal," Arty mutters, squinting after them.

"I agree it would be bullshit, but never underestimate human stupidity," Patricia says. Arty snorts dryly.

I hold Liria tighter. I know we are both wondering how the two of us will be able to keep battling so many enemies on our own.

Chapter 9

The wide, wooden floor of the loft is littered with sheets of canvas and small scraps of lumber, as if a fleet of tiny sailboats has exploded. Mr. Plath has moved us to a new place for the remainder of the New York show. It's even better than Morton Kopanis's, with gigantic windows looking out through the monstrous steel and glass pillars of skyscrapers holding up the smoggy Manhattan sky.

Tianna is bent over something called a miter box, sawing an angle in a length of wood with a hand saw. Arty has invited her over to teach me how to stretch canvases. I told Arty not to do that, but since I couldn't think up a good reason why she shouldn't, without creating hazardous situations by telling her that Liria is my girlfriend and is jealous, she did it anyway.

A sunbeam drapes over Tianna's back as she works, bringing out sparkling red glints in her puff-of-smoke hair. She tries to fill my mind with angles and instructions and advice as she saws, but I'm distracted by Liria, who is slumped on the couch,

173

her nostrils flaring while she pretends to read something on her phone. I hope I can get through this whole experience without any major violations of the girlfriend social dance.

Tianna finishes her cut and blows on it, spreading pine dust over the floor in a golden wave, and sending dust motes spiraling in a frenzied dance through the sunbeam. She fits the piece in with the others she's cut to form a rectangular frame, twenty by twenty-five inches.

"Hand me the staple gun," she says. She holds out her hand, palm up. I like how the pink skin of her palm contrasts with the brown of the rest of her. Her big eyes catch mine, and she smiles.

I smile back, and Liria fidgets on the sofa. I stop smiling, because I think Liria wants me to be surly and maybe to spit and yell at Tianna instead, but that sounds like an unpleasant and startling way to act and I don't want to do that.

Tianna is still looking at me as I try to figure out what to do with my face, one of her perfectly-shaped eyebrows creeping up, and I remember about the staple gun and pick it out of the clutter on the floor.

I lay it on Tianna's rosy palm. "Here you go."

"Thanks." She lays the butt of the gun against a joint in the wooden frame. "You staple the pieces together at an angle, like this." She pulls the trigger, and the gun goes *thwap* with a very satisfying sound. It sounds like when you find the perfect clothes for the day and all the vibrations fall into place. When she pulls the gun away, a staple is embedded neatly across the joint. It is very organized and pretty-looking.

"Some people use finishing nails," Tianna explains as she lays more staples, *thwap, thwap, thwap,* "but you really just need a good staple gun." She grins at me again, and I smile back more carefully this time, hoping it is not in the way Liria doesn't like. Liria doesn't look up from her phone, her foot wagging. Her vibrations are no angrier than usual for this situation.

Tianna chooses a large scrap of canvas from the remnants she's brought with her. She spreads it on a square of cardboard, then lays the frame on top of it and cuts the canvas around it with a scalpel knife, slightly bigger than the frame. "So, you sign the contract with Plath yet?"

"Not yet," I say. "I have only recently discovered the existence of something called an attorney, but now I have an infestation. They tell me my life up to this point has had so many legal complications it's a wonder I survived. My attorneys are now looking over the contract and sparring with rival tribes of attorneys, but they tell me it will be ready soon, once the dust clears and the casualties are hauled away."

Tianna laughs, and Liria shoots me a look, her lips twisted into what might almost be a smile. Since I hired Patricia's firm to look at the contract, she and her associates have organized my life into a precise, uniform grid so that there are no surprises and nothing to trip over. It is a strange feeling. I keep expecting one of them to show up and rearrange my sock drawer and measure my eyebrows to make sure they're exactly identical.

"I'm sure they'll get it worked out," Tianna says. "Mr. Plath is an amazing career-maker." She folds the edges of the canvas over the frame. "Anyway, then you take your handy staple gun again, and…" *Thwap, thwap, thwap.*

We have moved on to priming and sealing the canvas, Tianna discussing all the different ways to do it with different forms of goop for different textures, when the door to the loft opens and Arty and Stewart come in. Paper grocery bags crinkle in their arms, and I can tell by the happy glow on their faces that something good has happened.

"Did you get a message from Patty Harris?" Arty asks.

I feel around in my pockets and realize I've left my phone in the bedroom. "No."

"They're done with the contract negotiations." She grins even wider as she and Stewart set the bags on the black-and-blue-tiled breakfast bar. "It looks good, and apparently, she wants you to sign it. That's what my lawyer says, anyway."

"That's very nice," I say. Patricia made Arty get her own attorney, which was an uncomfortable situation for a moment, but it was resolved without major incident.

Stewart pulls bottles of booze and bags of pita chips from one of the bags. "Congratulations, Justin. You're going to be famous."

Liria and I look at each other. We're wondering if this strange thing could be true, and what it would mean for our battle with the butterfly's army if it is. "Thank you," I say.

"I got your prescription filled, Justin," Arty says.

She strides over, handing me a little bottle of pills. I take it and turn it around in my hands.

"The pills are different," I say.

"Dr. Schlopper upped your prescription, and the higher dosage looks different."

As she walks through the sunbeams back to the kitchen, there is a moment when the glare engulfs her. Arty disappears, and in her place is a vulture businessman with a gray suit and slicked-back hair.

My stomach cramps up. I shake my head violently, and when I look back, it's just Arty. She's in her jeans and t-shirt, her bobbed hair swinging around her ears as she unloads the grocery bags, and she is not a vulture businessman at all. I take a deep breath and let it out.

"Are you okay?" Liria asks.

"Yes. I'm fine. Just too much sunlight in here, I think."

But I don't know if that's true.

***

That night, we have a party in the loft to celebrate both the signing of the contract and the end of my show at Ms. Corinth's gallery. The show has gone very well, and they have had to work out complicated deals with buyers in order to keep my pieces for display while I work on new ones.

The setting sun peers through the gigantic hallway of skyscrapers glinting rainbows and gold off the crystal bowls on the catered buffet table. A raucous flock of art people crowd the room. Their jumpy, dancy vibrations tickle and prickle me and try to cause a ruckus in my body. I work on a painting to try to organize them into a manageable system, even though I think it is a violation of the social dance to paint during a party.

I use the small canvas that Tianna stretched for me, the acrylic gesso just barely dry enough to paint on. Tianna stands at my elbow, watching, munching a crunchy hors d'oeuvre and cradling a glass of red wine between her fingers.

"That's really beautiful, the way the colors sort of fade…" She makes swooping gestures with a toast point, mimicking my brushstrokes. "They melt into brightness. It reminds me of a creation story, you know? God creating something out of the nothingness."

"It's a little like that," I say. "It's a picture about the wonderful *thwap thwap* of your staple gun, because that sound is very definite and wholesome and scares away the unsettling feelings."

She laughs, munching the last of her toast. "You have the coolest ideas, and the coolest way of talking about them."

"Thank you," I say.

There's a buzz in the Dark Energy. Liria is sending me jealous glances while talking to a man with a strange, droopy mustache and a purple suit jacket with a pearly sheen like starlings' wings. She says something to him and they both come over and crowd around me with Tianna.

Liria's fingers alight on my back and gently graze down my spine. A crease dimples Tianna's smooth forehead. I think she sees in the Dark Energy that Liria is my girlfriend now. I wonder if

Liria is right about Tianna liking me in that way. It gives me a nervous feeling, because of how much trouble girls can cause when they like you that way.

The doorbell chimes and Arty goes to open it. It's Mr. Plath, and the atmosphere begins to shimmer and flow like expensive champagne as he stands in the entry shaking hands and greeting the other guests. He attracts people like the feeding truck attracts cows in a stockyard.

He detaches himself from the lowing crowd and strides over to me, grinning. "Here's my artist, hard at work even at a party."

I set my brush down and shake his hand. "Hello, Mr. Plath. It's good to see you this evening."

He pats me on the back, his sharp eyes traversing the lengths of my brush strokes on the canvas. Others flock over, trying to get a look too. The hum of their energy mingles with the gypsy-sounding music Stewart has on the stereo.

"This is more abstract than your usual stuff," Mr. Plath says. "It almost seems like you're painting noise."

"Yes," I say. "I'm painting the wonderful noise of Tianna's staple gun. She was very kind today and showed me how to make my own canvases, and so I got to hear it thwap things together."

Tianna is standing very quiet at my elbow, fiddling with her jangly bracelets, and she smiles shyly.

Mr. Plath laughs, and many in the crowd titter along with him. "That's wonderful," he says.

I poke one last dab of paint onto the canvas and turn to Tianna. "Tianna, this painting is for you, because you have been so nice, although it isn't dry yet."

Her eyes go big and her mouth opens for a while before words come out. "Really? That's really…thank you, Justin. I love it."

"Thank you for sharing all your wonderful knowledge with me," I say.

She puts her arm around my waist and gives me a quick squeeze. She has tears in her eyes which seems like an overabundance of emotion for this situation.

Some of her friends come over and look at the painting with her. Liria gazes at me over Tianna's head, and doesn't look happy.

Mr. Plath doesn't seem exactly happy, either. He looks like he has pulled the veil of his expression over a large number of thoughts, but I think I know some of them. My attorneys had to fight very hard to retain my right to give away my own pictures, because Mr. Plath didn't want me to have that right. I can't sell them myself, but I can still give them as gifts.

Mr. Plath lays a hand on my shoulder. "We need to get some food into you. I swear, you never eat. All you do is work."

We head for the buffet table. Liria comes with us.

"Tianna is just going to sell that painting and make a bunch of money that could have been yours, Justin," Mr. Plath mutters with a wry smile.

"I don't think so," Liria says. "You may know business, Mr. Plath, but I know women, and that painting is going right over her couch, or maybe her bed."

Mr. Plath throws his head back and laughs. "You may be right. Our boy does have a way with the ladies." He pours himself a glass of red wine, studying me with a smirk.

I fill up a plate with hummus and crackers. Liria holds a little pastry up to my mouth. "Try the fig brie tarts." I eat it from her fingers.

Mr. Plath's smirk burrows deeper into his face, his eyes sharp on us. I know people are wondering about Liria's and my relationship, but as long as Arty doesn't become homicidal about it and try to poison me again, I don't mind that they wonder.

Mr. Plath leans back against the counter, cupping his wineglass in his hands. "Well, Mr. Flaherty. Let me congratulate you on your stunningly successful show, and to express my profound delight that we were able to achieve contract synergy. I know our relationship will be long and fruitful." He raises his glass in a toast, and I toast him back with a pita chip, for lack of other immediate options. He sips his wine. "Our first step begins when we fly to Los Angeles. I have a client, a band called Astrograph...perhaps you've heard of them?"

Liria gasps, but it comes out more as choking, because her mouth is full. She struggles to swallow quickly. "They're awesome," she says.

Even I have heard of Astrograph, though I haven't heard of most things in the world.

"Well," Mr. Plath continues. "The extremely talented Justin Flaherty will be doing the cover art for their new album. I think the most effective way for him to grasp the vibe of their music and render it in paint is to spend some time in the studio with them."

Liria's eyes go wide. She wipes the crumbs from her lips, but she misses one on her cheek, so I brush it away gently with my thumb.

"He's doing the cover art for…oh my God, that's kickass!" she says.

Mr. Plath laughs. "I'm glad to hear you say so."

"I hope they like my artwork," I say.

"Of course they will, it's fabulous," Mr. Plath says.

I tuck back a lock of Liria's blue hair that has escaped from its clip. "When do we leave?"

"The day after tomorrow," Mr. Plath says. "I'll be going with you to L.A., so we'll take my jet."

Liria looks at me with an expression like she's about to take off flying around the room with a wet squeak like a balloon losing air. "Oh, my God."

"I'm sure a good time will be had by all," Mr. Plath says, giving her an amused look over the rim of his glass as he drains it.

The doorbell sounds again above the din of voices and music, and Stewart detaches himself from a cluster of guests to go open it.

Two middle-aged men stand in the doorway, their faces full up with bright-eyed business seriousness. They're members of one of the rival war parties of attorneys, I think, dressed in their full battle regalia of expensive suits and silk ties. They shake Stewart's hand, then hustle over in our direction. The crowd steps back to let them through as if they are afraid they'll be cut down by sharply-honed legal arguments.

"Mr. Plath," one of the attorneys says. "We're very happy about how the contract turned out."

Mr. Plath sets down his wineglass and shakes their hands. "So am I. Thank you for all your hard work, gentlemen."

The crowd has quieted and is watching us as if we are an important TV drama. Liria and I step closer together and take each other's hands.

"Gentlemen," Mr. Plath says, "This is the infamous Justin Flaherty, who has created all this fuss. Justin, these are my attorneys Marion Nalgas and Henry Pedos."

The men in suits turn to me. I put down my plate and wipe the hummus from my fingers before shaking their hands.

"I apologize for the fuss," I say. "Making trouble for people seems to be a disease I was born with."

They both laugh, as do many people in the crowd. "Not always a bad disease to have," Marion says. "It certainly doesn't seem to be such a bad thing in your case." He raises his eyebrows at Mr. Plath. "Where shall we do this?"

As if by magic, the clutter of glasses and plates disappears from the dining table as people in the crowd hurry to accommodate us. Marion sets his briefcase down and pulls out the contract. It is a pile of papers half an inch thick. I think that all those tens of thousands of words might have been better used elsewhere, like to describe the grand unified theory of the universe, and not just some business deal, but Patricia has explained that all those words are necessary in order to keep my life from collapsing around me into chaos and rubble.

My heart beats in my ears. The Dark Energy feels strange, but it seems like the Dark Energy always feels strange lately. I look at Liria, who gives me an uncertain smile.

I think this must be the right thing, since this is what the Dark Energy has been steering me toward for a long time.

"Do you want to read it before signing?" Henry asks.

I stare at the teetering stack of papers. Patricia has told me that it is a good contract and that I can sign it without worrying about my immortal soul being compromised or other bad things happening. But she says I can read it and call her with any questions if I want to. "If I read it we're going to be here until I'm dead, though."

The crowd titters. Henry offers me a pen and I take it. It is heavier than a pen should be and I wonder if it contains some secret attorney weaponry. I wonder if I press the wrong spot a hand wielding a judge's gavel will burst from the tip and bang me on the skull.

Henry points to the first page. "We'll need your initials here."

I handle the pen very gently and start signing in all the places he indicates, which is at least once on every page. Mr. Plath signs beside me each time. The stack diminishes as we go through, piling up again in a mess of signed papers beside my left elbow.

There are camera flashes, and I look up and realize that the crowd has gone completely silent. People are taking photos and video on their phones.

I glance at Liria. "I didn't know this was newsworthy." Everyone laughs again though I'm really not certain why this is funny. This seems like one of those things people generally think of as extremely boring.

"It's not every day a star is made," Mr. Plath says, and a little breath goes up from the people gathered.

Finally, after my hand feels like it's been punching people all night from the tenseness of so much signing, I put my signature on the last page. Mr. Plath signs below me then puts his arm around my shoulders while people take more photos. "Ladies and gentlemen," he says. "I present to you Justin Flaherty, the new king of the art world."

The crowd breaks into applause, cheers, and hooting. Liria's eyes find mine. She shrugs, then applauds with the rest, her lips quirking in a half-smile.

These people can have their king, if that's what they want. The Dark Energy can do whatever it likes with me, as long as I get to have Liria by my side.

Arty stands in the corner, watching me thoughtfully over the rim of her wineglass, and I wonder if she heard that thought.

Chapter 10

Mr. Plath's airplane is much different than the one we flew to New York in. It is sleek and shiny like a predatory bird, except for inside it is very comfortable, and I don't think it would be comfortable inside a bird.

Mr. Plath, Liria, Stewart, Arty, and I sit on soft, leather chairs around a small dining table while Mr. Plath's minions bring us lunch. Mine is grilled eggplant with garlicky gravy, tempura green beans, and whipped potatoes. Liria steals a green bean off my plate.

"Stealing is illegal, Christina," I say.

She bites the crunchy bean. "Arrest me, then."

"Perhaps I will. Perhaps I'll arrest you." I hold my fingers up to her temple in the form of a gun. "Get down on the ground with your hands up, somehow, even though it's very hard to do that without falling on your face! And then keep your hands up and do a very complicated backward somersault!"

Liria giggles, batting my hand away with her

greasy fingers. I have to clear the images of frightening police situations from my mind, which takes a while.

Liria's smile fades and she gives me a worried look as she piles a handful of her shoestring fries onto my plate. "Don't arrest me, Officer. I'm paying for the bean, look."

I blink away the last of the police thoughts and kiss her on her nose. We are not being careful in front of Arty anymore, because it is obvious in the Dark Energy that we're together, so she already knows. She has decided to not be any more murderous about it than usual, apparently.

"I hope you all were able to get some sleep last night," Mr. Plath says, cutting into his chicken. "I'm afraid there's another party to go to this evening."

"Sleep is overrated," Arty says. "Parties, however, generally aren't."

"My thoughts exactly," Stewart says, and they clink empty shot glasses. They are drinking through the airplane's entire complement of alcohol and watching the scene as if it were a darkly humorous movie. Mr. Plath seems to think they are a couple, which is a funny idea, but they have done nothing to disabuse him of it.

"I've arranged for a nice apartment for you all in Santa Monica, right by the beach," he says. "It has good light, and hopefully Justin will be able to get a lot of painting done."

Liria goes suddenly still. She makes strange, emotional ripples in the Dark Energy, and I see a worried look pass between her and Arty. A chill goes down my spine, and I wonder what dangerous situations there are in Santa Monica. I wonder if the gangsters are there also. The thought sends sweat trickling down my back.

Mr. Plath doesn't seem to notice the disturbance. "We'll be there for approximately three months. I've arranged a gallery show for you in Los Angeles, just to increase interest, since you don't have anything left to sell...unless you manage to produce a few more pieces by then." He smiles at me, but I hardly see it because Liria is staring distantly at her plate.

"Just give him paint and let him alone, he'll have twelve more pieces for you by tonight," Stewart says.

Mr. Plath studies me with a furrowed brow. "Everything all right, Justin?"

I blink and force my mouth into smile mode. "Everything is all right." I take Liria's hand under the table. "I just want to look out the windows, because being in an airplane is a very good view. Christina, will you look out the windows with me?"

She glances up at me from the corner of her eye, smiling faintly with a cocked eyebrow. I think I am not being very sneaky about my motives, actually. "Yeah, let's go," she says.

As we get up, Arty asks the minion to just bring the whole bottle of whiskey.

We go into the forward cabin, which is more like a regular airplane. It has six rows of seats, two on each side of the aisle. We sit in the bulkhead. Outside the windows, the land stretches flat and brown beneath a hazy horizon, broken sometimes by green squares of farmland. It makes me dizzy in a good way to be so far up, to feel all that empty space beneath me. I'm not scared of airplanes, it turns out, as long as no one with the sickness is scrambling my brain with wrong vibrations.

"What's the problem about Santa Monica?"

She grimaces at her lap. "I didn't know we were going there…I don't want to go there."

"Is it a bad place?"

The Dark Energy warps around her like a plastic bottle shrink-melting in a campfire. "No…it's an okay place. Lots of rich people."

"Rich people can be very disconcerting." She still doesn't look at me, and I take her hand, intertwining our fingers. "Liria, please tell me what's wrong."

She pulls her hands from mine and picks at her cuticles. "There's a guy there I'm afraid of running into."

"Oh." A small prickle of fear zings through the Dark Energy. "Who is he?"

"His name is Cyryl Czetski." She squints past me out the window, her face scrunched as if she has a bad toothache.

"You're related, I'm thinking."

She winces. "Not really. My mom told me all my life that he's my dad, but he's not."

"Oh," I say. Her foot taps against the floor, and she's digging at her cuticles like there's gold under them. "This guy who isn't your real father hurt you somehow."

She shakes her head quickly and smiles at me, slightly unconvincingly. "No, nothing like that. It's just…complicated."

I take her hands again before she makes her cuticles bleed. "Complicated like algebra, or complicated like I should run this person up a flagpole by his armpit hair?"

She snickers and gives me a little kiss. "More like algebra." She settles into the crook of my arm, gazing back out the window. "I just…I don't really want to talk about it right now."

"Okay, Liria," I say, though that isn't what I want to say.

***

We land in Los Angeles late in the afternoon, the sun confronting us with its chest puffed out, showing its Southern California bravado. I have already forgotten how much warmer and drier it is here. The air is soothing after the stickiness of New York.

When you travel with a very rich person, hordes of scurrying minions go before you, clearing away all traces of the real world like stagehands changing the set as you walk onstage. We don't have to wade through herds of tired travelers and stare anxiously at the conveyor belts, hoping our luggage didn't accidentally fall out of the plane on the way. Instead, we walk straight through the private terminal to a waiting Cadillac Escalade in front. Efficient people put our luggage in the back for us, and we are soon off and driving through the palm-lined streets, heading west for the ocean and the blaring sun.

Liria spends the whole drive gazing out the

tinted windows, still picking at her poor cuticles. I wonder if she is keeping an eye out for this Cyryl person, who might be strolling down the sidewalks. I imagine him wearing dark sunglasses and a tan sport coat, which he is careful to pull over the butt of his concealed handgun. I imagine him carrying briefcases full of money and illegal drugs, or perhaps documents stolen from the CIA.

We arrive in Santa Monica without car chases or gun battles, though, and pull up to a large, stucco apartment complex. It rises into the deep blue sky, the sand and ocean stretching at its feet. A warm, salty breeze wraps around us as we get out, but Liria huddles in it like she's cold. I put my arm around her tense shoulders. "This looks like a big town," I say. "It might be unlikely that you'll run into this man you're worried about."

"His condo is just right down the beach," she says in a tiny, shaky voice. "I think I could see it from here if the building weren't in the way."

"Oh," I say, my stomach cramping. "That is unfortunate."

We tromp into the elevator. Mr. Plath tells Arty and Stewart about a show he organized at one of his galleries in Spain. "The woman is an inspiring artist, she truly is. But she isn't, shall we say, easy to work with. For instance, in the last couple of days before the opening, she said she finished a new sculpture. She refused to let me see it because she wanted it to retain its 'mystique,' but was absolutely insistent that it go in the show. Threatened all sorts of legal action, got in a real snit about it."

Stewart giggles knowingly, covering his mouth

with his hand. The elevator doors open on the eighth floor and Mr. Plath leads us down the hallway. "Anyway," he continues, "the sculpture was six feet tall and weighed about fifteen hundred pounds. I had to hire people to move it out of her workspace and into the gallery, and it wasn't cheap since it was last-minute like that. I even had to transport a forklift to the site. Meanwhile, she still wouldn't let me see the damned thing. I have to admit, most of the reason I didn't pursue a release of the contract was that I was frankly curious, so maybe she was being very astute and business-minded and not just a nutjob, I don't know." He fishes keys from his pocket and unlocks a door. We step in, our shoes tapping on the white marble floors. We follow Mr. Plath through a wide archway flanked by marble pillars, and down three steps to a sitting room. A wall of glass looks out onto the ocean.

Mr. Plath tosses the keys onto a table of etched stone. "So, they finally hauled this thing into the gallery. It was the very last day before the opening, and we had to scramble to rearrange everything to fit it in. It was the size of a goddamned water buffalo, and all wrapped up in packing paper, so as far as I knew at that point it WAS a water buffalo. I almost wish it had been, considering."

He flops onto a blue linen fainting couch by the windows, and Arty and Stewart sit next to him in a love seat. Liria and I stand in front of the large French doors, squinting out over the balcony at the sun hovering low over the water.

"So, I had people tear the paper off," Mr. Plath

says, "and I finally got the grand reveal: it was a pair of gigantic, bare tits, made entirely out of half-melted sex toys. The nipples were a couple of neon green butt-plugs."

Stewart and Arty roar with laughter, and Liria snorts, shooting me an amused look.

"Oh, my God, that's amazing," Stewart says, clapping.

"Yes," Mr. Plath says, his voice rich with amusement. "Amazing. And that's not all. She didn't feel that the sculpture had enough artistic impact on its own. She insisted a woman clothed entirely from head to foot in black spandex, with holes over her nostrils so she could breathe, should stand alongside this tasteless heap and threaten patrons with a huge, floppy dildo. It was like something out of *A Clockwork Orange*."

Stewart presses his palms into his eyes, laughing wheezily. Arty is snorting in a way that is a lot more like Arty than Iris Pierson.

"Did you do it?" Stewart chokes out. "The dildo lady?"

"Yes," Mr. Plath says dryly. "What did I have to lose at that point?"

Arty and Stewart collapse hopelessly on their knees, almost frothing at the mouth. Then the door opens and the minions come in with our luggage and Arty and Stewart sit up, clearing the laughter out of their throats like adults trying to act mature when the kids come in.

A man in a gray suit comes over and says something in Mr. Plath's ear.

"Yes, thank you, Gerard," Mr. Plath says.

Gerard scuttles out, and Mr. Plath claps his palms against his thighs. "Let me show you around the place. Then we should go out and get some real dinner before our guests start to arrive for the party."

He takes us through another pillared archway and into a hallway lined with inset stone shelves. The shelves hold ivory carvings, old books, and worn wooden tools that are probably used to do some obscure thing I've never even heard of. I want to stop and talk to all the interesting objects, but Liria pulls me forward by the hand.

"I'm told you two share a bedroom," Mr. Plath says, his gaze touching curiously on Liria and me, "so this one is yours."

He pushes open carved wooden double-doors. We step through into a long room which is very large but somehow manages to seem like a cozy den. Soft wool earthy-toned rugs are spread on the marble floor. The low stone ceilings are bordered with geometric etchings. A king size four-poster bed sits at an angle against the far wall, and an easel stands in front of the gigantic windows, ready for me to paint. There is a private balcony, and a private bathroom.

"This is extremely luxurious," I say, as Liria stands blinking at it.

Mr. Plath smiles. "I hoped you'd like it. Iris, Stewart, your bedroom is this way."

Liria and I exchange a short smirk. The collateral damage of Mr. Plath believing that Arty and Stewart are a couple is that they have to share a bedroom. As they go out, they glare challengingly at each other behind Mr. Plath's back like two siblings preparing to fight over the last cookie once their parents aren't looking.

When we are alone, Liria grins and stands on her tiptoes to kiss me. I run my hands down her back and trace her hipbones with my fingertips, thinking about what it will be like to sleep in that huge bed with my beautiful girlfriend and go to rock star parties and play in the ocean. I'm thinking my life is too good right now. My scalp prickles wondering what trick the gangsters and the butterfly army are playing on me, because I know things this nice don't happen in real life.

After we're settled in with our luggage, we go to the restaurant. Mr. Plath, Arty, and Stewart decide we should walk, for exercise reasons, but I can tell Liria isn't happy about the idea. As we walk down the beach, she clutches my arm, her eyes touching nervously on the faces of the tan, svelte people around us. We can both feel them out there, the gangsters and butterfly army. The soldiers in California are different than in New York, but they still have the same rancid butter slickness and metallic stench. I don't know who they think they're fooling.

The restaurant is very nice; we sit on a patio that overlooks the ocean. Arty isn't drinking but is pretending she is, holding her glass of red wine decoratively and laughing a lot. Stewart sips a martini and tells funny stories about a cruise he took to Majorca. Liria stares out at the waves as the light of another day is absorbed into the darkness of space, the stars poking out and twinkling along with the fairy lights that dangle above us. Her soul seems curled in on itself, and I know the feeling. We're moving around through so many situations that it's difficult to know if we're where we are, or if we left ourselves behind somewhere else. I hold her hand and eat my cheese tamales.

When we get back to the apartment, it has been transformed into yet another strange place. Tall, fat white candles flicker everywhere, their flames swaying in the breeze from the open French doors. Bouquets of white-and-yellow flowers twist in graceful, organic poses in ceramic vases. A buffet table has been laid out in the dining room and there are crystal platters of hors d'oeuvres and dishes of dips of all colors. A man in a baby blue tuxedo stands behind a table laden with bottles of alcohol, ready to help you get drunk in any way you choose.

"You really know how to throw a party, Harold," Stewart says, and Mr. Plath laughs.

"Sometimes it seems that's three-quarters of my job."

There are minions everywhere, rushing around. They are so good at being inconspicuous, though, that I hardly notice them. Every so often someone comes to mutter something in Mr. Plath's ear. Someone puts music on—a band I've never heard before with a lead singer that sounds a little like Sylvester Stallone. I can't see where the speakers are. The noise seems to ooze from the walls.

Liria and I stand stiffly in the middle of it all. We are in the Dark Energy together, and so I know she feels the way I do, which is that it would be very nice to go into our room and shut the door and not come out again. But I think Mr. Plath and Arty would get complicated if we did that. "Let's go out on the deck," I say, and Liria nods.

We push through the French doors. The music is out here too, but there aren't any scurrying minions—they've already swarmed over the deck and done their magic. They've left stone lanterns and bouquets of LED fibers on the tables, and tasseled twists of linen and lights running through the railing.

We sit together on a lounge chair, our arms around each other. Liria presses her forehead into my chest, and we are quiet, just feeling the breeze on our faces. The stars over the dark, roaring ocean are peaceful to watch.

The French doors open. A sound of many voices tumbles out of the apartment as a man joins us on the deck. Through the windows, I can see that quite a few guests have already arrived, which is startling, since we've been cocooned in our quietness.

The guy shuts the door, drowning out the voices. He regards us with an uncertain smile. I think at first that he is an older man, but then I realize he is about my age but just dressed like he's old, in baggy slacks and a buttoned-up, V-neck cardigan sweater.

"Sorry, am I interrupting your glorious solitude?" he asks.

"Not at all," I say politely. "The solitude is even more glorious now that you are here."

He grins and fishes in the pocket of his slacks, coming out with a pack of cigarettes. "Okay if I smoke out here?"

"I don't object," I say. "You may want to ask Christina and the ocean if they mind, though."

The man laughs, and raises his eyebrows at Liria questioningly.

"Go for it," Liria says. She is watching him with bright eyes, and I take a second look at him.

He holds out his hand, and I shake it. "I'm Nate Hennessey."

"I'm Justin Flaherty."

"Oh! You're the artist."

"That's what they say."

He laughs again. His laugh is both hearty and giggly at the same time, and I like it. He shakes Liria's hand, too.

"I'm Christina Guzman," she says. "You're the keyboardist for Astrograph, right?"

"That's what they say."

We giggle. He leans back on the balcony railing and lights a cigarette, watching me with curious little eyes. "I've seen photos of some of your work. It's really amazing."

"Thank you, that's very nice of you to say. I'm a fan of your keyboard playing, as well. You play the right notes in the right places, and help create a wonderful vibrational atmosphere."

"That's probably the best compliment I've ever gotten." He turns to gaze out at the ocean, flicking his ashes over the railing. I can feel Liria's nerves humming. I know she is nervous about meeting rock stars, and I stroke her waist gently.

Nate exhales a puff of smoke. "This is a really nice place."

"Yes," I say. "Mr. Plath set it up for us."

198

Nate shoots me a sharp glance, then turns toward us again with his elbows on the railing. He is very skinny, his body almost lost in his baggy clothes. "What do you think of him? Harold Plath?"

Liria and I glance at each other. "He is a man with a lot of money," I say. "There are quite a few things one can think about him."

"You know him better than us," Liria says. "We just met him a few weeks ago."

"Your insight into his psychology would be valuable," I say.

Nate grins wryly, but he has a nervous crease between his eyebrows. "He's certainly made our career, but he's a trip to work with." He flicks his cigarette ash three times in a row and shifts on his feet. "It's like he turns everything into performance art, your whole life into a scripted screenplay, you know what I mean?"

Liria and I exchange a longer glance this time. I sit up a bit straighter. "I think I've noticed that about him," I say. "It's a little bit frightening, actually." A man like Nate is describing would have a powerful hand in the Dark Energy, which would explain how Mr. Plath controls the whole butterfly army.

"You mean he's running your personal lives too?" Liria asks.

"Not exactly." Nate shoves his square spectacles up his nose with his knuckles, the cigarette burning low between them. "He just makes sure we look larger-than-life when we're in public. I'm surprised by half of the things I read about us in the magazines, you know?"

"I'd be surprised to read anything about myself in a magazine," I say.

"But you've been in the *New Yorker* and a couple of others already, right?" he says. "We looked you up, because Harold was so insistent we let you do the cover art on this new album. I don't think he steered us wrong this time. Your stuff is ruddy amazing."

"Thank you," I say. I pick at the callous on my finger. No matter how many times Arty tries to train me out of it, I'm still nervous when people say things like this.

"Justin's just not used to the media yet," Liria says, snuggling closer against me. "This is all pretty new."

Nate nods. "You get used to it, kind of."

The French doors open again. A girl made entirely of legs, arms, and platinum-blonde hair strides out, giving us a goofy grin. She flings her unruly bangs out of her eyes, and leans against the railing next to Nate, nudging his foot with her booted toe. "Bum me a cigarette, Nate. I forgot my vapo."

Nate pulls the pack of Camels from the pocket of his baggy slacks, jerking his chin at us. "This is the artist, Justin Flaherty. And Christina."

The girl grins wider and strides gawkily over to us, holding out her hand, which looks huge on the end of her tiny wrist. "Hey! I'm Astrid Phillis. I'm so excited you'll be doing our cover. Your stuff is twisted."

Liria and I shake her hand. "Thank you," I say.

"Twisted in a good way, I mean." She collapses

into the chair next to us, sprawling out with her hand clutching her bony knees. She lights her cigarette and fixes me with a curious squint, her eyes gleaming under heavy makeup. "How did you learn to paint like that?"

I realize I'm picking at my callous until it hurts, and I clutch my hands together so I'll stop. "I haven't learned to paint yet," I say.

She laughs, a hoarse giggle, glancing at Nate. "Okay?"

"Justin never went to school, is what he means," Liria says. "He's just naturally amazing. He just started painting a couple months ago, actually. Before that, he just did pencil drawings."

Astrid and Nate both squint at me now. The sour, peppery smell of cigarette smoke curls around us. Nate nods. "Sometimes you meet people like that, who are just geniuses without any practice or training at all." He takes one last drag, then mashes his cigarette out in a crystal ashtray by a vase of flowers. "We all hate those sorts of people."

He grins at me, and Astrid laughs. Her eyes are huge and warm with candlelight glints as she examines me. "God, Nate, you're such a bastard. You know he's just joking, Justin."

"I'm glad he's just joking," I say.

Astrid's gaze flicks to Liria. "You're his girlfriend? Or wife, or what?"

Liria and I look at each other, blinking. We have gotten so used to hiding our relationship from Arty that we don't really know what word describes it. But we don't really have to hide anymore. "Girlfriend," I say. I like the sound of it, though it doesn't seem quite enough. Mina was my girlfriend, but Liria and I are in the Dark Energy together.

Liria nestles closer, and Astrid watches her for a moment with a strange look before taking a long drag of her cigarette, staring out to sea.

Chapter 11

It's midafternoon the next day when I walk into the studio where Astrograph is finishing up their new album. It is a windowless warren of instrument-cluttered rooms separated by double glass doors. Mr. Plath and I trudge through it to find the band in a room taken up almost entirely by a gigantic mixing board with rows and rows and rows of dials and faders which remind me of little toy robots lined up for battle.

All four members of Astrograph are there, lounged out in chairs and perched on stools. Two other guys I don't know are sitting at the board. One of them jabs a button as we walk in, extinguishing the bang and rattle of a drum kit.

"Hi, Justin," Astrid says, giving me a bright grin. "Hi, Harold."

"Heeeey," Patrick, the bass player, says, grinning wide and clapping jovially. "Here they are."

"Hello, all," Mr. Plath says. "I'm just here to drop off Justin for a while, so he can hear the tracks. I won't impose my presence on you while you're working."

There is a murmur of polite protest. "Stay and have a beer, Harold," Ivan the drummer says.

"Ah, I wish I could, but unfortunately I have obligations." He lays a hand on my shoulder. "They'll be bringing your paints in, in case you feel like working today. A car will come for you at eight thirty tonight, but call if you want to be picked up earlier or later."

I nod. "Thank you, Mr. Plath."

He pats my shoulder and waves goodbye to everyone. "Happy harmonizing."

He leaves, and I realize I'm standing there twisting my fingers together. I feel nervous without Liria around, but Mr. Plath said it wouldn't be appropriate for her to come. The studio is an "intimate atmosphere" is what he says, which is a concept that coats me with slippery weird disturbingness, like the time when I was eight and went into my mom's bedroom and found a bottle on her bedside table. It was the best color of purple, so I opened it and squirted some of the goo on my fingers. It was clear and as beautiful as liquid diamonds. The silky slipperiness of it along with the perfect purple of the bottle was so amazing, but then my mom came in and started shrieking and shrieking. I didn't know that it was sexual lube in that bottle, and that information made the wonderful situation slide into disgusting, insidious wrongness and I couldn't climb out of it for a long time, since there was no friction.

Astrid smiles at me and scoots over, patting the couch cushions. "Sit down, Justin."

I regard her, still twisting my fingers. Astrid's perfume smell and her punk-rock-dollishness drip down onto my soul, the niceness and wrongness of it somehow making each other more powerful by competing.

They are all looking at me. The thought of sitting by Astrid makes me want to run, but I know that would cause a horrible commotion in the social dance if I did. So I step over to the couch and sit down very carefully. I smile, even more carefully, because I don't want to risk sliding down into the pit. She smells like vanilla and cinnamon, like she has cookies in her pockets, but her leggings are so tight I don't know where she could hide them without me seeing.

"I have never been in a recording studio before," I say.

"It's always nonstop action, just like this," Ivan says. People giggle, breaking the ringing silence. Ivan gestures toward the men at the board. "Justin, I don't believe you've met our amazing sound engineers. This is Tom Rocher and Casey Everstein."

Tom nods at me. "Hello," he says. Casey waves and smiles. They are both very pale, like they spend most of their time in this windowless room.

"Nice to meet you," I say.

Casey looks over at Tom, raising his eyebrows. "We should just play through the tracks for him, let him see what it's all about, yeah?" He glances around at everyone. "That sound good?"

There are nods of agreement. Patrick the bass player grins at me. "See what pictures it makes in your head."

"The songs aren't done yet," Nate says, as Casey starts jabbing at the board. "We're doing overdubs right now. There are still a lot of flubs in a few of the songs."

"Yeah, like the part where it sounds like you fell face-first into your keyboard," Astrid says.

"That was purely intentional. I was making an artistic statement. Banging my head against the keyboard is a metaphor for railing against your authority."

Casey the sound engineer shoots a huge, crinkle-eyed grin at Nate. "I love that flub. I think we should leave it."

Nate pushes his glasses up his nose. "No way."

Casey taps at his computer keyboard. "I'll play the first track, called "Crayfish Revolution." He smirks at Astrid.

"Hey, don't judge my song titles," she says.

"I love it, it's rad." Casey swings around in his chair back toward the board. "Okay, here we go. It's a rough mix, but you'll get the idea."

A strong drum beat comes in, then guitar, then the song bursts wide open. Astrid sings a pretty but driving melody. Nate's playing beefy chords on a church organ, and the drums and bass bounce off each other perfectly. We all listen silently while Casey and Tom twiddle the knobs on the board, making subtle warps to the sounds.

The music surrounds me and makes the Dark Energy vibrate in a good way. I see Astrid trying to catch my eye, and I smile at her. "This is very nice," I say over the music, and she grins, looking very happy.

When the music ends they all glance at me, because the social dance requires my formal opinion. "That is amazing," I say. "The notes bloom into little star systems. You're populating the universe with your songs, and probably somewhere in space is a nebula made of your music which will someday coalesce into planets and asteroids and gas giants."

They all look at me a moment with wide eyes and little smiles. "Can we put that endorsement on the cover of the album?" Nate asks. Astrid giggles and pokes me in the ribs, which gives me a little shock, her cookie smell slipping all around me.

We listen through the tracks one by one, and they eventually seem to forget about me and fall back into working on things, which is interesting to watch because I've never seen how songs are created before. Someone will make a comment about something they heard, and Casey and Tom will stop the recording and listen to only the drumbeat, or the bass line, or whatever it was, trying to pinpoint what they're hearing that's wrong. Tom makes notes in a notebook so they can fix it later.

I like sitting and watching it all. It makes me comfortable to be with these people as they organize the universe with their musical art.

I'm so caught up with taking it all in that Astrid startles me when she speaks at my elbow. "Sorry, this is pretty boring."

Her eyes are very deep brown, a very striking contrast with her silvery hair. She isn't wearing as much makeup as she was last night. Her skin is creamy and perfect, almost translucent, with little freckles on the tops of her cheeks.

"This isn't boring at all," I say, picking at my callous.

She rolls her eyes. "Try being here for four weeks straight, making an album."

"Yes," I say. "That might get tedious, being down here, never seeing the sun. You're like coal miners, except you're mining for music instead. I'd worry about getting rickets, if I were you."

She laughs. "I don't want rickets; that sounds gross." Casey punches a button, and her words ring out into the sudden silence.

"What's this about rickets?" Ivan asks.

"Rick-ets," Nate says, pronouncing the word slowly. "Rickets. Rickets. Do crickets get rickets?"

Casey glances up from the board at Astrid. "That would be a good name for your next song: Crickets with Rickets."

She laughs. "Shut up."

Ivan slaps his thighs and stretches his muscly arms. "Speaking of yummy cricket rickets, we should go grab some food. I'm so hungry, I'm hung like a horse."

"Pttht," Astrid says.

"Don't get your dangles in a tangle, big boy," Patrick says.

They all get up. Astrid tugs at my sleeve with her long, slender fingers. Her fingernails are short and painted sparkly blue. "Come on, Justin, I'll buy you lunch." She smiles, and I'm in a cozy warm oven full of cookies, but then the Dark Energy squirts slippery wrong lube on me again and I have to stay very still so that I don't slide around in it.

They are all looking at me. "Okay," I say.

I stand up very carefully, so I don't slip. We wander back through the musical warren and out into the daylight, blinking and squinting. Everyone else fishes in their pockets and bags and pulls out sunglasses. I wish I had some, too, to shield me from the attacks of the villainous Los Angeles sun.

We crowd into a little taco restaurant just down the street, where the wait staff puts two tables together to accommodate all seven of us. Astrid sits next to me and tells me about their last tour of Europe, and the town in Ohio where she grew up.

"I'm hardly ever home anymore," Astrid says. "I miss having a cat, you know?"

"It's difficult, not having a center for your operations," I say. "The trick is to build a fort in your mind. Then you can take it with you." I think about it. "It would be very hard to keep a cat in there, though. Imagination cats are pretty good, but not as good as the real thing, I don't think."

She laughs, wrinkling her nose. "You're weird, you know. But I like it."

I stare at my fork. Astrid is assaulting me with her attractiveness, and it makes me want to hide under the table. I shake my head to dislodge the thoughts that come creeping, my mother's yelling voice and the sour smell of her anger mashed in with the good slipperiness.

As the waiters bring our food, two girls bounce up to our table, clutching napkins in their hands. They ask the band to autograph them. Astrid smiles and scrawls her name, then passes the napkins down to Ivan while the girls squeak like dog toys that really love Astrograph's music. After they wander away, tittering and waving, Astrid rolls her eyes at me, then stares down at her plate, pushing her enchiladas around with her fork.

I see her emotions around her in the Dark Energy. "It must be strange to be treated like that all the time."

"It is. It was cool at first, but now I just miss having normal conversations with people." She gazes at me distantly, chewing on her bottom lip. She doesn't have any lipstick on, and her lips are pink like the dawn in early spring; pale and cold and delicate.

I look around at the others. Ivan is holding two perfect curls of lettuce on either side of his face and asking Nate if he looks Jewish. Patrick and Casey seem to be trying to build a house of cards out of tortilla chips. And around at the other tables are a bunch of people who look like they spent a thousand dollars on their jeans and t-shirts.

I wonder how many of them are in the butterfly army. I wonder if any of the gangsters are here, waiting to strike. It's disorienting, and I have to take a deep breath.

I turn back to Astrid. "If you want to have normal conversations, I think that maybe you should not be a musician, and should not be in L.A."

Astrid laughs, and nudges my foot with hers under the table. "Good point." She sits there for a moment looking at me, her foot still next to mine, and there is a loneliness in her big, brown eyes that holds me still as my heart takes off sprinting.

Her pink lips curve into a gentle smile, then she presses them against my cheek. They are soft and warm and the cookie smell of her creeps over me along with another slimy wave of lube, goodness and badness and rightness and wrongness battling each other in bright clashes in my mind.

She sits back in her chair. My cheek tingles, and I am breathing a little bit fast and clutching the table.

"You're really sweet, Justin," she says. Her eyes fall to her plate and she picks up her fork, pushing her food around again.

"Thank you," I say, a little hoarsely, because I don't know what words could possibly come out of my mouth in this situation that would have true relevance. Astrid snickers, her eyes darting to mine briefly, her porcelain cheeks taking on a rosy tinge.

***

After we eat, we go back to the studio. The band keeps working on their songs, overdubbing parts they think are wrong, which involves playing little parts on their instruments over and over again.

I set up my easel in a corner and start to paint, because it seems like the best way to escape the lube.

As soon as I dip my brush into the colors I've mixed, I'm pulled into the interface between the Other Place and this one, flipping back and forth, the two dimensions stretching at one another. It makes me a little dizzy, but I like the interesting pictures it makes.

Astrid has turned into a puppet, with a stereo speaker in her gaping mouth, but there is another Astrid, who is human; I don't know if she's real or not, but she's sitting on a twisty tree branch above, holding the puppet strings which are all tangled up in a spider-web pattern. The human Astrid has a frustration face, trying to manipulate the puppet.

The other members of the band stand around, watching with concern, and Ivan is trying to help, tugging on another one of the tangled strings with a drumstick. In the crook of the tree, an insect looks on; it has a spider's legs and body, but butterfly wings too.

"That's *so awesome.*"

I'm startled completely back into the Physical World. Astrid is standing next to me, gazing at the painting with wide eyes and a slight smile.

"That bug reminds me of Harold Plath, though I don't even know why." She covers her hand with her mouth as she laughs.

I blink, coming back to myself. The other members of the band are in the control room, having some sort of argument about the drum set with the sound engineers.

"I think you're right, the spider butterfly is Harold Plath," I say.

"Oh, my God, don't tell him that, he'd puke." She slaps me gently on the shoulder, her smile fading. "Speaking of which, your car's here."

"Oh. Thank you for telling me." I quickly start digging in my bag for my brush cleaner.

"You shouldn't go. You should hang out. We can go for drinks or something later."

I give my brushes a quick cleaning with a rag. I'll do it properly at home, since I don't want to keep the driver waiting. "I'm not old enough to drink. And also I should get home and see Christina. She's stuck with Iris and Stewart, which sometimes results in severe discomfort."

Astrid taps her long fingers against her hipbone. "Okay. But you're coming back tomorrow, right?"

"Of course." I stand up, stashing my brushes and shouldering my brand-new art bag.

"Good," she says.

***

Liria is waiting for me in the apartment, which smells like garlic and onions and good things cooking. She throws her arms around my neck and kisses me as I come in, mixing her smell of sandalwood and cloves with the food smell. It is a comforting scent, and I sink into it, letting it wash away Astrid's slippery aura.

"I missed you," she mutters, her lips against mine. She grins and grabs my hand, pulling me toward the French doors. "I made dinner."

"You are an amazing person, Liria. Where are Arty and Stewart?"

"Out being dorks. Getting drunk and spending money or whatever."

She has set a table on the deck with a pretty blue cloth and fancy green plates. All around us, candles flicker in the balmy ocean breeze. All the flowers from the night before are arranged in pretty bunches on the deck and tables. She pulls out a chair for me, but I don't sit.

"I want to help you finish dinner and bring it out, and not make you be my waitress."

She shakes her head, kissing my nose. "Sit down. It's all ready. I'll bring it out. I want to."

She bustles back inside, her hips swaying, and I watch her until she's out of sight. I sit down and gaze out at the sliver of moon glimmering over the ocean as the last light of day fades.

Liria comes back with a platter piled high with steaming rice topped with green onions and chili peppers, sauce, and something else. "That isn't beef in there," I say, because Liria is respectful of my vegetarianism and wouldn't do that.

She wrinkles her nose. "It's gluten. Fake Mongolian beef." She sets it on the table and starts spooning some onto my plate.

"It smells extremely incredible. Did you make this?"

"I found the recipe on Pinterest and Laura— that's the personal assistant Mr. Plath assigned to us—went to get the ingredients."

She spoons food onto her own plate. Her golden-brown cheeks have a rosy tinge and her eyes are bright, which is a lot different than when I first met her. Even her hair seems thicker, the roots growing out shiny black and the blue ends fading to blonde.

"Liria, you are very beautiful and wonderful," I say.

"So are you." She leans over the plate and kisses me.

It is very nice to eat together on the deck overlooking the ocean, and her food is very good. The strange feelings of being in the alternate rock star reality with Astrograph seem far away as I tell Liria about their songs, and the painting I've started of the band. I tell her about lunch, too—about the girls asking for the autograph, and how it makes Astrid a little unhappy to be so famous. Liria stabs a piece of gluten repeatedly with her fork as she listens, which is a disconcerting amount of violence for peaceful food to have to suffer.

"Liria, why are you upset?"

She scowls at her plate. "Astrid likes you."

I twist my cloth napkin in my hands. "That seems an oblique conclusion to draw based entirely on the fact that she harbors a sort of ennui about her fame."

Liria gazes at me, and her frown morphs into a smirk. "You know a lot of words." Her smirk disappears. "But I'm right, she likes you."

My foot waggles and I press down on it with my other foot. "Why do you think that, Liria?"

"I saw the way she looks at you, that's all. And I'll bet she spent the whole time talking to you today."

I put my napkin down so I don't tear it apart. The food glistens on my plate, shiny brown sauce and bright green onions. I wonder if any of the onions get angry with the gluten chunks for ending up too close to other chunks of onion as I eat them. "It's really not the gluten's fault," I say. "It just ends up where I put it. I don't mean to mess with your universe like that. I'm just hungry."

"What are you whispering about, Justin?"

I tear my eyes from my plate and look at her. The slime is starting to trickle back in again, and I flinch and try to bat it away. "I was just apologizing to my food for eating it the incorrect way."

Liria gazes at me quirked lips, then hugs herself and gazes out at the darkness over the ocean. Her unhappiness makes painful waves in the Dark Energy, and my throat begins to close up. The slime pours in more and more until it's all over me. "I can't help the situations that happen, how people's vibrations slide all over you just because you're there, and I can't help that the slipperiness felt good on my fingers in the first place. I didn't even know it was some sort of horrible sexual lube. I thought it was lotion."

Liria's eyes snap back to mine, and she goes pale. "Hold on, *what*?"

My stomach is sick because now it's full of lube along with the Mongolian fake beef. Slime sloshes around inside of me and all over me, that good feeling along with the wrongness of my mother's smell, and she's screaming at me in my head again.

"I don't know why people have to yell at me and make things horrible like that, when it wasn't wrong in the first place because I didn't know what it was. It just felt good on my fingers." I stand up. "I need to run."

Liria's eyes glitter in the candlelight, deep and furious, and the Dark Energy around her is burning ice, but it can't melt away the slime which is all I can feel right now. "Don't you dare fucking run, Justin! You better stay and tell me what happened…what the fuck happened with the lube and fucking Astrid…"

But I can hardly hear her through the goop. "I have to run and clean this off of me, Liria."

She yells something else, but I'm dashing through the condo and out the door, down the steps, and into the salt-scented night.

I bound over the parking lot and down onto the sand. My sweat and the ocean and the moon wash away the lube and push the grossness of my screaming mother from my mind. I run up and down the beach for a long time, my muscles burning, my lungs pumping the contaminated bilge from my body. I don't know how long it is before the weight on me lightens, but when it does, a new feeling diffuses into the Dark Energy along with the memory of the hurt and anger in Liria's face and words.

I realize what Liria must have thought, and that she was mixed up about the nature of the lube incident. "No, no, no, Liria, I wasn't like that," I say. I turn my feet back toward home and run as fast as I can, tears blurring the stars and streetlights. "It wasn't like that at all, Liria."

I pound up the steps without waiting for the elevator, and burst through the condo's front door.

Arty and Stewart are sprawled on the couch in the sitting room, tumblers of iced scotch in their hands, the half-empty bottle on the teak table between them.

I stare at them, my chest heaving, sweat trickling in stinging trails down my back. Stewart nervously adjusts his glasses. Arty has her alligator look again, and there's a slight upturn to her mouth that makes a hard jitter run through me.

The condo settles around us, as if shrinking around the too-quiet atmosphere. There is an emptiness in the Dark Energy like someone has pulled all my guts out. "Where's Liria?" I ask.

Stewart shifts in his seat, his eyes full of pity.

"I'm afraid she's gone," Arty says quietly. There is a heavy sadness in her words, but it is too polished and perfect, like cheap jewelry with diamonds too large and glittery to be real. My ribcage sucks in against the emptiness.

"What do you mean she's gone? Where is she, Arty? When will she be back?"

Arty carefully pulls the corners of her mouth into a frown. "I'm really sorry, Justin. She was really upset about something…she said something about you and Astrid…I guess she was worried about you two, and then there's some photos on the internet of her kissing you…"

The sweat on my body freezes solid. I back up from Arty. "No, Arty. That was not what it looked like at all, it wasn't a romantic kiss…"

"Justin…"

"Where's Liria, Arty? Where is she?" She and Stewart go still, watching me with wide eyes, and I can feel this situation crawling all over me, the slime sloshing back in and creeping up my ankles, my calves. I shiver with horrible, sick jitters. "Go get her, Arty. Go tell Liria that it wasn't what it looked like and that it was a misunderstanding about the slimy lube situation."

"Justin," Arty says in that fake-sad voice,

"Liria..." She hides her face in her hands, and I wonder what her face is doing back there that she doesn't want me to see. Then she takes them away; I see the alligator look deep in her eyes. "Just let her go, Justin. She's bad news."

"No. No, letting her go is not a thing that is going to happen, Arty. And there's no bad news about her." I stomp out of the room because of how much I want to strangle Arty with her own guts right now. I have to stop in the doorway of my room because of how horrible that thought is. Is this how the Dark Energy makes you want to hurt people? Is this that test for me now? A moaning noise startles me, and I realize it's coming from my throat. I dig my fingernails into my neck to stop my body from doing things I don't want it to do. "I won't do that," I say. "I won't and you *can't make me* because *I'd rather be broken than find enlightenment that way.*"

I spit the slime from my mouth. I flip on the light switch in my room and go into my closet.

My paintings are there stacked in boxes. They've all been sold already, traded for the money that the butterfly will use to pay his army. It's what's been going on here all along. I've been sucked into this little game, and I don't want to play it, because there's no way for me to actually win. The game is too much. The tests are too much.

I open one of the boxes. The first painting I pull out is the one of the television-eyes butterfly. I lean it against the wall. It stares back at me with its horrible segmented eyes. They are staring slimy gross lube at me. "I definitely didn't paint enough obstacles."

There is a utility knife on the shelf that I use to cut canvas, and I pick it up. I flick it open so that the little, sharp triangle of razor shows, gleaming in the closet light.

It cuts through the painting with a very good feeling, like slicing through cold butter, and also like I'm cutting an air hole in the body bag I've been suffocating in. The two flaps of canvas separate and curl in a way that is beautiful and perfect. It washes the lube off and cleanses away all the feelings of wanting to hurt Arty. Arty is just another pawn. It isn't her I need to hurt. I take out another painting.

The soft sound of footsteps on the tile lets me know someone is approaching. They stop in the doorway. "What the...oh holy shit, Justin!" My scalp sears as Arty grabs my hair and tries to drag me away from the painting.

I push her off me with the hand not holding the knife. "Stop it, Arty. I'm done playing."

"What the fuck are you doing!"

"I'm winning." I turn back to the canvas. "I'm winning against the butterfly." I start to slice through the picture of Liria's struggles, and Arty lets out a wordless scream of rage and grabs my wrist.

There are running footsteps, and Stewart barges in. "Ohmygod," he gasps.

I try to yank my wrist out of Arty's grasp, and she bellows, "Hold him, Stewart!"

Stewart runs over wrenches the utility knife from my hand. I try to keep hold of it, but he gets it away. I yelp as it cuts through the skin of my wrist in the same way it cut through the canvas.

Stewart forces me down and sits on my chest. He is very heavy, and this is a really horrible situation. Maybe the worst situation ever. I keep struggling, even though I know there is no way I can win against this whole army. Not by myself. Not when Liria is gone.

Arty is talking on the phone in an agitated voice, but I can't hear what she's saying because my sobbing and Stewart's weight are pushing all my breath out. The lube is coming back and it's sloshing into my mouth and making it extremely hard to breathe. I try to get out from under Stewart, but I can't. He keeps saying, "It's okay Justin, calm down," but these are ridiculous words and I don't know why he bothers saying them.

There are more footsteps. I crane my neck around dizzily, my heart slopping into my throat. But it isn't Liria. It's Dr. Schlopper, Mr. Plath's hired psychiatrist, striding in with his grim frog expression and casual slacks. "Hello, Justin. I hear you're a little agitated, and I'm here to help you calm down, okay?"

I try to say something, but I don't have enough breath and only sputter lube all over Stewart's knees. Dr. Schlopper's face scrunches up more. "If we let Stewart get off you, will you promise to not hurt anyone, or any more paintings?"

I nod. Tears sting my eyes and I'm probably going to die.

Slowly, Stewart gets off me. I lie there trembling and gasping. "Oh, he's cut!" Stewart says. "Oh, Justin, I'm so sorry. Let me get a towel." He hustles out.

"I don't need psychiatry," I gasp. "I just need Liria back, Dr. Schlopper." My stomach is very sick and the goo is creepy-crawling into my veins. "Liria just thinks that the slime situation had to do with sexual things with Astrid, but it's a mistake. I need her back so I can explain about my mother and the lube, that I thought was lotion, and that it was just an occurrence in the aura and not in real life." Tears run down my face, and I'm choking on the goo now. "Please. Can you talk to her, Dr. Schlopper?"

"Okay," Dr. Schlopper says. "I'll talk to her if I can find her, Justin." He slides a hand into the pocket of his slacks and takes out a syringe.

I try to push myself away from him, but my head hits a wall. "No. Why…"

"It's okay, Justin," Arty says.

My heart is squirting the lube all through my body. I'm crying very hard, and my tears are lube tears, sliding nasty down my cheeks. "It's not okay at all, Arty, it's not."

"Justin," Dr. Schlopper says. He takes one step toward me and stops. He talks like I'm a kitten he's trying to lure out from behind the refrigerator. "Justin, I know this is very stressful for you, and I want to give you something to calm you down, so that we can get this figured out."

"Drugs aren't going to figure out this situation. No. Please."

Dr. Schlopper takes another step forward. "Let's talk about this."

My lungs can't inflate because my ribcage is collapsing even more. The slime pours over me and out of me, squirting from my pores. "There's no use negotiating with the butterfly army and the gangsters." Lube pours out of my mouth as I speak, and I gasp for air. "I can't…"

Dr. Schlopper lunges. I feel a sharp prick and burn on my shoulder, and the slime closes over my head, pulling me down.

Chapter 12

I dip my brush into the paints and lay a line of opalescent blue onto the canvas. I sense it as if it were being painted onto my body, smooth and slippery and cool, but in a different way than the lube. I can't feel the lube on me anymore, or much of anything, actually.

I am both in the painting and I am far away. I am not where my body is. The sound of Patrick overdubbing a bass part seeps through the control room's cracked-open double doors. It is echoey and distant, and has very little to do with me right now.

I woke up this morning in my bed, still in my clothes. I don't remember how I got there. I had a headache the size of the entire universe and Dr. Schlopper was standing over me with a syringe again. Before I could move or say anything, he gave me another injection. It made me throw up all over him, and there was a commotion of maids and of Arty and Stewart and the doctor trying to find all my pieces, clean them off, and put them back together again in time for me to be here today to paint. I don't know why they bothered, because the Physical World barely exists right now and so there's not much reason for me to pretend it does.

The medications have squeezed me dry like a paint tube. The thought of Liria being gone is there, but it is an inanimate object and holds only slightly more emotion than a loaf of stale bread does.

Arty says she is going to find Liria and talk to her today. She says she is going to explain everything, and I don't have to worry about it. That notion is not comforting. I think Arty is the one behind Liria and me being separated in the first place. I believe she poisoned me with the medication she had refilled for me back in New York, and that's probably why the lube situation happened. She is the one telling Dr. Schlopper to poison me, as well. Arty is not a trustworthy person.

I do not have enough presence in the Physical World right now to do anything about this situation. I'm a ghost and could probably float through walls if I wanted to.

Laughter bubbles out of the control room, and I glance up to see Mr. Plath sitting on the sofa beside Astrid, talking with wide gestures, trying to conjure the images of his story out of thin air. His sharp gaze catches mine briefly, and he falters and leans over to say something to Astrid. She looks at me, her smile fading.

I go back to my painting. I know that the commander of the butterfly army is making his moves, and that Astrid might be one of his pawns, but without Liria I don't know if it's worth fighting anymore.

I think I may have lost. I think I've failed this test completely. If that's true, I hope the Dark Energy absorbs me soon because I'm ready to be gone from this world.

The control room doors slide open and Astrid comes out, swinging her long legs, her fingers tucked into the front pockets of her tight, faded jeans. She grins at me, her face glowing like the delicate petals of a lily bathed in moonlight. Every part of her is too perfect to be real. She is probably a sex robot made by the butterfly army and sent to control me, actually.

She stands bouncing slightly on her Converse shoes. I try not to look at her. "Hey, Justin."

"Hello, Astrid." I can't feel the slipperiness of her aura today, and I wonder if it's the medication interfering with vibrations, or if maybe they reprogrammed her to make her different.

"Are you okay? You seem sad, and Harold told me you had a really hard night…that you and Liria had a fight or something…"

My guts cringe, but I'm too far away from them to really notice. "Yes. Liria was very upset about a picture that someone took of you and me together and put on the internet."

Astrid's eyes go wide and she claps a hand over her mouth. "Oh, shit. Goddamn, those fucking paparazzi…I mean, did you tell her…"

"I did not have a chance to tell her anything." I swipe another line of paint onto the canvas. The butterfly spider is in the process of squeezing a bottle of lube all over everyone in the band and on the Astrid puppet.

Astrid gazes at me with her plump lips slightly open, and sighs. "I'm really sorry."

"It is not your fault. I think it's probably just what you were programmed to do."

She fiddles with the long, silvery braid hanging over her shoulder and gives me a pity look. "Come on. We could go get a cup of coffee and just forget about it for a little while. If Liria's going to go running off like that, then she doesn't...I mean, if she really loves you, she'll be back."

I stir my brush around and around in the paint, watching the colors swirl and blend. I want to tell Astrid I won't go with her, but I can't seem to find the words inside me to say much of anything right now.

Astrid shifts on her sneakers. "Come on, you need a break from this anyway. They're going to be working on bass and drum overdubs for a few hours at least, and they told me it's cool if I leave for a while." She smiles with raised eyebrows, trying to burrow through the numbness that surrounds me with her kind expression. This kindness is probably part of her new programming.

I stir the paint for a bit longer. I want the butterfly army to defeat me as quickly as possible and get it over with, to tell you the truth, so I should just fall for all their tricks. "Okay, Astrid, I would enjoy having some coffee with you."

She claps her hands and does a little disco dance of happiness. She's a very well-programmed robot.

We leave the cool cave of the studio and emerge into the concrete oven of Los Angeles. The sun screams like a glam rock vocalist, the sound of its glare echoing off the terra cotta rooftops, gleaming luxury cars, and bleached sidewalks. It hurts my head very much, but I don't think it would shut up if I told it to because the world doesn't work like that for me.

We stroll down the busy street edging the neighborhood, past salons and boutiques. Astrid talks about a new song she's writing about one of her ex-boyfriends, but I can't hear her very well because of the noise of the sun.

We go into a café, and the air conditioning soothes us with its cool fingers. The waitress who seats us recognizes Astrid and tells her what a big fan of her music she is. She asks if she can take a picture of the two of them together.

Discomfort vibrates through the floorboards and creeps up my legs, which is almost a relief, because the Dark Energy seems to finally be soaking through my cotton prison of medication, but it's not really a relief. I don't want any more photographs. What if there is still a chance for Liria to come back, but she sees another picture of me with Astrid on the internet?

My heart pounds and my mouth tastes like the carrot I accidentally left in my sock drawer for two weeks. The waitress slides into the booth next to Astrid. They throw their arms around each other, grinning, while the waitress holds her phone out to take a selfie.

I fold my arms on the table and hide my face in them. The waitress thanks Astrid, and I hear her get up. Her excited voice comes from the back of the restaurant as she tells someone else about the photos.

"Justin, are you okay?" Astrid asks.

I wrap my arms tighter around my face. My foot taps very quickly against the floor. "I shouldn't have come here. I shouldn't have fallen for this trick, because what if I haven't really lost yet? What if Liria could come back?"

"It's okay Justin." I jump when her hand touches my arm. I press myself back against the bench seat, breathing hard and holding my arms tight against my sides so that she can't reach them.

"I shouldn't be here at all," I say. "This is a very bad situation. I can't believe I let myself be tricked like this." I get up. Astrid says something, but I am already out the door.

The sun starts screaming again as soon as I'm outside. It's screaming directly at me now. The world doesn't like me and is trying to push me out of it. "But I *won't give up*!" I scream back at the sun. "You can't make me! I just need to find Liria, because being together is what needs to happen!"

The sun just screams louder, and I press my hands into my ears. A woman on the sidewalk grabs her little girl by the shoulders and pulls her away from me. They are both dressed in very nice clothes, and I watch them closely as I walk by. "Don't attack me, you can't attack me," I say. "I'm stronger than you, even though Liria isn't with me, because Liria still exists in the world, and we are still a team."

I glance around at the boutiques and ice cream parlors, and at all the soldiers in the butterfly's army who are staring at me. I'm surrounded, and I don't really know where I'm going. I don't know where Liria is. "Liria, I'm right here. Please hear me and come find me. I'm very sorry about the lube."

Even with my hands pressed to my ears, I hear footsteps running behind me. I spin around quickly, my breath bunching up in my throat.

It's Astrid. "Justin," she pants. Her face is a very worried face. "Justin, stop."

I turn and keep walking. "I changed my mind about coffee, Astrid. I actually don't want to fall for the robot trick."

"Justin…" She trots along beside me. "Justin, please stop."

Tendrils of her silver-blonde hair are escaping from her braid and sticking to her perfect, sweaty forehead. I wonder how they make their robots sweat. "That is very good engineering." I keep walking. I consider running, but I don't know where I'm running to, and the army is everywhere anyway. "Liria! I'm right here! Please come back!" The sun's scream drowns me out. It doesn't want Liria to hear me. I wonder if the moon will be on my side tonight, and might help me and whisper to Liria in her dreams so she can find me. "I don't know if it works that way, because the sun and moon are opposite, or if maybe the whole world is against me."

"Justin," Astrid says, panting as she runs alongside, "you've got to stop. You're freaking people out, and I'm afraid…oh shit."

A cop car with its lights flashing pulls up to the curb in front of me. I spin around, almost running into Astrid. I walk the other direction. "No cops.

No, no, no."

"Fuck!" Astrid says behind me.

"Sir!" a cop voice yells. Another cop pulls up in front of me. They have me hemmed in now.

I stop and back up against the brick wall of a bakery. It smells like cinnamon and vanilla, like Astrid does, and I wonder if it is not a bakery at all. Maybe it's a robot factory.

"It's okay!" Astrid says. She runs up and stands beside me, glancing back and forth between the two groups of policemen. There are four of them approaching from either side, and I press myself harder into the wall. I wish I could melt through it, but the ghost medication has drained out of me and everything is very solid now.

"It's okay," Astrid says. "He's okay. He has a mental illness, but he's going to be okay, we just—"

"Step away from him, Miss," one of the cops says. He has his hand on the butt of his gun, which makes my heart trip over itself and my bowels clench. Another cop car pulls up directly in front of us. The butterfly's army of well-dressed people stands in a wide circle all around, staring at me, ready to move in.

I squeeze my eyes shut because I can't look at it. "Liria, where are you? I can't fight them all alone, Liria."

"Step away, please, Miss," the cop says again.

"No! Please!" Astrid says. "He's just...he has a mental illness. My brother has it too. He's not dangerous at all! He just needs help!"

The cops bark more cop commands, and the sun screams very loudly, but I build a bubble to try to block it out. I need to force my way into the Other Place, so I can find Liria there and talk to her. But the noise keeps punching through my bubble, and there's too much of the poison still in my veins. It's building walls to keep me out of the Other Place and grabbing at me with its insect feet and slippery lube fingers and pulling me back into the Physical World. I press my chin tight to my chest. "Concentrate. Concentrate. Concentrate."

The words conjure a vivid image of a can of orange juice concentrate, condensation dripping down its sides onto my grandma's kitchen counter. I can taste its sour, icy sweetness. I know what the Dark Energy is trying to tell me. It's telling me I need to concentrate my soul so it can fit through the cracks in the walls they've built around me. "Concentrate."

A calmness washes through me, and my chest expands with a deep breath. I hover above the can of orange juice, and see that it is actually a dark wormhole into the Other Place. I squeeze myself tight together so I will fit through.

"Flaherty!"

My eyes snap open. The wormhole disappears. I blink, and my chest tightens again. There are cops all around me now, so many of them. One of them holds Astrid back as she argues with him.

Arty is standing behind the thick wall of cops, scowling. "Flaherty! Listen to me!"

I blink again. There's something I needed to do, but there is only a hollow space where those thoughts were. Something about orange juice, but I can't remember. My hands curl into fists.

"Goddamn it, Arty! Stop stealing my thoughts!"

"Sir!" One of the cops says. "We need you to put your hands up!"

"Why don't you arrest Arty, who is a thought-stealer and a poisoner!" My anger fills me up and completely takes over the space where my thoughts once were. I shake my head to dislodge it. I was thinking about something very important and *I need to remember.*

"Justin!" It is Dr. Schlopper now, running up behind the line of cops.

I shake my head again until my brains rattle and tears fling from my eyes. "This army is ridiculous. It's *ridiculous* and I'm *so* tired, and I don't even have any thoughts to think with anymore! They've taken everything! What else can you possibly *want*?"

The cop in front has his gun out now, pointing at me, and a bullet of fear blasts through my guts. "Sir, put your hands up!"

Dr. Schlopper is saying something to the cops and trying to push his way through them.

I press my palms to my eyes. I want this to go away. I can't fight all this.

People are yelling at me. The sun is screaming. All of it is a confusion of noise. The vulture businessmen squawk behind it all. Their suit jackets flutter and flap as they gather around, waiting for me to die.

I hear Dr. Schlopper yelling my name, and the cops barking at him and me, but it is far away now. The vulture businessmen scuttle closer, smacking their lips.

Pain shoots through me, and my legs give out. I crumple to the hot sidewalk.

The vulture businessmen swarm forward on me as I fall, their patent leather shoes morphing into sharp talons that hold me down, their noses elongating into needle-like beaks. They pick apart my flesh, squabbling with each other over the choicest pieces.

Fluttering above on his grotesque neon wings, the butterfly looks on.

I've lost, but I don't care. I don't want to play the game anymore. The vultures consume me entirely, but I don't feel it. I've given up. It's really the end this time.

Chapter 13

Every so often there is a bubble of light, sound, and thought that presses against me. After a while, my mind arranges itself enough to have awareness of it.

There is sadness, and a sense of loss, and a million things that I don't understand, that I never understood and probably never will. There are just too many voices and ideas that it's extremely hard to stand back far enough to see the pattern.

The only cohesion is a singing heartbeat. It pumps life through the universe, the same life, the same heartbeat everywhere, even though the song is complicated and there are so many ways to hear it. There are no words to it, but I hear the words anyway. It's a song about the beauty that persists, the silvery thread of light that runs through the endless void. Love is real, even if it gets twisted by the violence of the Physical World and dies sometimes. We are real, even though we've made ourselves up. That is all there is to know.

The world is a complicated place, but it is

simple, actually.

There is a push and pull, a flash of pain, of urgent voices, of struggle. I cringe away from it, because it is too much.

But it is the way it is. We are all born in pain and into pain. Fighting it gets you nowhere.

The darkness lets me go, and I flow out of it and back into the light.

Chapter 14

I sit cross-legged in the grass, the wind hissing through the willow leaves and bringing the smell of rain and death. Clouds billow toward me, climbing over each other in the sky. Beneath them, far away across the plain and dark against the clouds, the butterfly army approaches.

I sit and watch. The wind is full of a wild peace, and it cools my cheeks.

The squabbling raucous voice of the army swells up on the wind as it gets closer. Thousands and millions of vulture businessmen, a monstrous flapping flock of gangsters. And in front, larger than a flying elephant and with blue lightning creeping along his DayGlo wings, is the butterfly.

They are angry, I think, because I came back to life again. But I am not angry at them anymore. They are just doing what the Dark Energy gave them to do. I don't know why it would give them such horrible things to do, and I hope someday they will learn that they can fight back against the Dark Energy. It shapes us, but we can shape it too.

237

Their noise takes over my hearing, pushing the peaceful roar of the wind from my ears. They screech like a thousand bulldozers tearing through rock, like a million chainsaws biting through wood, like the scream of wildflowers being smothered under concrete. Their smell of rotting meat and sour smog and tar coats me, and I can't smell the rain any longer. They're outrunning the clouds. The shadow of them blackens the earth.

I sit and wait as the grass and the willows dance. My approaching destruction presses against me, the tension of it building. I just watch them come. I am one man against a vast army. I am a tiny spark of enlightenment against a smothering darkness.

I feel a hand on my shoulder and look up. Liria is here, smiling down on me.

I smile back. "Liria, you're here."

"Of course I'm here." It's difficult to hear her above the noise of the army, because they are so close now. I stand and take her into my arms.

"I'm so glad you're here." I press my nose into her hair. They can trample me into dust, as long as I have the memory of Liria's arms and the scent of sandalwood and cloves to take with me.

Liria nestles closer. We watch the army approach.

They are about twenty yards away from us when the vultures begin to alight, coating the contours of the hills with their grey-suited bodies. The flock stretches back an impossible distance toward the horizon.

They fall abruptly silent. The wind hisses in the sudden silence. The clouds crawl closer, casting their shadows over our gathered foes. The butterfly stands in front, his huge wings spread wide, his television eyes on us.

Liria presses closer.

"Hey, honey!" We both turn. It's Lee Harvey, coming out of the willows. He shakes a paper bag, making it rattle. "I brought you something." He opens it up, and I'm staring at all the little rainbow pills inside, when Liria screams, and is torn from my arms.

The butterfly swoops up into the sky, clutching Liria in his spiny, spindly, creepy black insect arms. Her voice grows fainter as he glides away as fast as a jet, electricity crackling off his vast wings and dissipating into the clouds. "Justin!" she screams. "Justin!"

Lee Harvey giggles and pops some pills in his mouth. "Oh, my God. That's hilarious. Look at them go." He trots off after them on his skinny legs.

Even though my rage should be enough to fire me up like a rocket engine and send me shooting after her, I'm not angry. This is this way it is, and it is something I have to take care of.

I watch my girlfriend and the butterfly diminish to a speck on the horizon, and my heart diminishes with them. "Liria, I'll find you," I say, my voice whipped away by the wind. "I promise."

The army of vulture businessmen stands silently, their identical, pale, expressionless faces all pointed in my direction.

The army takes a step forward with a noise like a crack of thunder. Another step, and another, their pace quickening, each step concussing the earth and jolting my body. I stand motionless. I am one man, facing a vast army, but I'll fight them. I'll fight for Liria, because she is important.

***

I return slowly. My yellow-green nausea and nail-driving headache welcome me back. It's like Mom and David welcoming me home, except maybe not quite so uncomfortable as that.

My eyelids crack open. The light jabs me with needles of pain and I close them again.

"Mr. Flaherty?" It's a voice I don't recognize, a woman. She lays a cool palm on my arm. "Are you awake Mr. Flaherty?"

"I don't want to be awake, I think." My voice is rough, battered by its journey through my sore and swollen throat. "This is not the world I belong in right now. Maybe a little bit later."

The hand on my arm squeezes gently. "This *is* the world you belong in. How are you feeling?"

I attempt to open my eyes again. My head throbs. The sizzling glare of light resolves into the face of a square-jawed woman. She has gray hair in a ponytail and bunting bags under her eyes. The eyes are kind, the color of moss. Above her is an acoustical tile ceiling, and she's surrounded by an IV bag and monitors. A blue privacy curtain encircles it all.

"I don't feel very good, actually," I say.

Her lips push a dimple into one of her cheeks, and she pats my arm. "You'll feel better in a bit. You've been through a lot, but you're safe now. Do you have a headache?"

"Yes. And my stomach is not happy."

She nods. She takes her hand from my arm and moves off, disappearing behind the curtain. "Dr.— what's his name, Sloppy?"

"Dr. Schlopper," I mutter, wincing.

"Shhhlopper, yes. He gave you quite a medical cocktail, so I'm not surprised you're feeling a bit off. But we're getting fluids into you to help cleanse your system."

"Is that what happened? He poisoned me again?"

I hear the sound of water running in a sink. "I don't know about poisoned…"

I lift my heavy arms and peer around at myself, which makes me dizzy. I don't see any holes in me. "The cops didn't shoot me?"

"No," the woman says, her voice grim. "Dr. Schlopper was able to intervene." The water turns off. She shoulders her way back through the curtain and holds out a little paper cup and a couple pills. "Here. This should help."

I look at the little white pills on her palm, my stomach knotting up even tighter. My body goes clammier than a clam.

"It's just ibuprofen," the nurse says. "For the headache. I promise."

She looks like a very nice person. I don't believe she is part of the butterfly's army. My arm is floppy as I reach out and gather the little pills from her dry palm and take the cup. I am rigged up to all sorts of wires like a puppet, needles in my arm and suction cups all over me. I close my eyes and take a deep breath through my nose, trying to make my stomach calmer, before I bring the pills to my lips.

The woman puts an arm behind me and helps me sit up. My head throbs and sweat beads on my forehead, but I send the pills sliding down my throat, carried along by the apple juice in the cup.

I lie back on the pillows, closing my eyes and watching light shimmer and flash behind them. A worry scrabbles at the back of my sore brain, the ghost of a dream clinging to my neurons, but I'm worried I'll throw up if I try to think right now. "Why am I in the hospital if the police didn't shoot me?"

I hear the rustle of the curtain and the tap of her rubber soled shoes retreating, and I think she's not going to answer. But then I hear water run in a sink again, the squelch of her cleaning her hands. "You're in Olive Heights, a private psychiatric hospital, Mr. Flaherty. You were admitted by Dr. Schlopper as a psychiatric emergency."

"No, I'm not a psychiatric emergency. I'm just upset because my girlfriend has been taken hostage."

The water turns off and the nurse comes back. Her gaze skims my face and the monitors. She takes my hand in one of hers and uses the other to brush my hair back from my damp forehead.

"I really would like to go find my girlfriend now," I say.

"Shhh, Mr. Flaherty."

"I'm not crazy like they say. I'm just a person in a very bad situation, with people who have their own agendas that aren't very healthy for me."

"It's okay," the nurse murmurs.

I flinch, because I'm tired of being told that ridiculous thing.

Another set of footsteps approaches, heavier than the nurse's. The curtain whisks aside with a puff of air and another woman strides in, large and tall and serious. She has a mole like a dark nipple in the middle of one cheek and is wearing a white coat.

She smiles at me, but there is a furrow in her broad, clay-colored brow and her eyes do not smile. "Hello, Mr. Flaherty, good to see you awake." Her voice is like an indelicately played trumpet. She glances at the nurse.

The nurse squeezes my hand. "He's not feeling well because of all the medication, and I think he's frightened because of how he woke up here without warning."

The doctor nods, and she turns back to me. "Mr. Flaherty, I'm Dr. Copern. Listen, you're recovering from quite a high dosage of medication, and we'd rather not have to sedate you again, so you're going to need to stay calm, okay?"

My throat aches, and I wish so badly that Liria were here, but I squeeze my eyes shut and nod. One man cannot face an entire army in outright battle. I have to use tricks and guerilla tactics and sneakiness, instead.

"Good," Dr. Copern says, and the nurse squeezes my hand again.

The nurse and the doctor retreat behind the curtain and into the hallway where they mutter to one another. The doctor's heavy footsteps clomp away while the nurse comes back in. "Are you feeling any better?"

"Yes, thank you," I say, but my throat is still tight and that isn't really the truth.

"Poor thing. I'm going to order you some food. You haven't eaten in so long and it might settle your stomach. You going to be okay if I leave you here just for a bit?"

"Yes, I'll be fine."

She searches my face and nods faintly. "Be right back."

She trots out of the room, down the hall. I close my eyes. The world spins and my ears ring. I wonder what would happen if I got up out of bed right now and left. But I'm not sure that I can stand upright because of the medication. I don't think I could find Liria right now. And I think someone like Dr. Copern would probably shoot me down with a tranquilizer dart like a charging bear if I try to escape.

The nurse comes back. I realize I've forgotten to tell her about my vegetarianism as she positions a bowl of chicken soup on the tray table.

She pushes the button to scrunch my bed into a sitting position. I stare at the steaming bowl, wondering what to do about the food and things in general. The Dark Energy is far away, pacing around the blast zone left by the medication, but I can hear it whispering to me that I need to do the polite social dance. There is a roll with the soup, and a banana, so I pick up the roll and smear it with the little lump of butter that is sandwiched between two stamps of wax paper.

My stomach roars as the butter melts into the warm bread. I tear it apart with my teeth and chomp it down. Maybe if I get some food in me, I will be able to be a fast-enough charging bear to outrun the tranquilizer darts.

The nurse pulls up a chair and sits beside me as I eat the roll and the banana. She tells me her name is Nurse Julie and about how she took painting classes in college. "I haven't done much of it since then, and I was never anywhere near as good as you. I looked up your paintings on the internet, and…wow."

"I'm glad you like them." I swallow the last nub of banana and fold the limp peel next to the bowl. Nurse Julie watches me.

"You're not going to eat the soup?"

A little square of carrot floats in the golden broth, watching me like a chicken's eye. "No, I can't eat meat because of the way the animal bodies try to combine with my own and they don't fit together. The smell of their death is a force field that keeps me away, and I don't know how other people are strong enough to get through it, but I'm not."

"Why didn't you say something? I can get you something vegetarian…"

"It's okay. I don't want to be a complication in your life."

She blinks, and gives me a sad smile. She stands and fusses with my blankets before picking up the tray and going out. "You're not a complication. I'll be right back."

I trace the lines of the tray table's fake wood veneer. I wonder if my weapon of politeness is strong enough to break through the walls of this prison the butterfly has me in. It seems unlikely, but it's the only weapon I have right now.

***

Nurse Julie comes back with a vegetable omelet, which fills my belly so full that the sleepy weight of it pulls me down into the Other Place.

I rematerialize in what looks like a nightclub. It's full of lights and lasers and noise, and I'm sitting on a scalloped red velvet couch. I have a tall, neon pink cocktail in my hand, garnished with a whole roasted chicken leg. A black light shines above me, giving the cocktail a radioactive glow.

In the opposite corner, Liria sits on a red vinyl seat shaped like a pair of gigantic kissy lips. A black light dangles above her too, like a heat lamp over a plate of restaurant food. She is staring at the ground in a way that makes me think she isn't all here. Lee Harvey sits next to her, wearing nothing but a glowing neon yellow kilt held up by glowing neon green suspenders.

He reaches underneath his kilt and brings out a large paper grocery bag. He upends it in Liria's lap.

Pills spill out, glowing like multicolored fireflies in the black light, some of them as big as kittens and others as small as grains of sand. Liria frowns at them as they pile up tall on her knees and spill over onto the ground with a pittering noise.

My shoulders knot. I get up, wanting to evacuate her from the drug situation, but a half dozen vulture businessmen step out of the shadows, blocking my path.

I shift my weight from foot to foot. The vultures peer at me with shiny bird-eyes, their pupils expanding and contracting as if they're trying to size me up.

"Liria!" I shout, but she doesn't look up or give any sign that she's heard me. Lee Harvey is poking pills into her unhappy mouth with a long finger, and she swallows them without even seeming to notice what she's doing.

My fists clench, and I realize they're clenching around something. The neon cocktail has turned into a neon bazooka.

I take another step forward. The vulture businessmen scuttle and close ranks, ruffling their suits in readiness. I raise the gun and pull the trigger.

There's a popping noise, and a napkin folded into the shape of a swan flies out the barrel and into the face of one of the vultures. He squawks and scrabbles at his head, but he can't seem to get it off. He falls to the ground twitching, flailing his legs in the air. Black nylon socks peek from beneath the hems of his slacks. Another vulture materializes out of the gloom to take his place.

I fire again, spraying them all with chocolate truffles. Again, and they're splattered with bouquets of daisies and freesia. They croak and graak and mill about in agitation, all covered in sticky crème and flower petals.

My jaw tightens, and I raise the gun once more, feeling the power of it in my hands. I pull the trigger. A giant teddy bear explodes out the end with a boom, careening dead-center for the group of vultures like a bowling ball.

With a flash of blue lightning, the butterfly appears. He holds up a gigantic, plastic alligator, and the teddy bear bounces off it and ricochets in a spinning arc.

It tumbles through the air, straight for my heart. If I don't dive out of the way I'm done for, but I can't seem to move.

"Mr. Flaherty?"

I awake with a gasp. Odd angles, wrong colors, and different smells jar and muscle each other around trying to figure out an arrangement that makes sense to my brain. Then Nurse Julie's face appears above me, and my heartbeat slows.

"I'm in the hospital," I say.

She smiles. "Yep. And you have a visitor."

A mix of bright, hopeless hope and icy dread pour into me at once. Nurse Julie steps aside, and I sit up on my elbows, the hope blinking out of me in a second and the dread taking over completely.

It isn't Liria. It's worse than not being Liria. Arty sits in a chair against the wall, the curtain parted so I can see her faint smirk and the green of her eyes burning through her brown contacts. "Hi, Justin, how are you feeling?"

My muscles sear with pain because of how fast they tense up. "Where's Christina? Where did you fly off to with her?"

She grimaces slightly. "What are you talking about? I don't know where she is." She sighs, packing a whole conversation into that one expelled breath, but it's not a very good or believable conversation. "You need to let Christina go, Justin.

You need to get your head straight and recover. You have a show to get ready for, and more paintings to do. Thank *God* the sale on the painting you destroyed wasn't final yet, or you'd have a lawsuit to get ready for too. "

My hands clamp down on my sheets. "Stop with the stupid tests, Iris." The words blast from my lips before I can stop them, and I try to remember about anger not being useful.

"This isn't a test, Justin." She sighs again. "Look…Christina…I know you love her, but she isn't healthy for you. She's not the kind of person you think she is."

I close my eyes so the anger can't see me. "What person is she then?"

"Listen. That night she left, when you were out running, Stewart and I came back…we found Liria trying to pack up a bunch of your paintings and other stuff from the apartment. Apparently, she thought you were falling for Astrid, and thought the gravy train was drying up for her. She wanted to get out with what she could."

I keep my eyes closed and my face very still. "I don't think that's true."

"I've known her longer than you have, and she tricked me too at first. I loved her, but I know now she didn't love me back. She just wanted my money. As soon as she had some of it, she left. That's what she's done this time too. She left, and went back with that Cyryl guy, the one who's supposedly her father…except they don't act like father and daughter at all." Arty snorts.

I open my eyes. My teeth immediately clamp

together when I see Arty, and I have to pry them open like a live oyster. "I really think that's not true, Arty, and I want you to stop talking now."

Nurse Julie blinks. Arty fixes me with a hard stare before giving Nurse Julie a little, fluttering smile. "He calls me Arty sometimes. I think he mistakes me for someone else."

I take a deep breath through my nose, and blow it out. I close my eyes again. "If you're not going to bring Christina back, you need to retreat. Go away, Arty. *Go away.*"

"I'm afraid I'm going to have to ask you to leave, Ms. Pierson," Nurse Julie says.

Pounding footsteps approach from the hallway. I peek under my eyelids. Arty hasn't moved. She spears me with her sharp glare. I try to keep the bile from gushing out my mouth.

"Ms. Pierson," Nurse Julie says, her voice sharper than before.

Arty throws her hands in the air as she gets to her feet. "I'm going. I'm sorry. When he gets like this, there's just nothing I can do…"

Nurse Julie places a hand on Arty's shoulder and guides her toward the door just as two big men in blue scrubs come in. I close my eyes again.

"Everything okay in here?" one of the men mutters.

"The visit agitated him," Nurse Julie mutters. "Maybe he'll calm down now that she's leaving."

"I'm fine," I say. "No more medication, please. I just want *Ms. Pierson* to leave."

"I'm going," Arty drawls, and I flinch and clutch the sheets tighter.

Her boots clack slowly down the hallway and away, and my fists loosen. The two men approach my bed stealthily. I can feel the electricity of their presence. "No medication please," I say again. "I'm calming down now. I'm fine."

I open my eyes. The two men are watching me closely, and one of them is holding a syringe. I scoot away against the bedrail. "No medication please." His hand twitches, but he doesn't lunge.

Nurse Julie trots back in, and the two men step aside to let her through. "You okay, Mr. Flaherty?" she asks.

"I'm fine. I just don't appreciate certain people and their tests."

"Oh, Mr. Flaherty," Nurse Julie says, her eyes filling up with pity. She takes my hand and pats it. "You're going to be okay. No one is going to attack or trap you here, all right?"

My tight neck creaks as I nod. "I'm sorry I got agitated, Nurse Julie. You're a very nice person. Please don't let them drug me again, Nurse Julie."

She nods and turns to the men. "It's okay, you guys, I've got him."

"You sure?"

She nods again. They go out, and Nurse Julie pats my hand. "Let's get you disconnected from all this junk. Dr. Copern is going to do an assessment and then we'll get you into a room."

She pulls off the suction cups and yanks the IV needle out neatly, pressing a cotton ball to the puncture and taping it down. Some of the tension leaves my shoulders, but not all of it.

"Dr. Copern is the loud woman from yesterday?"

I ask.

"That was actually earlier today that she was in here, but yes."

I pick at the tape over my IV wound. Dr. Copern seems like a frightening person with very absolute ideas about what constitutes correct behavior. I usually can't do the social dance well enough for people like that, and they get very aggressive about it sometimes. "Could you do the assessment instead, Nurse Julie?"

She chuckles. "I'm not a doctor, so I can't."

"I'm worried that Dr. Copern will assess that she doesn't like me and things will go badly for me."

Nurse Julie gives me a pity smile over her shoulder as she washes her hands. "No one is ever going to assess that they don't like you, Mr. Flaherty. And I'll put in a good word for you, too. You don't have to worry."

"Thank you". Her shoes tip-tap the linoleum as she leaves. I pick at the tape on my arm until it curls up and tears off, the cotton ball flopping aside so I can see the little flower of dried blood on my skin. I wonder how I'm going to get Dr. Copern to assess that I am not a crazy person, so that I can go find Liria. The Dark Energy has me on a frequency that everyone says is crazy, so I don't have much hope in that regard. I'm going to have to think of some other way out of this situation.

Chapter 15

Dr. Copern comes in not long after Arty leaves. She pulls a chair up to my bedside and sits with her tablet computer on her splayed knees, asking me questions and watching me very intensely as I answer them. She wants to talk about Arty and Liria, and I get my fingers all tangled up in the strings on my hospital gown because I'm trying to unravel the complicated knots in the Dark Energy and answer the questions correctly.

"I'm told you called Iris Arty," she says. "Who is Arty?"

I try not to stare at the embarrassing nipple mole on her cheek. "Arty is another name for Iris. Arty is her real name."

"You mean that Iris is her middle name, or something, or a nickname?"

"No. I mean that Arty is her real name, and Iris is one she made up."

Dr. Copern's expression does not change. Her cheek nipple is staring at me steadily, along with her eyes. "Ms. Pierson says she has no idea who

Arty is, though. If it were her true name I think she would have mentioned it."

"Arty is not a very truthful person." I tug my fingers out of the cat's cradle of my gown strings, because they're starting to turn purple.

Dr. Copern squints at me silently. She's a machine that hurls questions at random, like the machines at batting cages that shoot baseballs. "Tell me about Christina. You think Iris—or Arty—is trying to keep you away from her?"

My headache is stomping its way back into my skull. "Christina is my girlfriend." I try to think of a way to explain the situation with Liria being kidnapped that doesn't violate the social dance, but I can't, and my fingers are turning purple again. "It's very complicated."

The questions go on and on like I'm the only contestant in a game of Jeopardy in hell. I can't see the window beyond the privacy curtain, but the splotch of daylight on the ceiling has faded from golden to orange by the time Dr. Copern snaps the cover of her tablet closed and stands up. "Okay, thank you, Mr. Flaherty. Nurse Julie will come get you settled in a room and give you some dinner. I'll write out my treatment recommendations this evening. You can start in on therapy tomorrow."

"Dr. Copern? Could I please call my girlfriend Christina? It is very important I talk to her."

Her lips twitch. "I thought she'd been kidnapped."

"Yes, but she has a cell phone and I'm thinking she might be able to answer it."

She squares her already square shoulders. "I'm

afraid I can't allow that. Your relationship with her was what put you here in the first place it sounds like, Mr. Flaherty. She isn't healthy for you."

My fingers clench around my sheets, but I keep myself from yelling because good things will not happen if I yell. "What are your recommendations, Dr. Copern?" I ask. "When am I going to get out of here?"

She tucks the tablet under a beefy armpit and shoves her fists into the pockets of her khaki slacks. "You've had a severe psychotic episode, Mr. Flaherty. This is a very good place for you to recover and get stabilized. Use your time here wisely, and don't be in such a rush to leave."

Before I can open my mouth to ask anything else, she rushes to leave.

A few minutes later, Nurse Julie brings in a maroon sweat suit, the shirt folded neatly on top of the pants like a stack of wrong-colored French toast. She sets them on the chair beside my bed. "Why don't you get changed out of that gown, Mr. Flaherty? I can take you to your room."

I stare at the fluffy squares of clothing. "Where did those clothes come from?"

Nurse Julie stops in the act of pulling the privacy curtain closed, and her hand darts up to tuck a tendril of graying hair behind her ear. "Ms. Pierson brought them in for you."

The sweat suit is the color of a tube of Mom's lipstick that she kept tucked in a little brass basket in her bathroom drawer. One day I could feel its creaminess from inside that drawer so strongly that I had to go and see it. I had to squish it between my fingers. I took a big bite of it, and it tasted like bitter roses and made my teeth tingle. When Mom caught me, there was upheaval and dire consequences.

I glare at Arty's handprints on the clothes. Bitter roses mingle with Arty's smell of coconut and anger. My teeth tingle so much they hurt all the way down my middle. "Those aren't the right clothes for this situation. I want to stay in my hospital gown."

Nurse Julie tries to hide a smile. "You can't wear your hospital gown out there, Mr. Flaherty. Everyone will see your backside."

"My backside isn't a catastrophic occurrence, but wearing those clothes would be."

Nurse Julie laughs. "Mr. Flaherty, you really can't wear your hospital gown. It's against the rules."

"I really can't wear that sweat suit. It would be a very bad idea to put that on right now or probably ever."

She gazes at me, and the bags under her eyes sag lower. "If I went and found something else for you to wear, would you wear that?"

"I think so," I say. "I think you're the sort of person that could choose the correct clothes."

"Wait here," she says. "I'll be right back."

She leaves, and I turn my face away from the sweat suit. It gives off waves of grossness and I have to plug my nose and shut my eyes to block them out. I wonder about Arty, and about Mom. Arty saved me from Mom, just so she could become the new Mom in my life, twisting things out of shape and trying to crowd me out of my own life. It wasn't a very good trade, actually. At least Mom used to love me, once, and Arty never liked me at all.

I forget about that sometimes, how Mom and I used to do nice things together, go to the beach and go swimming at the pool in Cambria. She used to smile and laugh, even though she was still mad at me sometimes. But things just got more and more messed up until mess was all there was.

Nurse Julie comes trotting back. "We had some things that might work. The shirt may be a little big, but the pants look about right for you." I risk a glance, and see her holding out another folded sweat suit, this one with gray pants and a shirt in a baby blue color that reminds me of the hat Mina gave me.

"They're clean," Nurse Julie says, her gaze focused on my fingers which are still pinching my nose shut.

I blink at the blue shirt, and let its soothing color seep into me. Mina is a very good person, and it's not her fault the Dark Energy wants us apart. "Thank you very much for your helpfulness, Nurse Julie," I say in my nose-plugged voice.

She grins and puts the clothes on the end of my bed. "No problem." She starts to close the curtain.

"Nurse Julie?"

"Yes, Mr. Flaherty?"

"Could you please take those other clothes away? They're really pushy and we're not getting along."

She gives me a half-smile and picks up the clothes before pulling the curtain all the way shut.

I unplug my nose and take a deep breath of the

cleaned-out air. My legs are wobbly and the ear-ringing darkness billows over my vision when I stand, but I manage to get the new clothes on.

***

Nurse Julie takes me to my room, which has a twin bed and a small wooden desk and chair. A tall window looks out onto a little courtyard with roses and a fountain, and I have my own bathroom, like in a hotel room. "This is very nice," I say, even though that isn't exactly true, because the situation of my having to be here is not nice at all.

She shows me where there is a button by the bed to call her if I need to, and says someone will come by to check on me every half hour. As she talks, I run my fingers along the curved edge of the desk. There are no sharp points in this room, because I suppose crazy people would want to do violent-type things with sharp points.

"Oh, and I have a surprise for you." She goes over to a cupboard by the door and pulls out a pad of very nice drawing paper and some charcoal pencils. "I talked to Dr. Copern and she said it was fine for you to have some drawing things. I thought it might help you pass the time. You're such an amazing artist."

I take the things from her, and stare down at them in my hands. "Thank you for making me so comfortable here."

She smiles, her thin cheeks lifting up her eye bags and making them not so noticeable. Then she tells me she'll be back later with my dinner, and goes out.

When she's gone, I put the drawing things on my desk and go over to the window. I expect it to have bars over it like in jail, but it doesn't. There's no way to open it, though.

There is nothing in my room that I could smash the window with. The desk and bed are bolted to the floor, and the chair is chained to the desk. I wonder if I could just launch myself through the window like the hero of an action movie when he's chasing the bad guy. The image of me leaping in slow motion through a flowering cascade of glass makes me giggle.

There's a man with a bald head like a pencil eraser sitting on a bench in the garden. His hand shakes as he smokes his cigarette. I run out of giggles. Heroes in action movies are never crazy people like us. We probably don't have the power to smash through windows like that at all.

I sit down at my desk and open my packet of pencils. My only power is making art, I think, but that's not a very good power. I don't see any way that I can draw myself or Liria out of our bad situations. In fact, my art was what got us in trouble in the first place.

I sink my teeth into the crackling soft wood of the pencil end, feeling the good ache in my teeth and tasting its dusty sweetness. It wasn't the pictures, really, that caused all these problems. It was Arty.

I take the pencil from my mouth. I lay the point to the paper and draw my first smooth, black line.

The square of paper is my window into the Other

Place, just like my bedroom window is my window to the garden. I draw Liria. She is curled on a sofa, hugging her knees. At her feet sits Lee Harvey, who is eating from a striped paper bag that says '*Hot Buttery Pills.*'

The butterfly is nowhere to be seen. It is just Liria and Lee Harvey, all alone. As my pencil continues to sketch, I recognize the huge, pillowy harem couch that they are sitting on. It's the one in Arty's apartment back in San Francisco.

My chest goes hollow as my heart transports itself to the far-away place where Liria is. I think that she has not only left town, but that she is doing drugs again. My fist tightens around my pencil. Arty and the butterfly must have done horrible things to her to convince her to leave. They must have made her think that I am really with Astrid, even though I don't know why she would believe something like that, since we are in the Dark Energy together. The gangsters and the butterfly army are capable of almost anything, I think.

I press my forehead against the cool wood of the desk. I wonder how I can get to San Francisco and to Arty's apartment. They won't let me out of here, and I don't have any money.

Plus, there are all my enemies. They would be able to foil a plan like that very easily.

Frustration pulls my drawstrings tight so that my teeth clench and my eyes squeeze shut. I need to think of another way fast, before they manage to take Liria away from me permanently.

Chapter 16

I sit across a desk from Dr. Copern as she flips through the drawings I've made on the sketchpad Nurse Julie gave me. I was up late drawing, and I am very sleepy now. This place has definite ideas about when you're supposed to wake up, and about how your life should be scheduled in general.

She flips to the next picture, examining them all very carefully, and I pick at the callous on my finger, wishing I'd hidden the sketches so she wouldn't have seen them when she came in to get me.

She looks at the last one then leans back in her chair and studies me instead. "Who is the woman in some of the pictures?"

"That's Christina, my girlfriend."

"And the man with her?"

"Her best friend, Lee Harvey."

Dr. Copern hunches over the drawings again, bringing a stubby finger up to absentmindedly rub her cheek nipple. I squirm uncomfortably because I can't help but wonder what that feels like, if it feels like touching a real nipple.

"And these other two pictures with Iris in them. She's always with a big butterfly. What does that represent?"

I flinch because I have picked too forcefully at my finger callous and peeled part of it away. "There's no reason to pretend in this sort of situation. I don't want to think about what else they can do to me for punishment besides kill me outright. I've never failed a test so badly in my life."

Dr. Copern's brow scrunches, and she leans closer. "Pardon?"

"No, nothing. I was just trying to decide how you want me to answer that question."

She gazes at me a moment, then picks up her stylus and makes a note on her tablet computer. I think I've gotten another red checkmark on the test. I take a deep breath and let it out. "The butterfly represents Harold Plath." She knows that already because she knows about the Dark Energy and it's obvious, but I suppose she wants me to say it out loud.

"That's your manager, correct?"

"He definitely manages. It would be appropriate to call him a manager."

"Do you think he is helping Iris, aka Arty, keep your girlfriend hostage?"

I can see the smirk hidden behind her no-expression mask. I squeeze my eyes shut and clutch my knees, letting my bubble of anger deflate. I try to catch the vibrations of the Dark Energy so I can see what it wants me to do, but I can't feel them, because of all the medication. The feeling of not being able to feel things correctly is very frustrating.

I open my eyes and pry my fingers from my knees.

"Do you feel like you can answer the question?" she asks, peering at me.

There is a framed print on the wall behind Dr. Copern's chair, of a little girl in a sundress walking barefoot on a sandy beach, the waves sliding around her toes. I wonder if that little girl's thoughts are peaceful. It is possible that, despite her surroundings, she is actually thinking about being chewed up by monsters, or remembering how her mom punished her for eating her lipstick by making her eat six more tubes of it until her teeth were all gummed up and her poop was pink.

I suppose it works the other way around too. I suppose that even though I'm in a not-peaceful place in the Physical World, I can still feel the peacefulness inside me.

I take another deep breath and let the soothing roar of the ocean fill my ears. "Harold Plath and Arty aka Iris have been working to separate me from Christina so that they can have more control over me and my situation. Christina is the one soldier in my army, and they don't want me to have even that, even though they have millions of soldiers in their own army. Arty worked very hard so that Mom wouldn't be able to lock me up in the mental institution and take all my money, and now she and Harold Plath have locked me up in the mental institution and are probably taking all my money themselves right now."

Dr. Copern stares at me and taps her stylus against her desk. Then she nods. "Okay, Justin. I don't think you're ready for group therapy yet. I'm going to keep seeing you individually for a while, and have you work with one of my colleagues, Dr. Varundi, on some grounding techniques."

She begins making more notes on her tablet while I picture another doctor in a white coat connecting me to the ground wire in an electrical outlet. This makes the giggles boil up in me. Dr. Copern raises her eyebrows, and I press my hand to my mouth.

"Sorry," I say. "Thank you for your help, Dr. Copern."

But she is not actually being very helpful, and I feel like I'm sliding into a bottomless pit, further away from Liria than ever.

***

The cafeteria is a round room with windows along the curved walls, and pyramid-shaped skylights above. It is like the hospital building is a convoluted silly straw, and the cafeteria is a bubble of sour-food-smelling air in the middle of it.

I stand in line between a woman with severely hunched shoulders and the man with the pencil eraser head that I saw in the garden yesterday. We slide our trays down a stainless-steel countertop while people in hairnets glop food on them. I get potatoes and little smiley wedges of steamed zucchini. At the next station, the guy hesitates with his tongs in the food bin and grins at me. "You're the new guy, right? Flaherty? The vegetarian?"

"Yes, that would be me." I eye the rubbery strips of chicken in his bin, but he takes the lid off a separate bin and clasps two beige pucks between his tongs instead.

"Here you go. Veggie chicken." He deposits the patties next to the potatoes, and I thank him, and move on for my cube of chocolate cake.

There are about ten round tables in the cafeteria, and they are mostly about half full. I look around, wondering which of the people here are the right kind of crazy for me to talk to, and not the scary kind. Nobody seems to be stabbing anyone else or talking to people who aren't there, though there is one woman who appears to be in deep conversation with her cup of orange juice, while the other two women at her table ignore her. There is a table in the corner that only has one person in it: a black man with glasses and a round face that I like. He has cheeks that look like they'd belong on a baby and not an ax murderer. I head over.

He looks up when I sit down, examining me with wide, curious green eyes.

"I hope it's okay if I sit here," I say. "My name is Justin, and I'm new, and I don't know if there are rules here about sitting with the cool kids at lunch, like in high school."

He wipes his mustache with his napkin and holds out his hand. "Not at all. My name is Edward."

I shake his hand, which is a little bit damp but feels friendly. Then I pick up my plastic spork and knife and begin cutting up one of the spongy circles

265

of not-chicken.

"Uh oh, new kid is sitting with Edward." It's the pencil eraser head man, who plops down with a slight groan and gives me a half-smile, jerking his thumb toward Edward. "You'd better watch out, kid. This guy will talk you out of your cake before you know what's happening. He's a heavy schemer."

Edward laughs and scoops up a forkful of potatoes. "I wouldn't say heavy." He eats the potatoes and swallows. "I'd only talk you out of a percentage of your cake, and it would be a fair percentage."

Pencil eraser guy fixes me with a knowing smirk, the tendons popping in his scrawny, flushed neck. "Eddie is a stock broker. They should have all of those guys in the nuthouse, if you ask me."

Edward grins and shakes his head, laying into his chicken.

Eraser Head nods at me. "I'm Cormac."

"Nice to meet you, Cormac. I'm Justin. And Edward can have a percentage of my cake if he wants. I don't object to a reasonable commission."

We talk as we eat. Cormac tells me he lives with his brother who is in the advertising business and has a house so big that it's actually two houses, so that leaves one left over for Cormac. He tells me that sometimes his brother gets jealous of how many women Cormac has sex with and so he sends him to this hospital so that he can have sex with them himself. I am pretty sure that Cormac is a real crazy person, because I'm thinking there are not many women who would want to have sex with a man with a pencil eraser for a head, but maybe I'm wrong.

Edward tells me his family sent him here because he was working so much that his brain sort of crashed along with the stock market, but he's starting to feel a lot better now.

I tell them about being a painter, but I don't tell them why I'm here because it's too complicated and tricky to talk about. They don't ask, but Cormac asks why I wasn't in the group therapy session that morning. "You got in a couple days ago, right?"

"Yes," I say. "I'm not in group therapy, though, because Dr. Copern thinks I'm not ready yet. She has me in individual therapy with a woman named Dr. Varundi."

Edward rolls his eyes and Cormac scowls as he scrapes the last traces of potatoes from the corners of his tray. "Dr. VaROONdee. What a quack."

"She didn't quack much," I say. "There weren't many ducks involved in our session. But it would have been more fun if there had been."

Both men laugh. Dr. Varundi is a woman that looks like someone has squeezed her middle until her eyes bug out. She spent a lot of time teaching me to notice things in the Physical World, like the couch I was sitting on, and the color of her blouse, and the texture of the carpet under my feet. It seemed like a strange thing for her to be paid to do, because I would have noticed those things were there even if she hadn't told me to, and I don't see how staring at and stroking the carpet and furniture is saner than what I do regularly.

After lunch, we have two hours of unstructured

time. Some of the patients, including Edward, head off to meet with visitors, but I told Arty not to come and Liria is sequestered in San Francisco right now, so I don't have visitors. I head to the recreation room with Cormac and the rest.

The recreation room has a television, a pool table, ping pong, and pinball. There are board games, packs of cards, and craft supplies on shelves along one wall. Open French doors lead to the courtyard. Cormac heads out to smoke a cigarette while I rifle through the craft supplies, looking for something to do.

"Justin Flaherty?"

I look around to see a man with a clipboard standing in the doorway.

"That's me," I say.

"You have a visitor that came in a little late. Come with me."

I get a gut punch of nervous anticipation as I follow the man down the hallway. I don't think Arty would have come back yet. I try not to hope that Liria might perhaps have escaped to come see me, but I can't help but hope just a little bit.

But when the man takes me through the door into the visiting room, the Dark Energy twists me into a weird shape, because Astrid is sitting at a table in the corner by the vending machines. She looks up from her phone and waves and smiles at me.

I don't know if it is a good idea or not for me to talk to Astrid. I don't know if she is really a robot or if I was maybe just confused. I haven't seen robots in the Other Place at all, and I think I would have if that theory had been true.

I look around for hidden cameramen. I don't see anyone behind the potted plants or concealed in the nook by the garbage can.

I realize I am standing in the doorway, and that Astrid and the man that brought me here are staring. I consider refusing the visit, but that would be a huge social dance violation, and Astrid has always been very kind to me despite the slippery lube incident, so I don't really want to do that.

I weave through the other tables, nodding at Edward as I pass him. He is visiting with a woman and a twiggy tween girl who I think must be his wife and child.

I sit across from Astrid. She is still smiling, but her skinny legs are crossed, her sneaker waggling, and there worry showing at the edges of her mouth.

"Hello, Astrid. I'm very sorry about the incident in the restaurant. I think maybe I had ideas that have proven to be incorrect."

She shrugs and holds back a smile. "Don't worry about it. It happens."

Astrid has a little pimple on her nose, hidden beneath her makeup, and it makes me feel better. They might make robots sweat, but I don't think they would give them pimples. "It is very surprising to see you here, actually."

"It shouldn't be surprising. I came as soon as I heard where you were." Her eyes wander around the room, full of sadness. "I hope they're treating you okay. You shouldn't have to be in a place like this."

"I agree that I shouldn't, but they are treating me

okay. They haven't strapped me to any tables or put electrodes in uncomfortable places."

Her grin creeps back, and she snorts. "Well, that's better than my weekend's going, at least."

I grin. "You are a very funny person, Astrid."

She ducks her head and taps her fingers on the tabletop. Her fingernails are painted bright yellow now. Next to me, Edward's daughter is feeding a dollar bill into the vending machine, but she keeps missing the slot because she keeps glancing at Astrid.

"Did Mr. Plath send you?" I ask. "Does he want you to tell me to hurry up and finish my Astrograph painting?"

Astrid rolls her eyes. "No. If he'd told me to tell you that, I would have told him to suck butt. The painting can wait. You need to get yourself healthy. Besides, we thought the painting was done. It's completely awesome." She laughs. "I can't believe you drew a spider squirting lube all over everyone."

I run my thumbnail along the plastic strip that edges our table. "That's just the way situations are sometimes."

"Harold has been talking about having you paint a bunch of posters for us after you get out. You know, band posters. We really hope you'll do it."

"That would be nice," I say.

She frowns at me, ticking her fingernails against the table. "Are you feeling better? I mean…" She grimaces.

I stare at her pimple just to make sure it's still there and wasn't some sort of trick. "I'm not actually sick. It's just that they say I'm crazy because of how I don't enjoy them kidnapping my girlfriend away from me. So if we're waiting for me not to feel that way about those sorts of things, it might be a long time before the posters get painted."

A sharp furrow appears in her brow. "Wait, what? Who kidnapped Christina?"

I dig my fingernail deeper into the plastic. I don't know if Astrid will listen to me any more than Dr. Copern does, but I guess I don't have much to lose anyway and it's nice to have someone to talk to about it. "Iris and Mr. Plath are keeping Christina away from me. Christina is back in Iris's apartment in San Francisco. I think they're telling her that you and I are boyfriend and girlfriend now, and maybe doing other things to keep her there too. She's my only ally, and they want to be able to take my money from me without any interference. But I don't care about the money. I just want my girlfriend back."

Astrid sits with her pretty lips hanging slightly open, her big hands splayed flat on the tabletop. "Whoa. Are you sure about that?"

"It's the only explanation that is consistent with events."

She turns her head away and gazes out the window, chewing on her lip. Edward's daughter is sitting back at the table with her parents, still shooting Astrid shy glances. Several other people are, as well. Astrid is extremely famous to the point where she glitters with the magic of it and draws attention everywhere she goes.

Astrid looks back at me, her brow scrunched deeper than ever. "I do know that Harold is being really super weird about you and your situation. He wanted to send a photographer with me on this visit. He tried to spin it as some sort of mental health advocacy bullcrap, wanting to show the public that a big-name musician accepts and supports someone with schizophrenia. But it seemed like more of his grandstanding to me, so I snuck off to visit you on my own."

My shoulders tighten up. "That's very kind of you. Photographers make me very nervous."

She shrugs and nudges my foot with hers under the table. "Christina isn't your only ally, you know, Justin." She gazes at me for a long while. "My brother has schizophrenia."

"I think I remember you saying that to the police."

"My brother is a great dude. It was really sad when he first got…sick, or whatever. He was this guy that everyone loved, a real leader, you know? He was on the basketball team, honor roll, girls were all over him…then one day…" She sweeps her bangs from her forehead with a twitchy motion. "He started washing his hands until they bled, because he said demons were making him touch them. He'd lock himself in his room and scream the scariest shit about how he was going to burn himself alive so that they couldn't torture him anymore. My mom broke open his door with a crowbar once, because she was afraid he was actually going to do it."

I concentrate on the pimple. "That sounds frightening."

She winces. "Once he got on medication and stuff, he got a lot better. He works now as a peer counselor, to help others who are going through the same crap he does. I'm really proud of him."

"He sounds like a very nice person."

Her face falls back into a frown. "You really think they're keeping Liria away from you like that? You sure it's not just she's, you know, jealous because of that stupid picture on the internet of us? Girls do get jealous sometimes, and they get all freaky and run off so that you have to chase them."

"I'm sure," I say. "Christina does get jealous sometimes but she always gives me a chance to explain myself, and besides…" I clutch the edge of the table, wanting to tell her what I saw in the Other Place with the butterfly carrying Liria off, but I don't. "Nothing, never mind."

Astrid quirks her lips. "You can tell me, you know."

I stare at her a long while, wondering if I can. I think I was wrong about her being a robot, but I'm pretty sure she doesn't know about the Dark Energy and would probably just be confused. I shake my head. "No, it's nothing."

She nods, then sighs. "I feel really bad for all this. It's sorta my fault, actually."

The plastic around the table edge is beginning to pull free, and I press it back again, trying to get it to stick. "It is not your fault, Astrid."

"It is, though." She covers her face with her hands for a moment, and I wonder if we are going to play peek-a-boo, but then she takes her hands away and she doesn't have a peek-a-boo face at all, just a very red one, and she won't look at me. "I shouldn't have kissed you, or anything. I knew you had a girlfriend."

I squirm in my seat. "It was just a cheek kiss and I think the vibrations were slippery and strange that day anyhow."

She breaks into a wide grin. "Yeah, you're right. The vibrations were definitely weird that day."

I smile back at her. "They're a lot better now, though. Thank you for visiting me, Astrid. You made me a lot more comfortable today."

Chapter 17

I stare at my little triangles of toast, but they don't make sense to me at all. The evening charge nurse got angry about how late I like to stay up drawing and attacked me with nighttime pills strong enough to completely explode my brain. I could have stayed up all night and been more present in the Physical World than I am right now.

I look up and realize that Edward and Cormac have been saying my name for a long time, and are staring at me with quirked lips. Edward jerks his chin back toward the doorway. "Nurse wants you, space cadet."

Nurse Julie is smiling at me with a clipboard in her hand. "Mr. Flaherty?"

I try to blink my brain into shape. "Yes?"

"You have a special visitor."

My gaze drops back to my toast. Their triangles are burned into my eyeballs now. I keep having visitors but it is never Liria. Nurse Julie says my name again because I have already forgotten about her.

275

I stand up and take my tray to the counter to be washed. Nurse Julie frowns at it. "You're not going to eat anything?"

I slide it across the steel counter, and a sweaty man in a hairnet takes it from me. I shake my head. "My mouth has forgotten how to eat right now."

"Are you feeling okay?"

"It was the nighttime pills they gave me and I'm not sure I remember how to be a human being."

She frowns harder. "I'll talk to them about that." She places a hand on my arm. "Come see your visitor."

She leads me down the hallway, but not toward the visitor's room. My thoughts try to wander in the correct direction to try to figure out what's going on. "Who is my visitor?"

She shoots me a cat-that-ate-the-canary glance from the corner of her eye. "A man who is obviously used to getting what he wants, and having the rules bent. It's not visiting hours, but we decided to allow the visit anyway."

My shoulders sink. "You're talking about Mr. Plath, I think."

Nurse Julie nods once. She opens an office door and holds it for me, a weird glazed-eye smile on her face.

It is Dr. Copern's office, and she is sitting behind her desk. She has a look of thwarted aggression, like she's a dog that tried to chase a cat only to have the cat corner her instead. Mr. Plath sits in one of the visitor's seats, licking his paws placidly. His legs are crossed and his posture is easy. He has a little polite smile that widens when he sees me.

"Justin," he says. "Nice to see you. They must be treating you okay, because you look a lot better than when I last saw you."

I twist the hem of my sweatshirt, the sand in my brain churning. "I must have looked very bad before, then."

His eyes get squintier.

I hear Nurse Julie shift on her feet behind me. "I'll just get back to the medical station."

Dr. Copern nods at her, but doesn't seem to want to take her eyes off Mr. Plath. "Thank you, Julie," she says.

Nurse Julie leaves. Dr. Copern's round, brawny shoulders tense. "Go ahead and sit down, Justin," she says.

I sit on the edge of the chair next to Mr. Plath, still twisting my sweatshirt. I don't care if I mangle it, because the squishy soft roughness of it clears my head slightly. "I want to know why you're here, Mr. Plath," I say. "You already have me locked up and have taken my girlfriend. I assure you there's no other injury you can do me right now."

His eyes squint even further, pulling his forehead into creases. His gaze darts briefly to Dr. Copern. "You think I took Christina from you?"

My anger swells my lungs like a bellows, and I force that anger-air out. It blooms from my nose into dangerous thundercloud, prickled with lightning. "I don't want to play this game. It is so pointless to do this social dance, when we all see what is happening in the Dark Energy and so there's no point in talking in stupid circles around it." Dr. Copern and Mr. Plath gaze at me in silence. I watch the anger cloud roll away and dissipate into peaceful sheets of cool rain. I blow it further off with a more relaxed breath.

Mr. Plath shifts slightly in his seat, and rests his chin on his hand, his elbow propped on the armrest. "I assure you, Justin, I didn't take Christina anywhere. It's my understanding from Iris that she went back to San Francisco because she was brokenhearted about your and Astrid's feelings for each other."

My body curls up like a prickly hedgehog, and anger thunder rolls in my ears again, vibrating my teeth. "My and Astrid's feelings are not for each other. No matter how much we may have slipped around in the lube, we never exchanged feelings like that. I only give my feelings to Christina, but you've taken her away and so I'm left holding the feelings-package and it's much too heavy for me."

"Justin," Dr. Copern barks, then seems to catch herself and talks in a fake-soothing voice. "I need you to relax right now. Remember the techniques Dr. Varundi taught you. Take a deep breath and pick an object to examine. Focus on it and give it all your attention."

I work at building a bubble around me. Dr. Copern's words bounce off its rubbery surface and ricochet right back into her face, and every time one of them smacks her, I feel a little better.

"Look at this picture," Dr. Copern says, picking up a framed photograph from her desk and turning it toward me. "This is my brother at his college graduation. Notice the color of his gown."

I do not look at the color of his gown. I watch

her words *smack bonk ping* into her face, and I contort the bubble so that it bounces them directly at her cheek nipple. I giggle slightly. "Bullseye."

Mr. Plath leans back in his chair, a calm spectator of this raging storm and volley of words. He taps his fingertips lightly on the chair arm. "You really care about Christina, don't you?"

"Of *course* I care about her, Mr. Plath."

He gazes at me a long time. There is something strange in his eyes that I haven't seen there before, but I don't quite know what it is. "She really helps you, right? Having her around helps…helps you to keep it together."

"Yes. Christina is very organizational for the vibrations." I hug myself. "I miss her very much, actually. Very, very much and I feel like all my pieces are falling apart right now. It was an unfair move to take away my one soldier when you have so many to begin with." I rock back and forth a little until the waves of loneliness have receded.

"Let me talk to Iris," Mr. Plath says. "I think she knows where Christina is. Maybe I can convince her that you and Astrid aren't together, and that it's all a misunderstanding. I'm sure she'll listen. Anyone can see how much she cares about you."

My neck muscles tense up, and I can't look at Mr. Plath. I know this is just another evasive move on his part to give me hope, so that I don't take matters into my own hands. He is trying to keep me locked up here, but it isn't going to work. I nod. "Thank you, Mr. Plath. I'm so grateful for your help."

He smiles. "Anytime, Justin. That's what I'm

here for."

Chapter 18

I sit with Edward and Cormac at the dinner table, all of us munching our pizza. The eyes of the other two are on me as they chew. Edward glances around to make sure no one is listening. "You really want to make a run for it?"

I nod, swallowing a doughy mouthful. "I really need to see my girlfriend."

Edward smiles to himself, shaking his head slightly. Cormac raises an eyebrow. "I don't blame you. There's not much going on in here in the way of pussy."

Edward laughs, shaking his head again.

I glance around the room at the women patients, and the female staff members standing along the walls. "Nobody's pussy seems to be doing much of anything, you're correct." Edward hunches over and laughs hard. "But it's not just my girlfriend's pussy I'm worried about. It's all of her. I think she might be in trouble."

Cormac nods and leans toward me. "Let me tell you a secret. I bust out of here sometimes too, when they're not looking."

I think he might be joking or that this might be part of his craziness, but Edward has a look like he's not surprised by the revelation of this secret, and I wonder if it is actually true. "Really?"

"Yeah," Cormac says. "They only let me have two cigarettes a day. They hide them somewhere in the nurse's station and dole them out to me during rec times, which is bullshit. So, I sneak out in the evenings after lights out to smoke. My brother, he gives me a little extra money to buy cigarettes at the store a couple blocks down, on the condition that I don't run away, like you're wanting to do." He munches a huge bite of pizza, sweat glistening on his very pink forehead.

"How do you do it?" I ask. "They lock our bedroom doors after lights out, so how do you get out?"

Cormac's eyes dart around nervously and he speaks at a whisper so I have to lean very close. "The locks on the doors are electric," he says. "They lock them all automatically, and don't check every door to make sure they're locked. So all you have to do is, when the door is still open, take off the little plastic cover by the handle, on the side that faces toward the hallway. Do it right after dinner, but before med call, when they're usually in the breakroom. Underneath that cover, there's one of those little round watch batteries, and all you have to do is take it out, turn it around so they don't get an alert at the station, put the cover back on, and your door won't latch." He shrugs. "Easy."

"Okay," I say. "I think I can do that."

Synchronicity

"That's not the only lock you have to get through, though," he says. "There's a keypad at the front entrance." He wipes his forehead on his wrist, takes another bite, and swallows. "You need the code to get out the front doors. I always watch the staff when they put the code in, whenever I can, because it changes a lot. A couple of days ago it was five-four-four-eight-three-two, but it could have changed."

"Five-four-four-eight-three-two," I repeat, and keep repeating it over and over in my head until the numbers dance Rockette-style in my mind, and know I won't forget them.

Cormac nods. He reaches into the pocket of his sweatpants, glancing around nervously again before he brings something out clutched tightly in his fist. He holds the fist out to me under the table, gazing at me significantly.

I put my hand out, and he deposits some sweaty, warm coins in my palm.

"That's some change left over from what my brother gives me. They actually have a payphone at the little store close to here, even though they don't have payphones anywhere anymore. You can use it to call a cab, or your girlfriend, or whatever."

I stare at the pile of quarters, nickels, and pennies in my hand. "Thank you very much, Cormac. That's very kind of you."

"Always glad to help out a man in love." Cormac hides his smirk behind another bite of pizza.

"You sure you want to do this, Justin?" Edward asks, gazing at me worriedly.

I nod. "I have to. Christina and I are not supposed to be apart, and horrible things will happen if I don't find her."

The two men gaze at me in silence for a moment, and Edward shrugs, leaning back in his seat. "Okay," he says. "Just be careful."

"I will," I say.

***

The night nurses' voices tumble down the hallway. They both have teenage sons and they are trying to outdo one another about whose boy left the grossest objects in the weirdest places. One of them says she found a half-eaten plate of chicken wings under her son's bed that had to have been there for at least a month. I can picture it there, glistening and fuzzy with mold in the half-darkness amongst discarded socks and tissues. I don't hear the other nurse's one-up because her voice fades as they head away from my room. Soon it's only bursts of accented syllables, the bouncing echo of a laugh, getting fainter all the time. I slide like a stealthy snake out from under my thin blanket and over the edge of my bed.

I slither along the floor, out the door of my room. The grit on the tiles rasps against my belly, but I am too slick to let it stop me because I am a snake with scales that glisten like water.

I slide down the hall, away from the nurse's voices. I keep close to the wall in the shadows. The doorways loom large above me in the gloom, and as I slip past Dr. Copern's office I see her hulked and hunchbacked shape crouching at her desk in the moonlight. I am worried she'll hear the hiss of my passage or otherwise sense my presence, but she doesn't move.

I slip through the kitchen, mice scampering away as I weave through the table's legs. The moon is huge, a dignified goddess, gazing through the skylights and leaving blotches and squares of rich silver on the linoleum.

The exit is just past the cafeteria—two wide glass doors which slide open on electric rails. In the parking lot beyond is a bus with half-lidded headlights like sleepy, glowing eyes. Above the windshield, neon letters scroll across the marquee: **"San Francisco Express."** I hope they have free tickets for snakes, because I don't have enough money.

As I approach the door, a shadow steps in front of the exit, its glowing wings spread wide to block my passage.

I freeze. The butterfly's television screen eyes gaze down on me dispassionately, the images billowing and flickering fluidly like the northern lights.

A shape in my peripheral vision draws my eye. Liria is sprawled in the corner, her loose limbs flopped on the ground. A syringe rests in one limp hand, and her eyes gleam wide and vacant in the light from the butterfly's commercials.

***

I wake up with a jolt, and the air squeezes out of

me. I am still in my bed, the sheets sticking to my sweaty skin. The night nurse forced another nighttime pill down my throat before lights out, giving it to me and then checking my mouth and under my tongue to make sure I'd swallowed it. It was a different type of medicine than the night before, because Nurse Julie talked to them about it, but it is still very heavy. It keeps pulling me down into the Other Place against my will. My spirit keeps trying to escape this place, but it forgets to take my body along with it.

The image of Liria's limp corpse sends shivers through me, and I clutch my blankets. This image is enough to keep me awake now, I think, and maybe keep me from ever sleeping again.

It can't be too late. Liria can't really be dead. I jump out of bed, and this time I know I'm here in the Physical World because of how the floor feels solid and cold beneath my feet. I step into my slippers and creep to the door.

I put my face close to the reinforced glass window and peer down the hallway both ways as far as I can, which is not very far because of the angle and how my breath keeps fogging up the glass. I do not see anyone. My heart bounces in my chest like an overinflated basketball.

I pull gently on the door. I let out a breath of relief as it slowly slides inward and open. Cormac's battery trick worked.

As I stand in the doorway, my ears ring and I'm dizzy. I'm scared of leaving here, of being caught and attacked with medication again and thrown into the hole, which is a horrible place Cormac told me about, or dragged away to jail. I'm not entirely certain how I'm going to get to San Francisco, so I hope Liria will answer her phone when I call and will have some ideas.

The vision of her blank eyes spikes through my brain again, and I force it away, outside my bubble. She is not dead. She can't be dead.

Tears fill my eyes, making the light bleed into prisms. No matter how scary escaping is, I need to find Liria. I need to explain things to her and hold her in my arms so that she doesn't feel alone and miserable, and doesn't have to do drugs anymore.

It is silent and still in the hallway. The murmur of the nurses' voices is quiet and far away. I slip out of my room and walk quickly down the hallway, my shoulders tense, my legs rubbery from the nighttime medication. The blood is rushing so fast in my ears that I don't think I could hear the footsteps if someone was coming after me. I glance over my shoulder, but there is still no one there. I pick up my pace. I'm almost running, prancing so that my slipper toes only make a light tap-tap on the tile.

I'm completely bathed in sweat by the time I reach the cafeteria, which is lit by emergency lights along the walls. No moon shows through the skylights above, only the night sky, the stars washed out by the orange glow of the city.

The exit is just ahead. There is no bus waiting for me in the parking lot, but shadows creep along my vision as I approach the exit. I keep thinking I see shapes, that the butterfly is going to jump out at me.

He doesn't. I stand in front of the doorway, my

chest heaving, and make myself glance into the corner where I'd seen Liria's dead body in the Other Place. She isn't there. I know that doesn't mean anything though, and I shut my eyes tight and gulp down my fear.

I need to not stand here forever, or someone will come.

I open my eyes and find the keypad next to the door.

I punch in the numbers with a sweaty finger, five-four-four-eight-three-two. The buttons beep into the gloomy silence like an intensely loud alarm going off.

The doors slide open with a whir, and I let out a breath.

Balmy night air rolls over me, smelling of exhaust and sour trash. Before I can think myself into a rusty hulk about it, I scurry out into the parking lot.

The door whizzes shut behind me. The parking lot is almost empty, only a handful of cars parked in random spots, and I head across it at an angle. Edward had described how to get to the convenience store with the payphone, which is only two blocks away.

I make it across the parking lot with no one catching me, but my scalp still prickles. There is the sound of a revving engine and squealing tires in the distance, and the faint thump of music comes from somewhere. An unsteady, drunken voice echoes down the alley, saying something about someone named Lori.

An ominous wave rolls through the Dark Energy,

making me crouch into the deeper shadows alongside a brick building. I lean against the wall and catch my breath, my eyes picking through the darkness. No one is around that I can see. I take another breath and start walking again.

I am very tense as I go out onto the sidewalk. The streetlights are like spotlights, and I feel eyes on me as I walk through them, even though there is only one other person out here and he has his back to me, walking away down the other side of the street.

I turn a corner and see the mini mart, with its glowing red lottery sign and faded beer posters plastered in the windows. As I get closer, I see the payphone under the awning, lit by dingy fluorescents, plastered with stickers and tagged with permanent markers.

I am shaking so badly that the phone rattles in its cradle as I pick it up. It is sticky in my hand, and the germs will kill me probably, but I don't have time to worry about that now. I will die if I don't find Liria, anyway.

The dial tone hums in my ear, stuttering as I put quarters in the slot. A wandering, harmonic melody plays through the receiver as I punch Liria's number in.

There is a pause, and the phone begins to ring. Once, twice, the phone slipping in my sweaty palm. Three times, four. My heart sags toward my feet. Five times. Then there is a click, and the female voicemail robot tells me I have reached the number I was calling but not the person that owns it.

I set the phone back in its receiver. I stare down

at my slippers on the stained pavement.

Maybe she's just asleep. Maybe she didn't answer because she didn't recognize the number and thought that it was a person even crazier than I am who is calling.

I don't hear the tires pulling up to the curb behind me until red-and-blue lights spin over my slippers like I'm at the worst dance party ever.

My stomach knots. "The police. Always the police." I turn.

Two police officers get out of their cruiser, their radios chattering, their belts hung with pistols and tasers and all the normal sinister cop things for bashing and shooting and electrocuting. They stalk over with their chins raised. "You Justin Flaherty?" They don't wait for me to answer. They grab me by the arms. "Come on, Mr. Flaherty, let's get you back where you belong."

I follow them limply and they put me in the back of the car, because I do not have the superpowers it would take to fight the police.

They drive me the few blocks back to the nuthouse, and I wonder if I will be locked up forever because I can't follow the rules of the social dance well enough. I wonder if I will ever see Liria again.

If she is already dead, though, it doesn't matter whether I'm locked up or free, because my only real escape will be into the Other Place, forever, to join her.

Chapter 19

Liria's friend Lee Harvey sits beside me tells me that I have to take a whole handful of pills to wake up, and then drink a cupful of thick, brown, sewer-smelling liquid if I want to see Liria ever again. The night nurses already lunged at me with flaming devil-needles of sleep juice after the cops brought me back, and I am not happy about even more medication. But I will do it, for Liria.

Lee Harvey pours the pills into my palm and hands me the cup of nasty stuff. I tip my head back to swallow the pills, but they turn into tiny, shimmering moths and flutter away before I can get them into my mouth. The cup of liquid has turned into a black stiletto heel, which would be difficult to drink especially under the circumstances.

Frustration squeezes my heart, and I look back up at Lee Harvey, hoping he will have more of the pills and juice. But Lee Harvey isn't there any longer, and I'm not in my hospital room anymore.

I'm on the plain again by the willow trees. The butterfly stands before me, his gigantic army of vulture gangster businessmen spreading out behind him for miles over the undulating hills. They cover the peaceful waving grass, their grey-suited bodies looking like an ocean of asphalt. It is as if the whole world has been turned into the butterfly's parking lot.

The butterfly spreads his wings, stretching them wide, wider. The neon-blue patterns squirm in a way that makes my teeth sweat but that I can't look away from. He brings up his first two hairy black legs and runs them along his proboscis tauntingly, watching me from the horrible darkness behind his television-screen eyes.

My hands dangle limp and empty at my sides. I have no weapons, no defenses. I am just Justin Flaherty, a person with a problem they call schizophrenia. I am a talented artist, is what they say, but that talent has brought me nothing but trouble, has driven away the woman I love, and earned me untold legions of enemies.

The butterfly raises his top right leg into the air. It is some sort of signal, I think. The silent air is about to rip apart from the tension like pants when you get too big for them. I stand trembling and hollow-chested, just wanting it to be over with. I have failed Liria, and have nothing else to live for.

The butterfly brings his arm down swiftly with a sound like a lightning strike. The noise blasts me back. I fly through the air at least a hundred yards, landing on my butt on the muddy stream bank.

For a moment, I think the noise has shorted my ears out and made them buzz, but then I realize that the buzzing is coming from the army. It starts low, grows to a rumble, and rises higher and higher until it's the sound of a million tea kettles whistling, a thousand train brakes squealing against the rails, and the wrenching, eye-watering sound of metal being tortured and twisted. I can't stand it. It's too much. I scramble back to my feet in the mud, wanting to run, wanting to be anywhere else but here, but I realize it's too late. I can't get away now.

The army rushes toward me, the butterfly gliding in front of them like a military bomber. The earth shakes with their thundering footsteps. They'll trample me soon, and I hope it doesn't hurt. I hope that Liria and I will get to be together in the Other Place when I'm dead.

A movement catches my eye. At my feet, flopping in the breeze, is a heart of faded red construction paper. I bend down to pick it up, and finally, the memory of what it is eases its way into my brain.

It's the valentine I gave Mom when I was six. It has **"I love you"** written gloppily in glue splattered with multicolored glitter. She gave me a big hug when I gave it to her, and it hung on our refrigerator for over a year.

I remember what that felt like, when Mom was happy, and had hugs for me, and when I wasn't a boy with problems yet, but just a boy.

When I was seven, Mom took off with some man and left me alone in the house for two days. That was when I had taken this valentine down and torn it to pieces. I'd stayed with grandma for a while after that, and Mom had gone in to get medication and psychiatric counseling.

I look up from the heart. The army is almost upon me. The butterfly glides closer, the army right behind him. He is fifty feet away. Thirty. Ten.

I look at the heart in my hand. Love is all I have I guess, though it doesn't look like much sometimes, to tell you the truth.

Maybe I shouldn't have torn up this heart, though. Maybe love is all Mom has too. She's the person the Dark Energy made her be. It's seriously hard to struggle against the Dark Energy to be something you're not.

But if you have love, it makes the struggle not so hard. If you have someone who believes in you, it twists the vibrations into beautiful patterns.

I hold out the heart toward the stampeding army. "Here, Mr. Butterfly, this is for you," I say.

There is silence.

The noise of the army ceases abruptly like someone turning off the way-too-loud television. The vulture businessmen have disappeared. The grass waves peacefully in the gusty breeze.

The butterfly glides down fluttering, and lands on the little paper heart. He is just a normal butterfly, with beautiful black-and-indigo wings. His tiny feet tap lightly on the construction paper, and his antennae wave curiously as he peers at me with his little, segmented eyes.

"Mr. Flaherty?"

Nurse Julie is standing beside me. She is wearing a firefighter's hat and a striped bee costume. I realize that somehow I am lying down, and I wonder how that happened. I try to sit up, but my body is too heavy.

"Come on, Mr. Flaherty, wake up. You've got a meeting with Dr. Copern."

"Did I defeat the army?" I ask. "Where's Liria? I can't have defeated them if Liria isn't here."

"You poor thing." She puts gentle hands on my back and eases me up, the world spinning into place around me. I'm back in the hospital. Nurse Julie isn't wearing a firefighter's hat or bee costume, just a red headband and a yellow smock shirt.

I have to sit on the edge of the bed for a while until the dizziness passes. "I need to see Liria," I say.

She hushes me, and I wince. I haven't defeated anyone. I am just the same Justin Flaherty, stuck in this terrible hospital doing this silly social dance. It is really disappointing. I am so tired. "Why do I have a meeting with Dr. Copern?" I ask.

"Well, we have to discuss your little escape incident last night." She gives me a sad smile. "You don't hate us that much, do you, Mr. Flaherty? Why did you try to run off like that?"

"Because love is important."

She is silent, blinking at me, then gives my arm a squeeze. "Come on, Mr. Flaherty," she says very softly. "Let's go."

We go out of my room and down the hallway, my slippers scuffling the linoleum. I almost trip a couple of times because I can't pick up my feet up high enough to walk like a normal person. The medication has given me too much gravity.

Nurse Julie takes me to Dr. Copern's office, and my heart is going to be sick all over the inside of me. Arty is sitting in one of the visitor's chairs, gazing at me with her mean, dangerous alligator look. I am so done with this situation. "I don't want her here," I tell my slippers.

"Mr. Flaherty," Dr. Copern says, "I know you have objections to her, but she is your guardian."

"She is not my guardian," I say to my slippers. "She is the opposite of someone who guards me. She is the one I need guarded from."

"She has started the legal process to become your guardian, based on my recommendation. Your trying to escape proves you need one."

I stand there, the anger in the Dark Energy slithering down into my guts. I look up at them, and they both have the same alligator look. "That look must be standard issue in this army."

No one replies. Nurse Julie puts a gentle hand on my arm. "I'll stay with you. Will that help?"

I look at her, at her kind green eyes with their tired bags underneath. I nod. "That would be very nice, Nurse Julie. Since I don't have any choice in these matters, anyway, I would like it if you would at least stay."

She smiles nervously and guides me to the chair by the wall. She sits between Arty and me. Dr. Copern leans forward with her elbows on her desk, gazing at me with her steely bugged-out eyes. "You put us through quite an ordeal last night."

"I don't mean for there to be ordeals for you," I say. "I just really need to go see my girlfriend Christina right now. It's extremely important and if you would just let me call her…"

"I'm afraid I can't support this unhealthy obsession," Dr. Copern says. "Justin, Christina left.

I know that's hard, I know it hurts, but she left you, and you have to move on."

"Someday you'll find someone who really loves you," Arty says in a voice greasy with fake concern. "But right now, you already have people on your side who care about you."

"I don't see much actual caring about me happening right now, except for perhaps Nurse Julie, who is very nice to me. The rest of you are attacking me. I thought I had defeated you with that heart, but I guess not."

Nurse Julie squeezes my shoulder.

"No one is attacking you, Justin," Dr. Copern says.

My anger makes me dizzy and sick, because it doesn't combine well with the flaming injections I got. "The butterfly's army is very well-trained and vicious and you're doing well enough defeating me without trying to convince me that you're on my side. Please don't play that game anymore, because it's extremely tiresome."

"Mr. Flaherty," Dr. Copern barks. "Listen. I know you're upset, but dealing with reality is part of your recovery. It is important that you learn to accept things the way they are, instead of how you want them to be. We're trying to help you with that, but it's very difficult if you keep running away."

I don't say anything. I twist my sweatshirt very hard and wish I could vanish and be out of this horrible prison of a situation.

"What I'm going to recommend," Dr. Copern says, "is that you be put in a more secure psychiatric unit for a while. After that, you can be moved to a long-term residential facility. You're lucky to have someone like Iris here to help manage that for you, because most people like you end up on the streets. We're going to make sure that doesn't happen, okay?"

The Dark Energy presses on me and I think I'm going to die. "No secure psychiatric units. No. Dying would be a relief, actually."

"Justin—" Arty says.

"No," I say. The fear and anger jitter up through my legs and I break into a cold sweat. Nurse Julie puts her hand on my arm, and it feels like a gigantic spider leg touching me. "No. Please, just bring Liria back, please."

Dr. Copern picks up her phone and starts dialing. "We need backup in here," she says into the receiver.

I put my head between my knees and rock back and forth. "Go away. Go away. Go away." The world presses in around me, and I realize it won't go away. I'm trapped here. I've failed the test. It's all over, and it's worse than I ever thought. I won't ever be able to escape to be with Liria in the Other Place. I'll be stuck in the Physical World, in a prison hospital.

This is what I get for fighting the Dark Energy. It probably wanted me to strangle Arty with her own guts for this not to have happened. But I suppose even a prison hospital is better than that.

There are running footsteps in the hallway, and stern voices. They're coming to attack me with their needles again, and there's nothing I can do. I gave away my heart and I have no more weapons left.

The footsteps stop at the door. I press my forehead into my knees, tensing up as I wait for the prick of the syringe.

"What the fuck?" Arty says.

"What are you doing to him? Why is he curled up like that?"

My head snaps up. I shake it until my eyeballs wobble, but she is still there. "Liria," I say, and I wonder if this is actually just another dream.

Mr. Plath and Astrid come up behind her. That battle formation makes no sense, and I open my mouth to warn Liria that she might be ambushed from behind, but Mr. Plath doesn't ambush her. He scowls at Arty instead.

"Justin," Liria breathes, and shoves her way into the office past Arty and Nurse Julie's knees. I take her into my arms with her half on my lap, and it is the best feeling ever. She smells like sandalwood and cloves, and something else I don't recognize that seems to not belong on her, but when we melt into each other it doesn't matter anymore.

"You're alive," I say. Tears run down my cheeks. "You came back. I'm very happy. I never was with Astrid in that way, Liria, and it was all a misunderstanding."

"I know," she says. "Astrid told me." She is crying too, but she wipes away my tears as if that is important. Then she turns to glare at Arty. "*Iris* here told me that you and Astrid were a couple, and all sorts of other things, but I know now that she was lying. She shipped me off to her apartment in San Francisco, told me I needed to get over you and move on, and not interfere with your career."

Arty's back goes rigid, and she opens her mouth to say something, but Liria plows through without letting her.

"And that bitch just happened to leave a bunch of bottles of fucking oxys and Vicodin in her medicine cabinet, because she knows I have a problem with that shit and that it's another way to control me. She was just trying to get me out of the way so she could do a guardianship petition and steal your money, just like your mom was trying to."

Dr. Copern sighs a disbelieving sigh. "Hold on here. We're trying to have a meeting, and I don't appreciate being interrupted with this—"

"Everything she's saying is true," Mr. Plath cuts in calmly, and I squint at him over Liria's shoulder because I'm still not sure he is real. "I believe Iris here has been doing some very manipulative things in order to gain control of Mr. Flaherty's finances. In fact, it seems perhaps she isn't who she says she is at all." He tilts his head up to look at her down his nose. His little smile is even more frightening than Arty's, and for a strange moment, I am proud of him, because Arty goes very pale and clutches the arms of her chair.

Mr. Plath steps aside, and two uniformed policemen come into the doorway. I clutch Liria tighter. "No, no police, not again."

But they aren't looking at me. "Artemis Kopanis?" one of them says, looking at Arty. Her alligator look has disappeared entirely so that she looks like a frightened little girl.

"Please stand up, Ms. Kopanis," the other cop says. "You're under arrest for the crime of

300

racketeering as defined by U.S.C. title nine-dash one hundred. You have the right to remain silent…"

"Oh," Nurse Julie breathes. The cops pull Arty to her feet and fix handcuffs around her wrists while reading her the rest of her rights.

I'm not completely sure what is going on here, but it doesn't matter. I gather Liria back in my arms and press my face into her hair. "I'm so glad I have you back."

"Me too," she whispers.

The cops take Arty out, leaving Nurse Julie and Dr. Copern to blink at one another with open mouths.

Mr. Plath appears again in the doorway, and clears his throat. He smiles and waves a piece of paper in the air. "I have an order from the admitting doctor, Dr. Schlopper, for Mr. Flaherty's release."

Liria grins at me.

"Being released from this situation sounds like a very good idea," I say.

Epilogue

My brush glides across the canvas. The pink sunset light rolls over the desert hills and through the window, making the paint look warm and cozy.

Liria sets a mug at my elbow and sits at the table, fiddling with the teabag in her cup.

"Thank you very much," I say. "It is very nice of you to make coffee for me."

I put my brush down sit down next to her with my warm mug. She puts her head on my shoulder, and we watch the sunset out of the windows of our new house.

Mr. Plath helped us find the house, and paid for movers to set it all up while Liria and I were on our honeymoon. He says it will be nice for me to have a quiet place to paint in between shows. My Astrograph posters were very popular, and it made me enough money for Liria and me to live on until the universe ends, I think, but he says it will be good for me to still do shows sometimes, just so Liria and I have something to do besides be all lovey-dovey with each other. We'd never leave the house if he didn't make us, is what he says.

Mr. Plath is actually a very good manager, it turns out. I think the butterfly was Arty, all along. Sometimes the Dark Energy can trick you like that.

I have enough money that I can send Mom some every month. She hasn't bothered me with more guardianship petitions, which is pleasant.

Arty is in jail, awaiting trial. Liria says she bets Arty hopes she can stay in there forever, because if she gets out, Liria's not-uncle Peter Czetski will murder Arty about fifty times because she was supposed to be dead in the first place. I guess we will never have to worry about Arty bugging us again, either way. And we won't have to worry about the angry mobsters murdering Liria, either, because her not-father Cyryl Czetski spoke up for her and convinced them Liria thought Arty was dead too.

Liria says we've defeated the gangsters and the butterfly army. She says we can just live quiet lives now. I can paint, and she can go back to school to be a psychiatrist, since we figure it would be nice if more good psychiatrists existed in the world.

I think she must be right, that we've defeated our enemies, because I am very happy with our nice little house and with Liria as my wife.

My situation is basically the best thing a person can ask for, and I think knowing that counts as enlightenment.

THE END

Acknowledgments

I'd like to thank, as always, my awesome editor, Laura Kemmerer, and the folks at Limitless Publishing.

I'd like to thank my parents, and my daughter, for convincing me to come home. Who knows what I was thinking? I'm happy here. A better situation does not exist for me, and I guess that counts as enlightenment. I'd also like to thank them for just being cool, and for putting up with me. I know it's painful, and draining. I hope you think it's worth it.

Phoenix: thank you for always knowing which clothes are the right ones for the day.

I'd like to thank all the people who stand up for neurodiverse rights. It seems like a new idea in the world, that neurodiverse people should have equal rights and protections; not be subject to involuntary commitment when we're not even in imminent danger of committing a crime; that we should be treated with compassion, especially by law enforcement; have control over our own lives and destinies…that our lives have value and beauty, and that we're not better off dead.

Being, and dealing with, a neurodiverse person can be very complex, both emotionally and legally. But I hope, if readers take away nothing else from this book, that they at least are able to see that Justin is a human being with thoughts and motivations like anyone else. Stimuli and emotions can affect him in ways other people don't understand, but that doesn't make him dangerous. And yet, the treatment Justin receives in this series is, if anything, better than most of us get. He has the privilege of having a great talent and being useful to people. Most of us don't have that privilege. It doesn't make us any less valuable, or any more deserving of your scorn or even of your pity.

Writing this series has helped me come to terms with myself and my own behaviors. It has helped me to not be ashamed of myself or blame myself for acting in ways others don't understand or want to put up with. They don't realize they do stupid and hurtful shit too...I'm no different than anyone in that respect. My style is just more flamboyant, I guess.

Writing this series has helped me to see how tenuous neurodiverse people's positions in society generally are. It has made me political. The pushback I've gotten for that has made me realize how much farther we have to go as a society in order to be accepting, not just of neurodiverse people, but of all those others that are fighting for their own civil rights.

I don't want to be political. It's hurtful, tedious, exhausting. But it's hard for me to turn a blind eye to some of the things I've realized about society. I hope that we can count on the support of some of you, even if it's only a kind word when you meet us on the street. It will make our burden that much lighter.

Thank you for reading, and for all you do.

About the Author

Elizabeth Roderick grew up as a barefoot ruffian on a fruit orchard near Yakima, in the eastern part of Washington State. After weathering the grunge revolution and devolution in Olympia, Washington, Portland, Oregon and Seattle, she recently moved to the (very, very) small town of Shandon, California: a small cluster of houses amidst the vineyards of the Central Coast.

She earned a bachelor's degree in Spanish from The Evergreen State College in Olympia, Washington, and worked for many years as a paralegal and translator. She went on to study chemistry, physics, and higher mathematics, with the goal of becoming a research chemist, but was eventually forced to concede that graduate school would require too much time away from her husband and daughter, and that–despite her good-enough grades–she was perhaps the wrong kind of nerd for such pursuits, being more the type that likes to dress in cloaks and hauberks rather than lab coats and goggles.

She is a musician and songwriter, and has played in many bands. She's rocked pretty much every instrument, including some she doesn't even know the real names for, but mostly guitar, bass and keyboards. She has two albums of her own, which you can listen to at pimentointhehole.com. She writes fiction novels for young adults and adults, as well as short stories, and keeps an active blog at pimentointhehole.com/blog

Facebook:
https://www.facebook.com/elizabethroderickauthor

Twitter:
https://twitter.com/LidsRodney

Website:
http://talesfrompurgatory.com/